The Promise of Love

Book of Love, Book Ten

Meara Platt

Text by Meara Platt
Cover by Dar Albert

Dragonblade Publishing, Inc. is an imprint of Kathryn Le Veque Novels, Inc.
P.O. Box 7968
La Verne CA 91750
ceo@dragonbladepublishing.com

Produced in the United States of America

First Edition June 2021
Trade Paperback Edition

The characters and events portrayed in this book are fictitious. Any similarity to real persons, living or dead, is purely coincidental and not intended by the author.

ARE YOU SIGNED UP FOR DRAGONBLADE'S BLOG?

You'll get the latest news and information on exclusive giveaways, exclusive excerpts, coming releases, sales, free books, cover reveals and more.

Check out our complete list of authors, too!

No spam, no junk. That's a promise!

Sign Up Here

www.dragonbladepublishing.com

Dearest Reader;

Thank you for your support of a small press. At Dragonblade Publishing, we strive to bring you the highest quality Historical Romance from the some of the best authors in the business. Without your support, there is no 'us', so we sincerely hope you adore these stories and find some new favorite authors along the way.

Happy Reading!

CEO, Dragonblade Publishing

Additional Dragonblade books by Author Meara Platt

The Book of Love Series

The Look of Love
The Touch of Love
The Taste of Love
The Song of Love
The Scent of Love
The Kiss of Love
The Chance of Love
The Gift of Love
The Heart of Love
The Hope of Love (novella)
The Promise of Love
The Wonder of Love
The Journey of Love

Dark Gardens Series

Garden of Shadows
Garden of Light
Garden of Dragons
Garden of Destiny
Garden of Angels

The Farthingale Series

If You Wished For Me (A Novella)

The Lyon's Den Connected World

Kiss of the Lyon
The Lyon's Surprise

Also from Meara Platt

Aislin

CHAPTER ONE

Taunton, England
June 1821

GENERAL AUGUSTUS MACLAUREN should have known better than to be drawn out of his bedchamber at the elegant Ashcott Inn by the feminine whispers and giggles just outside his door. But he was intrigued, his curiosity piqued.

The hour was not very late, only nine o'clock in the evening, and he'd just washed up before taking a book to bed. Bone-weary from his weeks of travel from the Continent to England, he had meant to retire early. He would have done so already had a noisy wedding celebration not been taking place in the inn's common room as he had arrived with a handful of his elite Scots Greys.

Augustus did not think it wise for these innocent misses to be spying on the wedding party. Some of these men were too deep in their cups to be relied upon to behave.

Concerned as to what these young ladies were about, he opened his door a crack to investigate. "Blessed saints," he muttered, for all three were beautiful, but one, in particular, was spectacular.

They were seated on the carpeted hallway floor, studying a book of some sort. It looked old, with a faded red leather binding.

"June," one of the young ladies whispered to the spectacular-looking one, "I told you it would work. See how that barmaid's bosoms are pushed up and practically spilling over? And look at those men? They are falling over themselves to gain her attention."

The guest chambers were one story up from the main rooms, where all the activity was taking place. The three of them were peering down at the rowdy revelers through the ornately spindled railing.

"Willow, it is just a coincidence. They're simply falling down drunk."

"Good heavens, look at that man," the third young lady commented. "Oh, dear. He is not behaving very nicely, is he? His nose is practically buried between her…endowments. It is just as the book said."

"Oh, Cammy. Don't tell me you agree with Willow."

"I do. Look at those dolts. See how eagerly they are handing over their coins to her as a gratuity? And what has she done other than jiggle her bosom in their direction?"

"Good for her is what I say," the one called Willow declared. "The young woman must be rich as Croesus by now. We must test it out. *The Book of Love* says this will work, and we've just seen proof of it. Show a man a little of your breast, and he will be in your thrall."

Cammy agreed. "Yes, and you must be the one to test it out, June."

The spectacular one gasped. "I will not jiggle anything at those men! Who's to save me if they make untoward advances? They are lewd and bawdy. We mustn't go anywhere near them."

"Oh, you have a point." Willow pursed her lips in thought. "But I know who would be a perfect test frog."

"Who?" Cammy asked, her eyes brightening.

"That old soldier we noticed walking in earlier. I think he was a captain or something. He seemed to be a gentleman, even if he spoke with a slight Scottish accent. His men obeyed him without question, so they obviously respect him."

Augustus sank back against his door frame, struggling not to laugh.

They were speaking of him.

He ought to have taken offense.

Old?

A captain or something?

Would he be tried for murder if he wrung their pretty necks?

The one called June spoke up. "He isn't old. I would describe him as battle-hardened. I thought he was rather handsome. He has a magnificent warrior look about him, don't you think? He looked like a man, not a pampered little boy. But what would a Scottish captain be doing here?"

Willow shrugged. "Passing through from Plymouth and heading north most likely. Which means we never have to see him again. It's perfect, don't you see? You're the one who's been complaining about being foisted on the marriage mart."

"Why should I not complain? I am two and twenty, not some dull-eyed ingenue."

Cammy nodded. "I understand your point about it being your first year out when most of the debutantes will be several years younger. This is why you must go in prepared with a battle plan. The sooner you gain a proposal of marriage, the sooner you can be done with the season."

Augustus choked on his laughter.

Were these girls demented? Were they seriously going to use him to test out whatever idiotic notions espoused in that book? What did they call it? Something about love? It should have been called *The Book of Ruin*, for this is what would happen to these silly geese if they went about exposing their endowments to strangers.

Well, he doubted June, the more sensible one, was going to do much more than give him a modest peek at the swell of her breasts. Did they think all men turned into babbling idiots at the mere sight of a shapely breast?

He glanced at the bed, suddenly no longer tired and decidedly curious to see what *Spectacular June* would do. He donned his jacket, buttoned it up, and realized he had not bothered to take off his medals yet. He did not usually travel with them pinned to his chest, but they'd stopped in Exeter for a formal meeting with several of Lord Liverpool's government ministers and hurried off immediately afterward.

No matter, they covered the expanse of his chest over his heart and would make him appear quite important now.

The display would likely dazzle these lovely rustics.

The three of them were once more huddled together, now peering between the railing spindles into the common room below. *Spectacular June*, he noted, also had a spectacularly shaped derriere.

He slipped unnoticed behind them and made his way downstairs, settling with a newspaper in one of the comfortable, leather wing chairs in the front sitting area. It was still too close to the wedding revelers for his liking, but several other travelers were seated there, and it appeared safe enough. The innkeeper and his sons were serving these tamer guests, a few of whom were husbands and wives, so June would not be the only lady present if she decided to muster her courage and approach him.

The innkeeper hurried over as soon as he had taken a seat. He'd purposely settled in one of the chairs that shared a small table with another similar chair. That one was empty for the moment, and he expected June to drop her delicious backside in it within the next minute or two.

He'd also purposely taken this seat to give himself the best view of the taproom if he glanced to his left, and of the upstairs railing if he glanced to his right.

"General MacLauren, would you care for a drink? I do apologize for the noise this evening. This wedding celebration is particularly rowdy, but it will break up soon. You won't be disturbed much longer."

"Thank you, Mr. Ashcott. A brandy for me."

The innkeeper rushed to fetch it for him and quickly returned with a fine crystal glass filled halfway with a dark amber liquid. Augustus sank into a relaxed pose, sipping his brandy and casually reading one of the newspapers placed in the sitting area for the convenience of the inn's guests.

It wasn't long before the young woman he'd taken to thinking of as *Spectacular June* sank into the chair beside his.

He ignored her.

She cleared her throat. "Excuse me, sir. May I sit here? You aren't expecting anyone to join you, are you?"

There was a lovely, melodic lilt to her voice that he hadn't expected or noticed when the three of them had been whispering upstairs.

"No, it is quite available." He smiled politely and returned to reading his newspaper.

She clasped her hands, obviously fretting as she glanced up at her companions for a hint of what to do next to gain his attention. She shook her head lightly and then gave an imperceptible shrug of her slender shoulders.

A moment later, she groaned softly.

Obviously, the girl was not used to talking to men. Nor should she be, he supposed. Even though she was two and twenty, she had an innocent look about her and could not have been out in the world much.

She cleared her throat again.

He lowered the paper, arching an eyebrow as he stared at her. "Are you ill?"

She blinked. "What?"

Her eyes were a stunning shade of cerulean, and her lips were an exquisite shade of rose. His heartbeat quickened. "You seem to have a frog in your throat. I cannot afford to be ill. I shall move away if—"

"No, I'm not ill. Good heavens, may I not simply clear my throat? It is rather dry in here, don't you think?"

"Of course." He set aside his newspaper and leaned forward. *Lord, have mercy.* Was there a more beautiful female ever created? "Where are my manners? May I order you something to drink? A lemonade? Or would you prefer tea? Perhaps with a little honey to soothe your throat."

"My throat is just fine," she said with annoyance but quickly recovered and cast him a hesitant smile. "A lemonade would be lovely. But I shall ask the innkeeper to put it on my account. It wouldn't be—"

"Nonsense. It will be my pleasure. It is merely a lemonade, surely that cannot be improper." Although he hadn't meant to offer her a drink or tell her it was his pleasure, but the pink blush on her cheeks and those deep blue eyes had suddenly turned his mind to boiled oats.

He silently berated himself for underestimating this girl. He'd expected to encounter a rustic, but she was elegant and her speech refined.

He also warned himself…whatever you do, do not look at her bosom.

Do not…

Oh, mercy.

She sighed, causing her chest to lightly heave.

He looked.

Just a glance.

She hadn't noticed.

Nor had her companions, he hoped.

Well, he wasn't going to look again.

Mercy.

He looked again.

She cleared her throat once more to regain his attention. "Well, thank you. Yes, I would indeed love a lemonade, if you don't mind."

"As I said. It is my pleasure, Miss…er…" She hadn't given him a name.

"Miss Monkton-Kidd," she said, tipping her head up as though daring him to contradict her.

"Delighted to meet you, Miss Monkton-Kidd." He raised his glass and nodded toward her, trying to smother his grin.

"Miss Tallulah Monkton-Kidd."

He'd just taken a sip of his brandy and now snorted it out through his nose.

Bollocks.

Tallulah?

Really?

He tried desperately not to laugh. He was a bloody general, one of the most highly decorated officers serving on the Continent. A top aide to Lord Castlereagh, no less.

Now he was drooling brandy out of the side of his mouth.

She handed him her handkerchief to wipe the dribble off his chin and patted him on the back as he fought to regain his composure. "Are you all right?"

He nodded. "Brandy…slipped down…wrong way."

"Oh, yes. That happens to me on occasion. Not with spirits. I am never allowed anything stronger than wine and rarely that. Your face is awfully red."

He shook his head. "I'll be fine. General Augustus MacLauren."

"What?"

He took a deep breath, coughed, and dared to take another sip of his brandy to ease the tickle in his throat. He sank back with a groan. "My name, lass. I am General Augustus MacLauren."

Her exquisite eyes widened in obvious alarm. "General? You are a general? As in the army? That sort of general?"

"I hadn't realized there was another sort. Aye, Continental commander of the Royal Scots Greys."

"You command an entire continent? Which accounts for your medals, of course." She had been bending over him, no doubt worried he was about to keel over dead at her feet, and completely forgetting about her mission to have him notice her breasts. But in worrying about his well-being, she was still bent over him, the exposed swell of her glorious mounds mere inches from his face.

He tried to keep his eyes from popping wide.

He failed.

June suddenly realized where he was looking, and her gorgeous eyes also widened. "I must be going," she said and turned to flee.

He caught her by the hand to hold her back. "Stay Miss Monkton-Kidd. I promise, you are safe with me." He quickly ordered the lemonade for her and was relieved when the innkeeper brought it over in a trice. "Are you any relation to the Monktons who reside in the neighboring village of Monkton?"

"Who?"

What harm could there be in having a little fun at her expense? After all, she had meant to use him as her dupe. "The village of Monkton. It is just over the hill from Taunton. I thought by your name, perhaps you had stopped here to visit relations of yours. The Monkton family is quite well respected in these parts." It was an utter fabrication. He had no idea whether such a family existed. But it was a way to ease her into conversation because—*mercy*—he did not wish for her to leave.

"Oh. Yes, of course. Our relations. But no, we do not speak to them. Our families do not get along. We are merely passing through from Barnstaple on our way to London."

"Pity, I rather liked old Binty Monkton. We were at university together. A most amiable chap. Do you know him? He is the one with the harelip."

She licked her own beautifully shaped lips. "Um, a harelip?"

He arched an eyebrow. "Surely, you must have noticed."

"Oh." She fidgeted with her hands. "I wouldn't know. As I said, we do not speak to that side of the family."

"Ah, indeed. Then you are not familiar with his brother either? Bunyon, we called him."

"Why?"

Gad, this girl was so gullible. "Because of his extra toe, of course."

"What?"

"He has six toes on his right foot."

She glanced up at the upper floor railing in panic. "Well, look at the time. I think I shall retire."

But the innkeeper chose that moment to pass by. "Is everything all right, Miss Farthingale? Did you not enjoy the lemonade?"

"It is perfect, Mr. Ashcott. Thank you."

"Good. Good," he said cheerfully and walked away.

"Farthingale?" Augustus stared at her, arching his eyebrow once more. "Then you are not Miss Monkton-Kidd?"

She began to squirm.

He saw every blessed thought passing through her panicked brain. Do I lie to him? Do I brazen it out? Do I simply admit the truth?

He leaned forward, watching her gulp down her lemonade, an obvious stalling tactic while she thought up a reason why she had lied to him.

"I don't suppose Tallulah is your real name either. In truth, you look nothing like what I would imagine a Tallulah would look like."

She set down her glass and blushed. "What would a Tallulah look like?"

"Older. Wearing a turban, perhaps with an ostrich feather poking out. Overpowering perfume." He eased closer yet. "No, your name is simpler. Something decidedly forthright. Ann. No. Mary. No…June, perhaps?"

She let out her breath in a deflated sigh. "You knew all along."

He nodded. "I heard you upstairs with your companions."

"They are my sisters. How much did you overhear?"

"All of it. I do not appreciate being used as a test frog."

"Then you weren't attracted to my…" She glanced down at her bosom. "You were only pretending to gape."

He grinned. "No, that part was real."

To his surprise, her eyes brightened. "It was? I mean, I only ask out of scientific curiosity. You see, we have a book that contains the secrets to making a man fall in love. Not that I am expecting you to do this, of course. We only wished to test out one of its theories having to do with the male eye and its attraction to the female…" She glanced at her bosom again. "The author insists it works."

"Apparently so. I just proved it, didn't I?" He glanced there again. Silently berated himself. And glanced again.

She smiled. "Do you wish to know why you cannot stop yourself from looking?"

He considered insisting that he wasn't looking, but his eyes betrayed him. "Yes, kindly enlighten me."

He ran a hand raggedly through his hair.

Blessed saints.

What had he just gotten himself into?

"First of all, the book says that all men look at a woman's…attributes first when making a determination of her worthiness as a mating partner."

Should they be having this conversation? She did not know him. For all she knew, he could be a depraved fiend. But she was talking to him as though they were in a laboratory and had just conducted a successful scientific experiment.

She did not see him as a man but as her test frog.

"My gowns tend to be modest, so you cannot clearly see all you wish to see of me. Because of this, your eyes are compelled to fill in whatever it is that is hidden from your view. You cannot help but continue looking until your eyes are satisfied. It is your base instinct taking over. This is what the book claims."

He stared at her, his mouth agape. It wasn't his eyes he was worried about, but the lower part of his anatomy that seemed to have developed a mind of its own. "What do you call this book?"

"*The Book of Love*." She blushed. "I know it is forward of me. I cannot imagine why I would ever hold such a conversation with you. But there is something quite trustworthy about you."

He leaned in closer, his manner as severe as he could manage. *Mercy, again.* He was making a fool of himself over this beauty and responding with heat to the sweet timbre of her voice. "Now see here, *Tallulah*. You are going to get yourself ruined if you speak to men this way when you are in London."

She frowned at him. "My name is June. Juniper, actually. Have you forgotten already?"

"No, I haven't forgotten." He could never forget this exquisite girl. "I am trying to subtly make a point."

"And that is?"

"Do not trust men. Ever. We are not eunuchs. We will respond to the sight of a beautiful young woman. Given the opportunity, those less disciplined males among us will behave badly. Quite badly." He glanced at the young men now stumbling out of the taproom.

A few of them noticed June.

Damn it.

He did not like the way they were ogling her.

She was paying no attention to them and still going on about that stupid book. "This is what the author says, as well."

"June, we are going to walk upstairs now. I want you to take hold of my arm and not let go of it until we have reached the landing."

She frowned. "Why? Do you want me to show you the book? Or do you think I am an utter nodcock and will foolishly follow you into your bedchamber? I assure you, that will never happen."

He rose as the young men brazenly approached. "June, get behind me now."

"Ain't she a pretty morsel. Keeping her all to yourself, mate?"

She finally realized what was happening and scampered to his side. "Oh, dear. I'm so sorry. I did not realize…"

He wanted her to run upstairs but saw that one of the men had positioned himself to block the staircase.

He'd spent the past five years on the Continent working alongside Lord Castlereagh, handling all manner of sensitive diplomatic missions and, on occasion, flexing Britain's military muscle as commander of his elite cavalry regiment, the Royal Scots Greys.

His assignments required tact, intelligence, and a quick wit, for he was often up against the greatest minds in Europe. He had handled his missions effortlessly, moving in the highest circles of society, often a guest of the most powerful royal families. His name had been tied to exquisite, sophisticated women, some of them princesses.

To now be taken down by a wide-eyed innocent from the Devonshire town of Barnstaple was simply unacceptable. It would never happen.

It *could* never happen.

Nor was he going to let these three drunken arses get the better of him.

As soon as she was securely behind him, he turned to the one who appeared to be their leader. It was a simple tactic, take down the leader and the minions will flee. "That is my wife you are leering at. Take yourselves off before I toss you out of here."

Odd how easily the reference to June as his wife tripped off his tongue. But he gave it no more thought as the first young buck attempted to take a swing at him.

He easily parried, twisting the oaf's arm and shoving him back at his friend, who was standing by the staircase, purposely hoping to anger him and draw him away from it so June could make her escape up the steps.

Where was the innkeeper? His own men had retired early, and he was loath to wake them now. Besides, he could handle these three drunks.

They came at him all at once, one of them picking up a chair and managing to hit him over the head with it while he was making quick work of the man's two companions. But the chair leg caught him in the face, splitting his lip and momentarily stunning him.

He managed to subdue the last man with a quick slam of his fist to his jaw.

The others were now back on their feet, but before he could get to them, June grabbed a fire iron and swung it hard at the back of one man's knees. He flailed and fell hard to the floor. She turned and jabbed the iron into the other man's privates.

Oh, lord!

Even he felt a sympathetic ache to his bollocks as the man yelped and fell even harder than his companion had done.

"Move a muscle and I shall hit you both again," June said, holding the fire iron upraised with two hands, as though it were a claymore, and looking like a magnificent warrior queen.

Her chest, of course, was heaving.

It did not bear mentioning.

The innkeeper and his sons finally heard the commotion and hurried to his aid. "General MacLauren! Are you all right? My apologies!" The innkeeper's eyes were rounded in alarm. "Do you need a doctor?"

"No, I'll be all right in a moment." His head was now pounding, and he was seeing double. But his gaze came sharply back into focus when he felt June's soft hands suddenly on him. She pressed her body to his as she tucked her shoulder under his arm to hold him steady.

"Why did you not tell me those louts were behind me all this time?"

"I preferred not to alarm you."

"Nasty fellows. I wish you had told me. I am not a porcelain doll. I could have helped you fight them off sooner. Oh, that first blackguard landed a nasty blow to your face. What a dirty fighter to hit you with a chair. Do you think you are seriously hurt?"

"No." He did not mean to growl at her, but it irritated him that she had bested these men without so much as getting winded.

She smiled at him. "I heard you tell them I was your wife. That was wonderfully protective of you. And they still came after you. They are despicable."

He set aside his wounded pride and caressed her cheek. "As long as you are all right."

She let out a shaky breath. "I am. But please let me help you upstairs. Where is your room? I shall walk you there and see you safely settled. Your lip is swelling. It is also cut and bleeding."

He glanced up to see two young faces still peering down at him.

"Those are my younger sisters, Willow and Camellia. We call her Cammy. Let me help you into bed."

He moaned. "You will do no such thing."

"You are a stubborn Scott, aren't you?"

"Where is your chaperone?"

"Our Aunt Charlotte retired early. Travel does not agree with her. We are not keen on it either. We were quite happy at home. Have you ever been to Barnstaple? It is a lovely town. But our parents are determined to have us make brilliant matches, apparently something we cannot do there. So, we've been shipped to London to accomplish the task."

He held on to the stair post as he climbed, irritated that June was helping him and even more irritated that he seemed in need of her help. "What sort of man do you hope to snare?"

"General MacLauren! I am not a hunter out to trap an innocent rabbit. I don't wish to *snare* anyone. What I hope to do is find love. Which I doubt will happen if those oafs are representative of the crop of London bachelors. I don't suppose you will be—"

"I'm riding north to Scotland."

"Oh." She motioned for her sisters to open his door.

Augustus growled to chase them away. They quickly backed off but remained in the hall, peering in as June led him to his bed and nudged him onto it. "You are a cantankerous fellow, aren't you? Sit there and don't move."

She bustled to the ewer and basin on the bureau, grabbed the cloth set out beside the ewer, and poured water on it. She returned to his side and began to gently dab his lip. "As soon as Mr. Ashcott comes up here, I'll ask him for some brandy to apply to the injury. You have a nasty cut, and it needs to be more thoroughly cleansed."

"I'll take care of it myself."

"Why will you not let me help you? May I not return the favor? You saved me from those awful men."

"No, you may not return the favor. What you had better do is leave my bedchamber immediately."

She leaned closer, determined to tend to him. "Your door is open. My sisters are standing just outside of it. Well, they were just outside. They are probably looking at what's going on downstairs. They'll return in a moment. So why must I leave?"

"Because I am in danger of kissing you."

She laughed. "You wouldn't. You are a gentleman."

"Aye," he said, "but I am still going to kiss you if you insist on staying."

She gasped. "Are you suggesting you are attracted to me? That my bosom ploy worked? That is fascinating, don't you think? How long will you be here? May I…oh, I suppose you and your men will be riding out first thing in the morning. Well, if you change your mind, would you—"

"No, I will not agree to be your test frog. And stop smiling at me in that soft way."

"How else should I smile at you?"

"Are you not paying attention? You should not be smiling at me at all. You should not be touching me. Nor should you be alone with me in my chamber."

"Because you are in a low-brain frenzy to kiss me?"

"A what?"

Her breath held, and she stared at him with her big, blue eyes. "Are you irresistibly and compellingly attracted to me?"

"Stop spouting that damn book."

"You are very handsome, you know. And I rather like the idea of experiencing my first kiss with a Scottish army general."

"Damn it," he grumbled, "your first?"

She nodded, holding the damp cloth to the cut on his lip. "Others have tried, of course. But I think I am a hopeless romantic. I wanted it to be special. A kiss that I shall dream on for the rest of my life."

He had bedded princesses, countesses, courtesans, all of whom were experienced in the art of pleasuring a man. They had indeed pleasured him in every physical way possible.

But none of them had ever given his heart pleasure.

He stared at June.

Spectacular June.

It wasn't merely her looks that had him in a heated frenzy; it was her charming, and yet incredibly irritating, innocence. "And you've chosen me? A complete stranger?"

Her smile faded. "You are right, of course. What was I thinking? We don't know the first thing about each other. And yet…I cannot explain it. There's a little voice inside of me that is telling me it must be you. Truly, I am sorry. I'll go now."

"Wait." He drew her down onto his lap and lightly wrapped his arms around her waist. "I never said I wouldn't do it."

He waited to the count of five, expecting her to protest. He would release her, of course, if she demanded it. When she didn't, he cupped a finger under her chin, lowered his mouth to hers, and kissed her. Properly…or improperly, it depended on how one looked at it.

His lip hurt.

He didn't care.

He was surprised by how lovely her mouth felt against his.

And then *Spectacular June* did the unthinkable.

She kissed him back with innocent ardor and…

What was the name of that book she had been spouting? *The Book of Love?* He had to get his hands on it.

There was no way on this green earth…not a chance that…*Spectacular June/Tallulah* could not possibly…no, she could not…and certainly not with a first kiss.

She could not have stolen his heart.

Could she?

CHAPTER TWO

"CRUMPETS!" JUNE CRIED as General MacLauren stood up suddenly and would have sent her toppling to the floor had he not kept his arms around her.

They were muscled arms and quite magnificent, circled protectively around her so that she felt like a butterfly enveloped in a warm cocoon. That he did not appear to be delighted was irrelevant. "Miss Farthingale, you had better go."

"Why? Because I kissed you back?" She knew it was foolish to respond with indignation, but she intended to stand firm and not allow him to avoid the fact that it had been a wonderful kiss. Indeed, so brilliantly executed, she simply could not bear to leave him yet.

Obviously, he did not feel the same way. He had shot off the bed and was now eyeing her as though she were an unruly pup who needed to be grabbed by the scruff of her neck and carried down the hall to be dumped at her guardian's door.

His eyes were blazing. Well, they were smoldering, really. It was an exquisitely steamy look. Perhaps he wasn't angry so much as wanting to peel the gown off her body and explore every inch of her. One could only hope his thoughts had strayed in this direction because hers certainly had regarding him.

She would not mind peeling his clothes off and…

"Miss Farthingale." He shook her gently to gain her attention. "Must I toss you out? I dinna mean to insult you." His brogue was more pronounced, a sure sign she had affected him. "But you cannot behave this way around men."

"I am only behaving this way around you. Surely, you cannot believe I would ever consider entering another man's bedchamber or kissing another man." She tipped her chin up in the air, daring him to accuse her of having loose morals, which she supposed she had when it came to him. "As I've mentioned, you have a very trustworthy and reassuring look about you."

"And as I've mentioned, you do not appear to know anything about men."

"Yes, I heartily agree. Hence the book." She nibbled her lip, now fretting she may have been too forward. Of course, she had been. Was there any doubt? But she had been so caught up in his kiss, was it her fault she may have shown a little too much passion? How was she to know it would be so enjoyable or that she would respond to him this way?

He might have warned her.

After all, he had done this before.

She was a complete novice.

She sighed and shook her head. "I'm sorry. I have been behaving very badly, and I appreciate your trying to remain a gentleman. In my defense, I was swept away by you. I should have realized it was dangerous to kiss you, for you are worldly and experienced. But you are also irresistible. Have others told you this?"

His smile was one of wry amusement. "No."

"Oh. I'm surprised. I thought surely…" She knew she ought to shut up now. No good could come from this conversation. But her lips were tingling, and so was her body. This, apparently, had the effect of loosening her tongue and making her chatter. "I've read about these forbidden feelings in those books our parents do not ever permit us to read. We inhale them like chocolates, of course. Who can resist? The point is, no one teaches us about passion, so we are caught off guard when suddenly enveloped in its enthralling waves and swept away."

"As you are now?" His smile was also devastatingly appealing, filled with warmth and affection. Well, perhaps tolerance was a better word for it. Not affection. He could not possibly feel anything for her now that she had behaved like a wanton goose.

She nodded. "Your kiss was quite exhilarating but also frightening. I wish one of our elders had discussed this with us, warned us of this surprising whirlpool of feelings the touch of one's lips to another could stir."

"Did the book you and your sisters were huddled over not mention it?"

"*The Book of Love*? It is a serious scientific analysis of the components of love. Although it discusses the five senses, sight, touch, taste, hearing, and scent, it does not quite prepare one for the impact of them. Did you enjoy the kiss, General MacLauren?"

He folded his arms over his chest, which only served to accentuate his size and strength. "Yes, Miss Farthingale. I did."

She released a breath in relief. "I hoped you would. Too bad you must leave tomorrow. Well, we will also be leaving. And then we shall never see each other again. It is a shame, don't you think?"

He did not bother to respond.

She sighed. "I would love to show you *The Book of Love*. Do you suppose we might have time tonight? But you must give me your oath not to mock me or the book."

"Miss Farthingale, you have my word as an officer and a gentleman that I would never mock you. More importantly, you have my word as a Scot. However, I doubt we shall have time to look at it tonight. My men and I will be heading to Bath in the morning. We leave at sunrise, and I am quite spent from our journey."

"We are off to London later in the morning, assuming Aunt Charlotte is feeling well enough to travel." She tried not to show that her heart was sinking, for he did not seem to be broken up over their parting, and she did not wish to look even more foolish than he already believed her to be. "Are you sure it is too late for us to talk now?"

"Quite sure. Even if it were not, I am no one's test frog. But you will find cooperative bachelors in London who will not mind being used as your dupe. The town is teeming with titled idiots." He nudged her closer to the door as he spoke. "You'll have your choice of frogs, toads, and every manner of brainless society creature once you reach town."

She paused at the door and turned to face him. "First of all, the book does not refer to men as brainless. It claims men have two brains, the low and the high. The high brain is the one that allows you to fall in love with one woman and protect her and her offspring."

"And the low brain?"

"It is your thoughtless brain, the one that acts on instinct. It is as much a part of you as the beat of your heart or the flow of your blood. It is as innate to you as your will to survive."

Since he had not kicked her out yet, she continued. "Not only to survive but to leave your mark. This is why men have the urge to populate the earth with their offspring. In this regard, you are no different from all male beasts. Rams, lions, chipmunks. But I digress. It is the reason why your eye was drawn to…" She glanced down at her bosom. "Because you wish to breed strong, healthy offspring. This is why you could not help assessing my own…suitability as a breeding partner."

He arched an eyebrow. "Is this what you think you are to me?"

She nodded. "But only at the low-brain level. This is what the author claims. It is why you were compelled to look at my healthy…" She glanced down at herself again and sighed, knowing she was irritating him. "This is how you determine whether or not to mate with me."

He groaned. "It is my fault. I should not have let you go on about this."

"But this is exactly my fear. I cannot discuss its teachings with just anyone. The man has to be intelligent and thoughtful. I am not looking to attach myself to an idiot, no matter how wealthy or elevated in rank. This is why I am being such a nuisance to you. You are a man of rare quality, General MacLauren."

He gave her cheek a light caress. "I've just kissed you. Please call me Augustus, at least while we are alone in my bedchamber, which had better not be much longer."

"To be precise, we are now at your doorway. Surely, that is not improper."

"With you? It is." He gave her cheek another light stroke, gently running his thumb along the line of her jaw. "June, you do not need to use any of the tricks in that book to lure a man and make him fall in love with you. Just be yourself, and they will drop at your feet. You are a young lady of unusual quality, and it shows."

She laughed gently. "Oh, I shall take it as a compliment, although I am not certain you meant it as such. But thank you."

"You had better leave now." He ran a hand through the waves of his dark hair. He had nice hands. Big and powerful. They were obviously used to rough work and yet had felt exquisitely gentle when holding her and caressing her cheek. "It was a pleasure to meet you. And an even bigger pleasure to kiss you."

He placed an arm around her waist to guide her down the hall.

She liked the feel of his arm around her. "I enjoyed our kiss very much, too. I suppose I've made no secret of it. Thank you, Augustus. Truly. I shall always dream of you, and this moment we shared. Please remember me."

He spoke softly and with a wrenching ache. "Rest assured, I will not soon forget the night I met Miss Tallulah Monkton-Kidd."

She rolled her eyes and winced. "Will you never let me live this down?"

"No." But he was smiling again, and the smile reached into the depths of his emerald-dark, utterly captivating eyes.

It was extraordinary. The thought of parting from him left her physically pained. Her heart felt taut, as though caught in a vise. Her brain was shouting at her not to let him go. She wanted to obey, was desperate to see him again. But how? He was off for Bath and then Scotland in the early morning, and they would never meet again unless he came down to London over the next few months. "Well, goodnight then. Safe travels to you and your men."

"Thank you, June. Safe travels to you and your sisters as well."

She walked thoughtfully to the guest quarters she shared with her sisters, feeling his gaze upon her, for he had remained standing in the doorway to make certain she reached her chamber without incident. But when she opened the door and entered, she noticed the room was empty.

Of course, her sisters must have gone to tell Aunt Charlotte what had happened. She hurried to the unlocked door between their adjoining rooms and knocked lightly before walking in.

"Aunt Charlotte…" She stopped and glanced around, now confused. "Where are Willow and Cammy? I thought they were in here with you."

"They left several minutes ago. Do go away, June. I have a pounding headache and just took some laudanum to help me sleep. Leave me in peace, child."

She eased toward the door. "Yes, I'm so sorry."

Where were her sisters? Had they been foolish enough to run downstairs? She had to find them, but after the incident with those three drunkards, she dared not search on her own.

She waited a few minutes, hoping they would return.

When they did not, she grew worried.

"Oh, he's going to hate me," she muttered and headed straight back to General MacLauren's bedchamber to knock on his door.

When he did not respond, she knocked more urgently.

"Bloody blazes, what—" He had flung the door open, obviously not expecting to find her standing there, for he had removed his jacket and unbuttoned his shirt, leaving her to stare at his exquisitely rock-hard and superbly chiseled chest.

Mercy.

Her heart shot into her throat, and butterflies began to flutter in her belly as she stared at the spray of dark curls across it and the thin line of dark hair that ran down his sleek torso to disappear below his navel into his trousers.

He was a big man, powerfully built.

Oh, nothing soft about him.

His shoulders were broad. His legs were long and lean, his thighs muscled.

His stomach was tight and rippled.

"Why are you back here?" He quickly buttoned his shirt and cast her a quelling glance when she attempted to step in. "Are you trying to compromise me, *Tallulah*?"

She frowned at him.

Would he never let her forget that harmless, little fib? "No. My sisters are missing." She clasped her hands together and began to rub them in a fret. "They are not with our aunt. They are not in our bedchamber. I'm worried they went downstairs. I want to look for them, but I dare not go down there alone."

He turned away to tuck his shirt into his trousers. "Go back to your quarters. I'll search for them."

"I'm coming with you." She cast him the stubbornest look she could muster. "I won't stay in my room. I'll just follow you down, so you may as well let me go with you. It will be safer for me, and you might need my help again."

He growled softly. "I dinna need yer help the first time."

She grinned, liking the arrogant Scot in him better than his facade of a sophisticated, mannered gentleman. "Yes, you did. Come on. We are wasting precious time."

They hurried back downstairs and glanced around. No sign of her sisters in the sitting area. The common room was mostly empty now, but there were several men standing by the bar in the area that served as the taproom. "Stay out, June. Let me go in alone."

She did not argue, for those men did not appear to be the polite sort. Probably more local gentry from the unsavory wedding party. They had that disdainful air of entitlement, as though the circumstances of their birth gave them the right to be rude and unruly.

Augustus returned a moment later, frowning. "Neither the bartender nor the serving maids have seen them."

June's hands began to shake, so she clasped them again. "Where can they be? They were with us only moments ago."

"Might they have gone to the inn's kitchen?"

"Why would they?" But she nodded. "Let's look there."

They encountered her sisters strolling out of the kitchen, each with a glass of milk and plate of apple pie in hand. June placed a hand over her heart. "Thank goodness! What are you doing down here? You gave me the scare of my life. How could you wander away after what happened to General MacLauren? Those horrible men might have come back and hurt you."

Willow had the good grace to appear remorseful. "We went down the back stairs so those sots would not see us. In any event, they're not here. They were taken to the magistrate's house, which is just next door. He's a big, brute of a fellow. You should have seen the way he stormed in and dragged the three of them away."

"With the help of a deputy," Cammy added. "That man was big as an ox and just as daunting as the magistrate. Oh, my. One would have to be a fool to dare take them on. Anyway, all the excitement made us hungry."

June was glad to hear those well-heeled churls had been hauled away, but she still remained tense. There were others in their party who were staying over at the inn and could not be trusted to behave. "General MacLauren will escort us back upstairs now, and you must promise not to leave our room again. We've disturbed him enough for one evening."

Her sisters smiled at him.

"Thank you for defending June's honor," Willow said, her smile more of a smirk.

"You were brilliant, General MacLauren." Cammy was now gaping at him quite inanely. June wondered whether she had looked as foolish. "The magistrate mentioned he was going to come around first thing in the morning to speak to you about those men."

"I expected he would," he said with a nod. "But we'll be leaving Taunton quite early. I had better stop in to see him before my men and I ride off."

When they reached their guest chamber, he waited for them to go in and close the door. June put her ear to the door to listen for his fading footsteps, but the hallway was carpeted, and he had a light tread despite being big and solid, so she really could not hear anything.

She waited a few moments longer, then moaned and fell onto her bed. "Isn't he the most divinely handsome man you have ever beheld in your life?"

Willow laughed. "He is nice looking, June. You are obviously in raptures over him."

"How can anyone not be?" She moaned again and glanced at the door. If she stared at it long enough, could she will him to return?

Willow hopped onto the bed beside her. "What happened after we left his room? I'm sorry we abandoned you, but we thought it would be safe enough. His door was open, and he was bleeding. Nothing was going to happen between the two of you. Then there was a sudden commotion downstairs when the magistrate and his deputy strode in."

"We were curious and wanted to see what else would happen." Cammy walked over to the bureau and picked up *The Book of Love* to tuck it safely back in June's travel bag. "We felt it was our duty to see those drunken sots properly taken into custody and tossed behind bars for the night. We wanted to offer our statements to be helpful in putting them away. But the magistrate and his deputy were too busy subduing them to pay us any notice. Those horrid men were still belligerent."

"You would think they would be repentant for the trouble they'd caused," Willow added. "But they weren't in the least. They attacked the magistrate and his deputy, too. Can you believe it? Only monumental fools would dare tangle with those two. You should have seen them, June. What was the magistrate's name? Brayden or something like it. Maybe I am just thinking of the men our cousins married. But his name sounded something like that. Well, he and his deputy were strong as beasts and easily hauled those scoundrels off. Hopefully to a dank chamber with iron bars. Cammy, did you notice the muscles on him?"

Their youngest sister nodded. "He was all right, but what about his deputy? Have you ever seen anyone so big and frightening? Quite handsome in a brutish way, didn't you think?"

"If you say so. I did not get a good look at him." Willow shook her head. "Come on, we had better get ready for bed."

June helped her sisters out of their gowns and then held out her arms while they helped her out of hers. "Aunt Charlotte did not look well. I went to her chamber thinking to find you both there. Then General MacLauren and I returned downstairs to search for you. I had better check on her first thing in the morning. She took laudanum for her headache."

"She was in a foul temper when we tried to tell her what happened." Willow took the pins out of June's hair and then handed her the hairbrush. "She growled at us when we entered, so we tiptoed out of there. Since you weren't hurt, we decided there was no harm in waiting until morning to bother telling her the news."

"That was wise. We needn't upset her." After donning her nightrail, June took a moment to braid her hair. Her sisters had already done the same and were now climbing into bed. There were two beds in their pleasant chamber. Cammy and Willow shared one, and she had the other all to herself. Aunt Charlotte liked her privacy, so she had insisted on her own room throughout their journey.

June made certain the door was securely latched, then blew out the candles and climbed into bed. Instead of leaning her head against the pillow, she clutched it to her chest and pretended she was curled around General MacLauren. Being held in his arms had felt surprisingly good, and she still ached for him.

His kiss had been exquisite.

She had experienced only one in her entire life, his. So she could not be certain whether kisses from other men would ever compare. Yet, she sensed they would not. Having been quite satisfied with his, she did not wish to look any further for a suitable match. Why should she when he was obviously perfect?

However, he did not appear to be nearly as taken with her. It seemed a terrible shame that her wish would never be granted. Having to look for someone as fine as General MacLauren when she reached London seemed an insurmountable task. Did such another man exist? She did not think so and suspected her season would be a failure.

She closed her eyes and resolved to stop thinking of him since he would ride out of her life at daybreak, and she was not about to chase after him. Besides, how could she hold strong feelings for him after knowing him less than an hour? *The Book of Love* spoke of connections and expectations, of threads of experiences shared by two people to bind them to each other.

She and the Scottish general had nothing in common.

So why could she not stop thinking of him?

After much tossing and turning, June finally fell asleep and was awakened at dawn by birds chirping outside her window. She rose to peer out, her thoughts immediately returning to General MacLauren.

She did not see him in front of the inn, nor anyone else for that matter. But it was early yet, and he might have delayed his departure in order to stop at the magistrate's office first. She opened the window to poke her head out of it. The light breeze felt warm against her face, and although the sun was only now rising above the horizon, it promised to be a fine day. No rain in sight, at least not for the morning.

Feeling restless, she donned her robe and slippers, unlatched the door, and walked quietly down the hall in the hope of peering over the railing to see if the Scottish soldiers were awake and perhaps gathered downstairs.

Her heart fluttered, for there they were, six of them quietly seated at a table in the common room having their morning coffee. She preferred tea, but the aroma of those roasted beans wafting upward toward her was quite heavenly.

She studied the men while they quietly chatted among themselves. They looked rugged in their uniforms, but none as handsome as General MacLauren.

She refused to think of him as Augustus, for that made him seem too real and approachable.

As though sensing her presence, he suddenly looked up. Her heart shot into her throat. He was ridiculously attractive, even with the slightly swollen corner of his lip and the noticeable bruising around his eye where the chair must have caught him. It hadn't been obvious last night. She hoped it did not pain him too badly.

Indeed, he looked magnificent, and she looked as though she had just stumbled out of bed. She hadn't even thought to brush her hair before walking out of her chamber, just left it in the loose braid she always fashioned before retiring for the evening.

However, he did not acknowledge her beyond a devastatingly piercing gaze before turning to one of his companions and whispering something to him. The man, who was a good bit older and more portly than the others, glanced up and smiled at her. It was an unexpectedly kind smile and caught her by surprise.

Uncertain what to do, she responded with a genuinely warm one of her own.

After that brief exchange, the kindly soldier and the magnificent man of her dreams simply returned their attention to their companions and thought no more of her. She stepped out of their line of sight, emitted a shaky breath, and leaned back against the wall for support as her body shuddered.

"Forget him, June." She closed her eyes and swallowed hard in an attempt to restore her composure.

What did she think would happen when he saw her again?

This battle-hardened, sophisticated army general had merely been tolerating her idiotic behavior last night. His stony expression this morning was a clear indication he wanted nothing more to do with her. She kept her eyes shut as she struggled to hold back her tears, not even understanding why she felt like crying over a veritable stranger.

They were nothing more than two travelers passing in the night, destined never to meet again. "Stupid book," she muttered, wishing she had never been given *The Book of Love*. She had read it and was keenly aware of the power in its words.

How could she now undo this understanding?

Having opened herself up to meeting the right man, she did not know how to shut her heart down now that she had met him. She knew it for a certainty. Everything about Augustus MacLauren drew her in, all five senses overwhelming her at once. The handsome look of his face. The masculine scent of him, leather and musk and clean, male heat.

And his voice…oh, that deep timbre and the hint of a brogue. He could read off a shopping list, and she would melt in a puddle just hearing him speak.

Not to mention the touch and taste of him when he'd kissed her, those strong arms swallowing her up and holding her close, and the taste of brandy on his lips as he'd deliciously explored and nibbled hers.

Sighing, she returned to her quarters. Her sisters were awake now, so they helped each other to dress, then packed their belongings and prepared for their own departure. Once June had finished, she went to check on Aunt Charlotte. "How are you feeling this morning?"

Her aunt was still abed, she noted with a frown. The shades were drawn to block out all the light. "Dreadful, June. I fear I cannot leave today."

She immediately went to her aunt's side. "What's wrong? A fever?"

But her forehead was merely warm to the touch, nothing out of the ordinary and certainly no cause for alarm.

"Just a headache, my dear. Perhaps it is the impending storm."

"What storm?" June frowned. "The day is sunny and clear."

"Not for long, according to the pounding in my head. My lumbago's acting up as well. Do be a dear and order breakfast brought up to my room. I won't be getting out of bed today. Will you make arrangements with Mr. Ashcott for another night's stay? And do let the ostler and our driver know not to prepare the carriage."

"Very well. Shall I also ask Mr. Ashcott to fetch a local doctor for you?"

"No, dear. Just let me rest."

June nodded and went to the door. "We'll take turns checking on you. I'll see if they have a bell for you to ring in the event you take a turn for the worse."

"Nonsense, that clanging will split my head in two. No need for a bell."

"All right." She was reluctant to leave her aunt in this condition, but sleep was often the best medicine, and Charlotte did not appear otherwise distressed.

She returned to her chamber to let Willow and Cammy know where she was going, then went downstairs and requested one of the maids to bring her aunt's breakfast up to her. "She prefers cocoa in the morning rather than coffee or tea."

"Right away, Miss Farthingale," the girl said with a pleasant smile.

"Thank you." June took a moment to glance around. The

common room was beginning to fill with other travelers ready to get on the road, but the Scottish soldiers, including General MacLauren, were gone.

She shook her head in silent admonition and went in search of the innkeeper's wife. She was in charge of the kitchen's busy staff, and this is where she found her. "Mrs. Ashcott…" She quickly relayed the situation and asked for all her aunt's meals to be brought up to her. "Please have the maids tread softly around her so as not to disturb her. My sisters and I will take turns checking on her, but if any of your staff notice she is in distress, please have them summon us immediately."

"Never you fret, Miss Farthingale. We'll take good care of her."

"Thank you, Mrs. Ashcott." She then found the woman's husband and asked about extending their stay.

"Of course," he said, obviously quite proud of the inn he ran. "Most of that noisy wedding party are clearing out today. We don't have another major affair until next week. There won't be a problem. Stay as long as you need."

She thanked Mr. Ashcott, as well, and then walked outside to enjoy the cool morning air. A light breeze surrounded her and ruffled the muslin of her travel gown. She brushed back a stray wisp of hair, for the breeze had also managed to blow a few curls out of place. But she did not mind, for, all in all, it was a glorious day. The sun was shining, and only a few tufts of white clouds hovered overhead to break up the vibrance of the blue sky.

No sign of this rain her aunt was predicting.

"Mr. Geoffries," she said to the ostler, who hurried out to greet her as she approached the stable, "my aunt is not feeling well. We are going to remain at the inn for another day. Will you please let our driver know?"

"Yes, Miss Farthingale, I will. 'Tis a pity Miss Charlotte is feeling poorly. Not everyone enjoys the bumps and jolts of the journey. M'own wife never could travel. Always upset her tender stomach. Ye let her know I hope she's feelin' better soon."

"I will tell her, thank you." She meant to return to the inn to meet her sisters for breakfast but lingered a moment longer to clear her head. However, she dared not tarry too long, knowing her sisters would worry about her.

After last night's incident, they were all on edge.

The enticing aroma of eggs, sausages, and freshly baked muffins from the inn's common room wafted outdoors and tickled her nostrils. It was far more tempting than the scent of horseflesh, hay, and stable muck. She realized she was hungry and could not wait to dig into the fare prepared by Mrs. Ashcott's cooks.

"Miss Farthingale," someone called to her as she made her way back to the inn.

She paused to glance behind her and was surprised to see General MacLauren striding toward her. Her traitorous senses exploded all at once. The mere sight of him had her heart caroming like a billiards ball upon the gaming table, crashing and reeling from side to side and knocking over everything in its path.

This man was simply too handsome for words. It wasn't merely his physical appearance, which was enough to have any woman's heart throbbing riotously. There was a depth of intelligence in his eyes and a quiet air of confidence about him, a reassurance that anyone under his protection would be safe.

It was an inner strength that sprang from his soul and could not be faked or denied.

It was there in his confident, commanding stride.

"General MacLauren," she said in a whispered breath, unable to contain her smile despite every effort to appear cool and unaffected.

Drat.

This was her obvious weakness, this inability to hide her thoughts and feelings. The words 'blank expression' could never apply to her. She showed everything, which is why she was considered a dreadful card player. One had only to look at her face to know whether the hand she held was a winner or a loser.

Since she hadn't been able to contain her smile, she allowed it to come forth with the full blast of its warmth. She was not ashamed of her feelings for him. Quite the opposite, she considered herself to be showing remarkable intelligence in selecting him as the man she wished to marry.

Goodness!

Perhaps she was rushing things a little.

More than a little.

She only wished he would show similar intelligence, not in offering to marry her. Of course, it was much too soon for that. But did he not wish to pursue their acquaintance in the hope it might turn into something more?

Crumpets. He did not appear to be considering her in this way at all.

Even the smartest men could be utter dolts when it came to love. "What happened, General MacLauren?" she asked, maintaining her smile as he strode toward her. "Where are your men? And why are you still here?"

CHAPTER THREE

AUGUSTUS HAD HOPED to run into June and at the same time dreaded seeing her again for the havoc she wreaked to his heart. What was it about this girl from Barnstaple that shook his foundations?

She was giving him that wide-eyed look of adoration again.

The very one that made him want to kiss her…deeply.

But years on the battlefield, followed by years in command of the peacetime Continental forces, had trained him to reveal nothing of his own thoughts. "My men rode ahead to Bath while I stopped next door to speak to Magistrate Brayden."

"Ah, to give your account of what happened last night," she said with a knowing nod, her head now slightly angled so that the sun glinted upon her lush, dark curls and brought out the sparkling blue of her eyes. "Brayden," she said with a pensive purse of her lips. "My sister mentioned his name last night. Several of my cousins are married to Braydens. I wonder if they are related. Probably not. The name is common enough."

"They could be." He tried not to stare at the fullness of her rosy lips, but it was hard to ignore them while she nibbled the gorgeously plump lower lip.

Which brought his mind reeling back to the kiss they had shared last night.

That kiss.

He'd thought himself so clever, expecting her to dart away

like a scared rabbit when he had proposed it, warned her it would happen if she did not scurry off. Too late, he had learned an important lesson.

June was no scared rabbit.

Indeed, she did not flinch nor did she so much as bat an eyelash when he took her in his arms and slowly dipped his head…and now, having tasted the honey sweetness of her mouth, all he wanted to do was kiss her again and again.

What was it about this girl that had him so beguiled?

He shook out of the thought. "I told the magistrate about the oafish behavior of those drunken sots toward you."

"But they did not manage to lay a hand on me because you stopped them. What about their attack on you?" She cast him a gentle look of censure. "I hope you did not make light of it. Although I expect you did if your stubborn expression is any indication." She reached up and lightly touched his face near the bruising around his eye. "I suppose the damage to your face told him all he needed to know. Does it hurt?"

"No."

She smiled wryly. "Would you admit it to me if it did?"

He chuckled. "No, I suppose not."

"I thought as much."

He tore his gaze away from her sparkling eyes and glanced toward the stables, knowing he ought to bid her good day and ride off if he wished to catch up to his companions before they reached Bath.

He should not be dawdling by her side.

"General MacLauren, will you—"

"Augustus." He brushed back one of her windblown curls and tucked it behind her ear, trying not to caress her cheek as he did so.

But he had no discipline when it came to June.

His knuckles grazed her soft skin.

She sighed. "Augustus, will you need to return to Taunton to give additional testimony?"

"Yes, it is likely. Ordinarily, the magistrate would consider it merely a drunken brawl, hold court, and impose a light sentence on those belligerent sots. But those scoundrels have been terrorizing the citizens of Taunton with impunity for several years now. This is his chance to have them bound over and tried in a Court of Assizes."

"Because they attacked you? Of course, you are the king's man. Continental commander. Attacking you is an attack on the king."

He nodded. "The assizes are held in Taunton only during the Lenten term, not usually in the Midsummer term, but these defendants are of sufficient stature and connections to warrant a special proceeding. The magistrate wants the trial held here in Taunton, not in Exeter as it would normally be held. Apparently, this magistrate is quite influential in the area and has already started making arrangements for court to be held here. It is not out of the way for the Ridings judge."

Her ensorcelling gaze had him riveted to the spot. Worse, she had no idea how beautiful she was or the effect she was having on him. Despite his best efforts, he found it impossible to summon the will to leave. "For this reason, he has asked me to return once I've concluded my meetings in Bath."

"Obviously hoping your testimony will finally allow him to punish those churls and put them behind bars where they belong." June frowned. "Will their families allow it? Are they not well connected?"

"I imagine they will raise bloody hell, pardon my language. But those men deserve to be taken down a peg. Even if they are set free, at the very least, they will be heavily fined."

"What makes you so certain they won't escape monetary punishment as well?"

"For one thing, my testimony cannot be dismissed or ignored. No one in their family will dare intimidate me for fear of being summoned before the king. I am not merely one of his highest-ranking representatives. He and I are on quite good terms."

June's eyes widened. "You are?"

He nodded, now irritated with himself for mentioning it. He was no green youth hoping to impress a beauty by boasting of his royal connections. He had only meant to indicate that those knaves and their connections paled in comparison to his own. "His Majesty and I have known each other a long time."

"You are friends?"

"I would like to think so. Perhaps he considers me more of a trusted confidante. We dine together often when I am in London. But I would never involve him in something so petty, nor would I ever ask him to intercede. Those oafs don't need to know it. Quaking in fear over the possible consequences will do them good."

She laughed.

Gad, even her laughter was charming, like a soft ripple upon the breeze.

"I hope those wretches are now on their knees casting up their accounts," she joked. "They ought to be trembling in their boots. Serves them right for terrorizing innocent guests."

"Well, if the judge won't impose a harsh enough sentence, I'll set you and that hearth iron loose on them again. You wielded it with fiery magnificence. Better than any Viking shield-maiden. Better than my best dragoons could ever wield their swords."

"A bit of an exaggeration, don't you think?" She blushed but was obviously pleased by the compliment he had not meant to give her. It seemed his brain turned to boiled oats where June was involved. "Thank you, Augustus."

He caressed her cheek again, yet another thing he had not meant to do, but he did it anyway. Yes, boiled, grainy oat mush for brains. "I had better be on my way. I suppose you will be leaving soon for London."

Her expression turned thoughtful. "Not today. Aunt Charlotte isn't feeling well, so we will be here at least another night."

"I see. Has a doctor seen her yet?"

"No, she claims to be merely suffering a megrim and does not believe there is anything to be done about it. She'll rest today and hopefully be restored by tomorrow. My sisters and I will keep close watch over her to be sure there isn't something more serious going on."

"I hope there is nothing more. As for you and your sisters, be careful walking around town. Do not wander off on your own. The magistrate may have no choice but to set those oafs free pending trial."

"We'll be careful and stick together. I doubt we will stray far from the inn. If we do go anywhere, we'll make sure to have our driver accompany us."

He ached to kiss her. "See that you do. I wouldn't like anything bad to happen to my *Tallulah*."

She gave a laughing groan. "I am starting to hate that name. I shall issue the same warning to you. Be careful on your travels. I would not like anything bad to happen to my test frog." She placed a hand on his arm. "Oh, Augustus, please do not be angry with me. But I cannot keep my feelings bottled in."

His blood caught fire.

She did not need to tell him anything, for he could see into her heart as though she were made of delicate glass, her every feeling, her every hope and dream open to his view with crystalline clarity. "Please look me up if you happen to come to London. We are staying with our Uncle John and Aunt Sophie on Chipping Way. The Farthingales of Chipping Way. Will you remember this?"

He nodded, for he was not likely ever to forget a thing about her. "Yes, June. But do not hope for things that cannot be. After my meetings in Bath, I will return here just long enough to give testimony, then I am bound for home. Caithness. Do you know where it is?"

"No."

"In the Highlands. North of Edinburgh. North of Aberdeen. North of Inverness. A lifetime away from London."

"I see. Then I wish you safe travels and a happy life, Augustus. I do not think I shall ever find a better replacement for my test frog. I am glad to have met you, even if it was for such a short while. I had better not stand here any longer, or I shall make a fool of myself and cry." She turned abruptly and hurried inside the inn.

He felt her absence like a stab to the heart.

He was going to miss his *Tallulah*.

The ostler brought out his gray as he strode to the stable. "General MacLauren, it was a pleasure to meet ye, sir. And Titan here is one of the finest horses I've ever beheld." He patted the big gray affectionately. "Beautiful, massive beast."

"Yes, he is a champion. Kept me alive in battle, for certain." He mounted, feeling quite at home in the saddle, as any soldier in the Scots Greys would. Their horses were an extension of themselves, man and beast moving as one on the battlefield, instinctively understanding what the other needed, darting and dodging, keeping each other alive. "I'll be back in a few days, Mr. Geoffries."

"I look forward to tending Titan again." He stroked the horse's nose. "Too bad Miss Farthingale and her family will be gone by then. Pretty thing, she is. And she seems to have taken quite a fancy to you. But I suppose all women do."

He bid Mr. Geoffries good day and rode off, unwilling to engage in further chatter, especially about June. He was already wondering whether he had made a serious mistake in not pursuing her.

But he dismissed the possibility.

One did not change the course of one's life over a chance meeting.

Still, the notion of her toting that big, red book around and trying out her experiments on anyone else had him frowning.

He would have enjoyed being her test frog.

Perhaps if she were still in Taunton when he returned…

He caught up to his men not far from Glastonbury.

They merely exchanged brief greetings before riding hard toward Bath. Since Augustus hoped to reach the lively resort town before darkness fell, they saved their chatter until stopping at a roadside watering spot to rest their horses and grab a meal for themselves.

Augustus was pensive as he handed his mount to the ostler at the Red Rose Tavern. "See that all the horses are properly watered and fed."

"Aye, General MacLauren. Ye need have no worries about these grand beasts. They'll be well-tended."

Since the day remained sunny and pleasant, he led his men to one of the tables in the tavern's garden and ordered ales and cottage pies for all of them. The tavern owner had boasted his cottage pie was the finest to be found in England.

"He's right," said Augustus taking a bite once the dish had been brought out to them. "This is delicious."

"The ale's decent, too," said Jock Sinclair, a colonel in the Scots Greys and his highest-ranking aide among his own retinue. "Not bad for an English libation."

"Still piss compared to our Scottish brews," grumbled another of his aides, a weathered old soldier with bright red hair and a portly build by the name of Angus MacKay. He was one of his best sergeants, strong as an ox and still as spry as any of the younger soldiers within the regiments under his command. With the added benefit of his experience, Augustus had come to value his advice above those of his other aides. "What did the magistrate have to say to ye, laddie?"

Augustus waited for the serving maid to bring another round of ale and leave them to themselves before responding. "Magistrate Brayden wants me back to give testimony when the judge arrives in Taunton at the end of the week. I'll return there once our business in Bath is concluded."

Angus nodded. "And I'll come with ye."

His other four companions agreed.

Jock nodded. "We'll all come back with ye. A few more days

delay in getting home won't matter."

Hamish Sinclair, the youngest among them, took a swig of his ale and then smacked his mug down on the table. "Aye. We rode into battle together, and we'll ride home to Caithness together."

Augustus held up his hands in surrender. "Very well. But I will not hold it against any of you if you happen to have a change of heart."

Angus tossed him an irreverent look. "We're not abandoning ye."

"Fine. Didn't I just agree?" He arched an eyebrow at the old soldier who ought to have retired from service years ago. But Angus was not the sort ever to set roots, so the army had become his home.

They left the tavern and rode fast the rest of the way to Bath, reaching it by late evening. With the hottest months of the year approaching, the town was already filled with Londoners settling into the elegant crescents and tree-lined squares to enjoy the waters, assembly halls, and other entertainments offered in the lively town each summer.

His thoughts once again turned to June and the fun they might have had if he had brought her here. Of course, that was never going to happen.

In any event, taking the waters would be something done more for their amusement than for treatment of medical ailments. However, her Aunt Charlotte might have benefitted from a sojourn here.

He considered bringing back a few bottles of the spa waters for the aunt, but June and her family would be long gone by the time he returned to Taunton. "Botheration," he muttered, silently chiding himself for allowing the beautiful Barnstaple lass to steal into his thoughts yet again.

He acquired lodgings for himself and his men not far from one of Bath's popular pump rooms. Once settled in their quarters, he and Angus went next door to a pub called the Landsdown

Quarry to slake their thirst. Their younger companions joined them for a round and then set off to find themselves women to slake their other desires. "Ye needn't stay here to keep me company, lad," Angus said as the others rose to leave.

"You're not holding me back, Angus." But this could prove to be an even bigger bother, for he found himself having no desire for female companionship. Well, he would not have refused June's company. In truth, all he wanted was her company.

This would pose a problem since he was not likely ever to see her again unless he did something about it.

"Ah, it's the pretty lass with the dark hair and big, blue eyes ye left at the Ashcott Inn that ye're wanting something fierce." Angus patted him none too gently on the back. "Ye know where to find her. She gave ye her direction in London, did she not?"

"I'm returning to Caithness."

His crusty companion shrugged. "What does it matter if ye delay yer return another few weeks? Caithness is just a big pile of rocks and valleys, cold enough in winter to freeze the cheeks off yer arse. Seems to me, the lass is worth pursuing."

"No, I need to get home and see Grandda." The man he called Grandda was actually his granduncle, the Earl of Caithness. He'd taken in Augustus and his brother, Thad, when they were younger, raised them after their parents had died. Well, Thad was his half-brother, the offspring of their father and his second wife, a good woman who had treated Augustus as though he were her own son.

He had been fortunate, for losing his own mother had been hard on him. Then to lose Thad's mother as well, soon followed by the loss of their father, had been difficult on all of them. His cousins Malcolm and Robbie had experienced a similar loss.

The Earl of Caithness had taken them all in, treated the four of them as though they were his sons. He could not insult the earl by going to London instead of returning home to the Highlands.

He could never be disrespectful to his grandda.

Angus, sensing the finality of his decision, did not belabor the point. Instead, he turned the conversation to tomorrow's meetings. They would no doubt center on more discussions about Lord Castlereagh's declining health and hints of his paranoia.

Augustus had already been in contact with Lord Liverpool about Castlereagh's growing liability to England, not only at home but on the Continent where efforts to maintain peace were vital and already strained, especially with the Austrians and the Russians.

In truth, he was worried that tomorrow's meetings would result in a command to immediately return to Vienna. He would refuse if this were so. He needed to return to Caithness. Short of a declaration of war, he would not be dissuaded from going home. Besides, even in poor health, Castlereagh was more competent than most politicians in their prime.

He gulped down the last of his ale and left the tavern with Angus.

Women approached them.

Angus succumbed and left with two of them.

Augustus returned to his quarters alone, suddenly wondering whether he should have been so quick to dismiss June from his thoughts.

He laughed at the notion, his voice echoing in the dark.

Obviously, she had not been dismissed so easily, if at all, since he was still dwelling on her.

Not merely dwelling but bordering on obsessing over her now that he was no longer in her company.

He undressed and fell naked into bed, his body aroused and his heart feeling emptier than it had ever felt.

What in blazes was he going to do about June?

He had always expected to marry, perhaps had put it off longer than necessary. But as top aide to Castlereagh, and possibly about to take over Castlereagh's duties as foreign minister in addition to peacetime commander of the Royal Scots Greys, he could aim much higher than Miss Juniper Farthingale from Barnstaple.

Several European princes from long-established royal families had already indicated willingness should he offer for one of their daughters.

In truth, he could have done so at any time over these past few years. Offered for an Austrian princess and sired little archdukes and duchesses, for even though he was not in the royal line, the princess he would take as his wife was likely to be.

He settled on his back and gazed up at the old, beamed ceiling, barely making out the outline of the wooden beams in the drenching darkness.

He never minded the darkness, for he liked to think in the quiet of the night.

It was a habit gained on the battlefield when all he had to remind himself that beauty still existed were the abundant stars and the silver glow of the moon shining overhead. He would look to the sky on those cool, crisp nights and momentarily forget the pain and hardship of war, the senseless brutality and losses, the stench of death.

The truth always came out in the inky blackness.

But not all truth was bad.

At times, he would recall memories of his youth, of happier days spent in his beloved Highlands. Those memories kept him going, kept him sane.

Those early years came back to him now, the carefree life he enjoyed as a boy when he and Thad would clamber up the hills like mountain goats and spend hours looking out across the rugged crags and green, grassy glens. They'd watch hawks circle overhead in hunt for prey and boast to each other about what they would make of their lives.

Thad had been the fiery one.

He had always been the deliberate one.

Perhaps too deliberate.

Yes, that had been him. Always too cautious. Never leaping before he had thought everything through.

Thad's fire had made him an excellent field general, while his need to consider every angle to the last detail had made him an excellent strategic commander and now a Continental diplomat.

He sighed and threw one arm over his brow.

"Damn it," he muttered, knowing what was going to happen tomorrow. The high-ranking government ministers present at the meeting would ask him to take over Castlereagh's foreign ministry duties immediately. There was no other reason why he had been ordered to Bath instead of allowed to ride straight home.

He would accept, but not until he first spent time at home.

His soul was empty.

He felt it acutely now.

The war had damaged him, just as it had so many men. His heart was torn and his body in need of nourishment that could only be provided by loving family and a return to clean, mountain air, the drafty, stone walls of Dornach Castle, and the tang of salt air off the North Sea.

He wanted to be surrounded by ornery Scots who spoke in thick brogues even he would have trouble understanding after all these years in cultured society. He was eager to drink bootleg whisky and eat oatcakes and haggis till his stomach revolted.

And yet, as his thoughts wandered from Europe to the Highlands and back to here, June kept popping up and seeming to fit in wherever his life had taken him and would ever take him.

He hardly knew her.

They had shared one kiss.

One breathtaking, irresistible kiss that had his heart pounding at the mere recollection of her soft, pliable lips pressed to his, at first with hesitancy and then with wonder. Yes, it was her sense of wonder, the innocence and delight shimmering in her bright eyes that had made their kiss memorable and spectacular.

The delightful feel of her body, too.

"Stop thinking about her," he muttered, knowing he needed to dwell on tomorrow's meetings. He had to hone his strategy when dealing with these English politicians, for the slightest misstep, and they would box him into a corner.

He managed to spend most of the night pondering what he would say, anticipating the questions likely to be posed, and laying it all out in his mind like a chessboard. If Lord Havestock said this, then he would respond with that. Same for Lord Ballinger, one of the highest-ranking ministers in the Exchequer. That lord was a sharp one, and it would take all his concentration not to be trapped by him.

After having played out the chess game in his head, he allowed his thoughts to drift back to June. His low brain, as June had described from her silly book, was still in a frenzy over her. Lying alone in bed, his mind awhirl and his body unfulfilled only made his ache for her more acute.

Lord, he would be eaten alive tomorrow if he did not get her out of his brain. Low brain and high. He needed to banish her from his thoughts completely. "Hah, that is no' going to happen."

He fell asleep with his body in taut, raw torment.

He woke up early the next morning, washed, dressed, and went downstairs to the inn's common room for breakfast. He did not bother to wait for one of the serving maids to attend to him, instead grabbing the nearby pot of coffee and pouring himself a cup to clear his head.

He was on his second cup by the time his men staggered down one by one.

Jock groaned and collapsed on the chair beside him. "I'm getting too old for this."

Augustus merely arched an eyebrow, not bothering to chide any of his companions over their ragged state. They had been too long without women and obviously overindulged last night. There was no harm since only he was to meet with Lord Liverpool's ministers an hour from now.

His men would have the day to themselves to recover from their excessive revelry. "Behave yourselves, lads. I may have need of you before the meeting's end."

"We'll be all spit and polish," Angus assured him, casting a frown at each of their companions. "We'll be waiting here for ye, dressed in our uniforms and fit for presentation."

Jock laughed. "Aye, wouldn't dare contradict old Angus."

"Old, am I?" He set down his coffee cup with a clatter. "Come outside with me, and my fists will show ye just how much life there is still left in me."

Augustus rolled his eyes. "That is exactly what I am talking about. Behave, all of you."

The MacKays, Sinclairs, and MacLaurens were all neighboring clans within the Earl of Caithness's holdings. What had once been bitter rivalries were no more than friendly jesting now, and Augustus meant to keep it that way.

The war against Napoleon had bound them together. So had their years in Vienna after the war while on their diplomatic mission. But now that they were returning home, their Scottish natures were coming to the forefront. Without a common enemy to bind them, they would descend into petty squabbles unless he kept them in line.

"See you later." He finished his breakfast and rose to meet Lord Ballinger and Lord Havestock. They were waiting for him at Lord Ballinger's magnificent townhouse on one of those elegant crescents.

They'd obviously started their meeting earlier and had been discussing him if their guilty looks as he strode in were any indication.

Damn.

"Good morning, my lords. I can see this will be more than a general discussion of Lord Castlereagh's failing health or our foreign policy aims. Shall we get right to the point? What are you going to demand of me?"

CHAPTER FOUR

"How is Aunt Charlotte feeling now?" Willow asked June the moment she walked out of their aunt's guest chamber with her lips pursed and frowning.

"Her headache is gone, but she now claims she has put out her back and cannot travel by carriage over those bumpy roads." What had started as a day's delay had now turned into three with no hint of them ever resuming their journey to London because of Charlotte's ever-shifting ailments.

Cammy had also been standing outside their aunt's door and now chimed in. "One would think she is purposely stalling."

June nodded. "It seems so, doesn't it? But what reason would she have to keep us in Taunton? It isn't as though there is anything for us here."

Cammy and Willow exchanged glances.

"What?" June folded her arms across her chest, impatient for their response.

Willow spoke up. "General MacLauren is due back, perhaps as early as today."

"Everyone knows how taken you were with him," Cammy added.

She groaned.

Yes, of course.

Her inability to hide her feelings.

Everyone at the Ashcott Inn had to know by now and be

laughing about it. The thought of General MacLauren reciprocating her feelings was ludicrous. He had been amusing himself at her expense by claiming that kiss.

Well, she had been the one to push him to it.

He was an honorable man and would not have kissed her had she not put herself forward shamelessly. That his low brain was obviously approving of her meant nothing. He would have kissed any number of women had any of them behaved as foolishly as she had done.

Getting him to accept her at the high brain level was the impossible task.

It did not matter whether he would be back today or tomorrow or not return at all. He was not keen to see her, nor was she eager to make a fool of herself over him again.

She returned to their bedchamber and took out *The Book of Love*.

Cammy giggled. "How many times have you read it since General MacLauren left us?"

Willow snickered and gave her a playful nudge. "Don't wear it out before it comes to me."

"Nonsense. The two of you have already been reading it over my shoulder. And we've been discussing it, dissecting it, studying it 'til the words are pouring out of our ears."

Willow took her hand, her manner more sympathetic. "Has it helped you?"

"I don't know. I thought I would use the time to try out some of the theories on someone other than General MacLauren, but my heart simply is not in it. No one appeals to me. Not even the magistrate or his deputy, and they're both handsome men and probably quite trustworthy." She sighed. "But they aren't *him*. Oh, what am I to do? This is hopeless."

She tried to hand the book to Willow. "Here, perhaps you can make better use of it."

Her sister refused to take it. "No. It is still your turn."

"Did you know the magistrate and his deputy are brothers?"

Cammy shoved the book back at June when she tried to hand it off to her next. "And he isn't really his deputy. Apparently, he is merely visiting. He is an agent for the Crown. Isn't that exciting?"

Willow rolled her eyes. "Thrilling. But he cannot be working in secret since everyone seems to know what he does."

"Fine, be sarcastic. He isn't a spy. He's a tracker. As good as any bloodhound, they say. But they are handsome men, aren't they, June? Especially the magistrate's brother. His name is Lorcan Brayden. He's a bit of an ogre. All he does is frown at me whenever I try to talk to him."

Willow laughed. "The magistrate is no different. He grunts whenever I try to talk to him. No wonder Aunt Charlotte is always warning us that men are apes. Who can be married to a man whose only conversation is to grunt at you? At least General MacLauren can string two words together in a sentence."

Cammy nodded. "I tried to ask Lorcan if he was related to the London Braydens who married our cousins, but he ignored the question. Can you believe it? Well, I'm not going to ask him again. If we are somehow connected through marriage, I would rather not know it."

"Enough about men," June said with determination and tucked the book back in her travel bag. "There are plenty of other things to occupy our minds. Let's enjoy the day. Mr. Ashcott mentioned at breakfast that there will be a Midsummer's Eve party held here tonight for the inn's guests. He thought it would be fun for all of us to participate. We are all to wear masks, and there will be musicians and dancing. It is safer than the wilder celebrations certain to take place in town this evening."

Her sisters hurried after her as she marched out of their chamber and went downstairs.

"Shall we go into town this morning as we planned?" Cammy gave a slight shudder. "I don't like the thought of those three rogues who attacked you and General MacLauren being on the loose. Did you hear? They've been released. I suppose the magistrate had no choice but to set them free after the Earl of

Monkton intervened and demanded it."

"This is why he is hoping General MacLauren will return," Willow added. "Whether he does or not, we cannot remain in hiding forever."

June nodded. "I agree."

Those churls, having been set free, would likely be up to more mischief tonight. Hopefully, it would only be harmless mischief since they were to stand before the judge in a matter of days and could not be so foolish as to add more charges against them.

She had learned the names of these miscreants when Magistrate Brayden had come by to take her testimony. He'd told her a little about them. Their leader was Lord Belfy, brother of the Earl of Monkton. The other two were his cousins, Lord Mercer and Lord Hurst. All three of them had been sent down from Oxford, apparently due to their insatiable enjoyment of pranks and debauching instead of attention to their university studies.

Rumor had it the Earl of Monkton was livid with the three of them and had now cut off their allowances. No doubt those wastrels were too busy trying to get back in his good graces to dare cause more mischief. Not that she believed them to be truly repentant. They would behave themselves only long enough for their lives of ease to be restored.

One's true nature did not change. Zebras did not magically lose their stripes, nor leopards lose their spots. These men were what they were, and no polished facade would hide their wicked hearts.

June wanted nothing to do with them. If she encountered them in town, she would cross the street and walk in the opposite direction.

It was a beautiful day, much nicer than the last two, which had been constantly raining. Aunt Charlotte's megrim had not been a ruse after all, although June was still suspicious of the other ailments their aunt had come up with.

She and her sisters needed to get out and stretch their legs a bit. "Let's do a little shopping. Perhaps pick up a trinket or two for tonight's party."

Cammy clapped her hands. "An excellent idea. I'd love a stroll along the High Street. We can browse the shops and stop for a lemon ice afterward. I wonder if any shops carry faerie wings."

Willow nodded with enthusiasm. "Oh, yes! Such fun. Would it be too scandalous if we wore our hair down for the party? After all, it is Midsummer's Eve, and we would have our masks on."

June laughed. "I doubt we shall fool anyone with our disguises. But I see no harm in it if we are to remain at the inn."

She patted the tight coil of her hair, eager to take out the pins and shake it loose. Not now, of course. They had to look proper while in town. They would take their carriage driver, Mr. Pierson, with them as an escort, of course. That ought to keep them safe enough.

It was not long before she left the inn with her sisters and Mr. Pierson. The four of them made their way past the magistrate's office on their walk into the heart of town. The Ashcott Inn was conveniently located close to the main shopping streets, so they did not have very far to walk.

Magistrate Brayden was just coming out of his office as they passed by. He strode toward them. "Good day, Miss Farthingale," he said, politely greeting her first and then turning to her sisters. "Miss Willow. Miss Cammy. Where are you headed?"

"Just down the street to the shops." June took his arm when he held it out to her. "Were you going that way, too?"

He grunted but said nothing more.

She smothered a chuckle and took it for a yes.

Willow and Cammy walked in front of them, and Mr. Pierson trailed slightly behind. He wasn't used to serving as chaperone, and it was obvious to all that he wished to be anywhere but herding young ladies out for a day of shopping.

Willow did not look all that happy either. She kept glancing back at June and the magistrate. June smothered another chuckle, knowing her sister all too well. Despite referring to the magistrate as a grumbling ape, Willow liked the man. Of course, she would walk over a bed of nails before admitting it. But it was obvious Willow wished to be the one holding onto his arm.

Well, it was a good, solid arm.

But it wasn't Augustus MacLauren's arm. Nor did June respond at all to his good looks or muscular frame. Odd, really. Shayne Brayden had dark hair and attractively dark, silver-gray eyes. She ought to have felt something, shouldn't she?

Her lack of response only made obvious what her heart had known from the first. She was in love with General MacLauren. It still did not bear admitting to anyone, for how could she be so certain considering their short acquaintance?

Willow glanced back again.

Poor Willow.

Was it worth the effort to think up a way to change places with her when they had such a short way to go?

Yes, of course, it was. She would do anything for her sisters. "Oh, Cammy! I just remembered…" She turned to the magistrate and eased her arm out of his. "Please excuse me a moment."

She dragged Cammy further ahead, purposely leaving Magistrate Brayden no choice but to offer his arm to Willow, which he did because he was a gentleman at heart.

One did not have to be glib or speak in flowery prose to be gallant. Shayne Brayden was the protective, taciturn sort who usually grunted instead of spoke full sentences, but he was never going to leave Willow to walk on her own.

He was the sort of man who would risk his life to protect the weak and vulnerable should harm befall them. Not that she, Willow, or Cammy fell into that category. They had been raised to think for themselves and not cower from a fight.

Cammy laughingly snorted as they hurried ahead. "You are shameful, June. I'm sure Mr. Brayden knows exactly what you are doing."

"Does he appear miffed?"

Cammy accidentally dropped her handkerchief as a ruse to

look back. "No. His face is expressionless. How do men do this? For all we know, he could be madly in love with her, or he could loathe her beyond reason. His face gives away nothing. And ours show everything."

June pulled Cammy along as soon as she had tucked her handkerchief back in her sleeve. "Some women are good at hiding their feelings. I'm sure we'll encounter many of those cool, sophisticated Incomparables once we reach London. I think we must practice those looks. You know, that slightly glazed stare, as though looking beyond one's partner in conversation and seemingly bored with the world."

"Oh, yes. Let's practice that look. Do it now, June. Look at me as though I am beneath your notice."

The attempt was ridiculously unsuccessful.

June tried; she really did. But it took less than the count of three for her to burst into laughter. She gave Cammy a hug. "Oh, abject failure!"

"What are you doing?" the magistrate asked.

"Trying to look sophisticated," Cammy blurted before June could stop her.

He almost cracked a smile in response. "Cold and imperious is not sophisticated."

"Then what is?" Willow asked.

"Grace under pressure. Kindness. Courtesy. Compassion." He cast all three of them a stern glance. "Just be yourselves. Do not pretend to be someone you're not."

Willow pursed her lips. "What are you saying? That men will fall at our feet if we show no polish? How can that be? We'll be laughed out of London."

"I'm not saying that at all. I'm suggesting that if you wish to find the right man for yourself, then just be yourself. How will he know to find you if you hide who you truly are?"

June stared at her sisters, the three of them looking a bit sheepish. What he had said made more sense than anything the three of them had been spouting just now. "Thank you, Mr.

Brayden. I suppose you've noticed we are completely out of our depth and not happy to be pushed onto the marriage mart."

He nodded. "Just keep your eyes open when in London. I've seen enough of these supposedly elegant gentlemen to know they are not to be trusted."

"And are you to be trusted?" Willow asked.

"Depends." Steel glinted in his dark gray eyes.

"On what?" Willow persisted.

"The situation."

Willow stared back at him. "Care to elaborate?"

"No."

Willow looked outraged, but June and Cammy could not help but laugh. Apparently, he was done talking. Having dropped his pearls of wisdom, he was now back to merely grunting.

He left them in front of a quaint ladies' shop, warned them once more to be careful, and proceeded to wherever he had been going before encountering them. Mr. Pierson remained standing outside the shop while they browsed along the aisles.

"May I help you, ladies?" A pretty woman of middle age and lightly graying hair scurried out of the back room to greet them.

Cammy smiled at the woman. "We were looking for faerie wings."

"Or perhaps just some pretty clips for our hair," June said, suddenly thinking their idea of dressing up might be rather silly, even for Midsummer's Eve.

"Don't back out now, June. It must be faerie wings for us." Willow cast her a stubborn look before turning back to the shopkeeper. "We are guests at the Ashcott Inn. Mr. Ashcott is having a quiet party for the inn's guests and will be handing out masks to all of us. We thought it might be fun to add a touch of magic."

The woman smiled amiably and clapped her hands. "Oh, that is lovely! I don't have any wings ready-made but I have these lovely bolts of cloth just received from the Farthingale mills. They make the finest cloth in England."

June grinned at her sisters. "We know, Mrs…er…"

"Albright. Mrs. Lucinda Albright's the name."

"A pleasure to meet you. We happen to be quite familiar with these mills. You see, we are Farthingales, as well. As a matter of fact, we are on our way to London to stay with our uncle, John Farthingale, and his wife, Sophie. Do you perhaps know our Uncle Rupert? He's the one who does most of the traveling for the business."

Her eyes brightened. "Indeed, I do. A very fine gentleman. Always fair. Never cheats his customers and never provides inferior goods. A man of his word, he is. Come, have a look. The fabric is as light as gossamer, and I can easily make wings out of them. What color gowns do you plan on wearing tonight?"

"Mine is a bluish-green, like the color of the ocean," June said.

"Mine is lilac," Cammy added.

Willow spoke last. "Mine is tea rose."

The woman drew out the bolts to match their gowns. "I'll add stays at the top so your faerie wings will hold up. All you will need to do is clasp the wings to the back of your gown. Here, I have some lovely, jeweled clasps for you to peruse. They aren't real gemstones, of course."

June smiled at her. "Oh, they're perfect. And look at these shiny threads. We'll take some of these seed pearls, too. We can wind the pearls and glittering threads in our hair."

"And make circlets of flowers, too," Cammy said. "I noticed a meadow beyond the Ashcott Inn garden. We can pick wildflowers there."

"What about Aunt Charlotte?" Willow asked. "Should we have wings made for her?"

The three of them burst out laughing.

June wiped a mirthful tear from her eyes. "Good heavens, no! Can you imagine Charlotte in faerie wings? As it is, she'll grumble at the need to wear a mask."

"Assuming she is able to make it downstairs now that she has supposedly thrown out her back." Willow nibbled her lip. "Oh, that is mean of me. But I cannot help feeling that her ever-shifting illnesses are contrived."

June agreed. "I think so, too. But do we really mind the delay?"

Willow shook her head. "No. I like it here."

They returned their attention to the shopkeeper, who was once again fussing around them after bringing out more wares to sell.

Cammy selected a bracelet, and Willow chose a necklace.

June removed her coin purse from her reticule and paid for everything.

"I'll pack up your purchases and will have the wings ready in two hours, perhaps sooner. Enjoy the rest of your shopping, in the meanwhile. Mrs. Guinn runs a lovely tea shop just down the street if you find yourself hungry later."

After thanking her profusely, the three of them walked out, chattering excitedly. Cammy raised her arms and began to flit like a butterfly. "I cannot wait to see the wings, can you? We'll have such fun tonight."

June cast her an indulgent smile, for their youngest sister had always been a bit of a free spirit. Of all of them, Cammy would be the one to feel most confined by the rigid rules of London society. This assumed they would ever make it to London since their Aunt Charlotte had endless excuses to keep them in Taunton.

They walked along the street, Mr. Pierson obviously bored but dutifully staying close to them. After browsing a few more shops, they stopped at Mrs. Guinn's charming tea shop. Mr. Pierson went across the street to a respectable enough looking tavern for a pint of ale.

They happened to encounter the magistrate as they left the tea shop. He was walking back to his office and accompanied them to pick up their purchases along the way.

He frowned at Mr. Pierson, who appeared to have imbibed quite heartily. "Your responsibility was to guard the ladies."

"And that's just what I did, yer honor," he said defensively, although his hiccups somewhat diminished the effect of his indignation.

"Go back to the stables and sober up, Mr. Pierson. I'll escort the young ladies back to the inn." He watched as their driver stalked back to the tavern instead, muttering something about not being hired as a governess.

Magistrate Brayden was livid when he turned to June and her sisters. "Come to me if ever you wish to go into town. I don't think your coach driver can be trusted to protect you."

"We are not delicate flowers," Willow insisted. "We can take care of ourselves."

He folded his arms across his chest and scowled at Willow. "You don't know those men as I do. Lord Belfy in particular. He's a nasty one. I would not like you to learn your lesson the hard way."

"You're right, of course," June said, also scowling at her sister. "We have no intention of running off on our own. Do we, Willow?"

"No," she muttered.

Mr. Brayden said nothing, merely arched an eyebrow, then led them into the shop. He greeted the shopkeeper and tried not to laugh when he learned what it was they had come back to retrieve. "Wings?"

"For Midsummer's Eve," Cammy said. "We wanted to get into the party spirit."

June cast him a wry smile. "Will you be stopping by the inn this evening?"

He managed another of his almost smiles. "I think I must, if only out of curiosity. But only for a short while. I am certain to have my hands full with the revelers who will be out in the streets tonight."

Cammy frowned. "Can you and your brother manage an entire town on your own?"

"Lorcan and I will manage just fine. We've handled rougher assignments."

"You have?" Willow's eyes brightened. "Here in Taunton? It does not seem like a wild town. The townspeople we've met have been quite nice, other than those three miscreants my sister and General MacLauren encountered."

"It is a quiet town for the most part. No, my assignments were elsewhere. Lorcan and I were agents for the Crown. Lorcan is still on active duty, but I retired from service several years ago."

"Why is that?" Willow asked.

He shrugged. "I got tired of getting shot at."

Cammy put a hand over her heart and gasped. "Oh, my. That is dangerous."

"It is one thing to be shot at on a battlefield. One can understand the enemy shooting at you. But to be home and encountering English traitors, men who would betray even their loved ones for coin…" He shook his head and sighed. "My anger almost got me killed on that last assignment. Took me months to recover from my wounds."

"And now that you've recovered, you serve as Taunton's magistrate," Willow said with a nod.

"Something like that," he muttered. "I'll also have my regular force on night watch duties this evening. They are all good men and trained. But this does not mean you should venture out. Stay at the inn tonight, and you'll be safe."

The magistrate insisted on escorting them inside the inn when they arrived. June noticed he was frowning as he bid them good day. "What's wrong, Mr. Brayden?"

"I just don't like that driver of yours, Mr. Pierson. The man is a tippler, that's all. Not unusual in his line of work. Still, I don't like the idea of him being responsible for delivering you to London."

She cast him a wry smile. "We're here for another few days if Aunt Charlotte has any say in the matter."

He cast her a genuine smile. "Ah, I noticed her shifting illnesses. Well, don't forget my offer. I'll be busy this evening, but if any of you ever have need of an escort, just pop next door to my office. One of my men or I will walk you to wherever you need to go."

"Thank you, Mr. Brayden." June spared a glance at Willow to silently warn her not to spout off again about how capable Farthingale women were in defending themselves.

Perhaps he was being a little too protective since even he had admitted Taunton was for the most part a quiet town. But she appreciated his attentiveness. Lord Belfy and his cousins were not harmless. She did not want Willow forgetting those unpleasant gentlemen had been released from custody and were now on the loose.

They could not be trusted even if they were unlikely to cause more trouble now that the Earl of Monkton had cut off their funds. They were obviously weasels and not averse to causing mischief if they thought they could get away with it.

That the judge would be here in a day or two to mete out punishment would not hold them back.

She bid the magistrate good day, resolving to have a more extended conversation with him after this nasty affair was over. Since Lorcan had not been forthcoming at all with Cammy, they had not probed further about their connection to the London Braydens who had married their cousins.

No matter, she would ask him before they left for London.

She made her way up to the chamber she shared with her sisters, her thoughts immediately turning to Augustus now that the shopping excursion was over and no longer distracting her.

How soon before he returned to Taunton?

She hoped it would be tonight. It seemed silly, but she wanted him to see her in her faerie wings and mask, to see her with her hair loose and flowing, and silken threads wound through her curls.

Would he enjoy the sight of her in her costume?

Was he thinking of her at all?

Her sisters followed her upstairs. They dropped off their purchases, and all three went to visit their Aunt Charlotte. She was sitting up in bed, appearing quite comfortable as she read a book and leisurely sipped her cup of hot cocoa.

She did not seem to be in any discomfort.

June eyed her dubiously.

"Ah, girls. Did you have a nice time in town? Show me what you purchased."

Cammy hurried back to their room and returned with their packages. "Will you join us downstairs for the party later, Aunt Charlotte? We thought about buying wings for you as well—"

"My dear girl! I am far too old to be cavorting as a faerie. I may come down for a spell, but at most, I shall be sporting the mask delivered to my room earlier today. Mr. Ashcott has a basket full of them in all shapes and colors beside his desk. Pick out the ones you like, but I suggest you go down right away before all the good ones are taken."

"I'll go," Cammy said. "I'll choose the perfect ones for us."

She came back a few minutes later with three masks in hand. "The emerald green one is for you, June. This gold one is for Willow. I found this beautiful lilac mask for me."

"Oh, they're lovely." June couldn't wait for the party to start. "This will be so much more fun than those stuffy London soirees."

Her mind was already in a whirl, thinking of all the fun they would have tonight.

But mostly, she was thinking of Augustus.

Would he return this evening?

In time to kiss her under the moonlight?

CHAPTER FIVE

"MIDSUMMER'S EVE, LADDIE," Angus said to Augustus as they reached the Ashcott Inn shortly after ten o'clock in the evening and handed their mounts to the inn's ostler. They had made good time returning to the inn since this was traditionally the summer solstice and the longest day of sunlight in the year.

But the sun set as they rode into Taunton.

It was dark now, and yet one would believe it was midday for all the activity going on in town and at the inn. "I hear music. There must be a party going on in the inn's garden. Will ye stop moping over the lass and join in the celebration?"

By *join in*, he knew Angus meant find himself a willing maid to ease his ache for the evening. "You go on ahead. I'll see to our rooms."

Jock remained by his side while the others strolled into the garden to grab themselves a drink and perhaps share a dance before heading into town to engage in more serious revelry. He cast Augustus a wry grin. "The party is likely a dull affair, suitable for the well-heeled guests, but a bit too tame for us. I think we need something a little…heartier. And by heartier, I mean pagan."

Augustus chuckled. "Maybe. I'll think about it."

Jock arched an eyebrow. "Ah, ever the diplomat. Don't forget, I know ye Augustus. Ye're giving me the brush off. I willna force ye. But give it some thought. If ever there was a night to indulge in the pleasures of a woman, this is it. The lass ye canno' seem to stop thinking about is surely in London by now. Ye mustn't pine for her forever."

He did not bother to deny he was missing June.

Not that it was anyone's business but his.

However, his companions seemed to have turned into gossiping hens. They were all keenly aware he had not sought out the comforts of a woman while in Bath.

Not only aware of it but knew the specific reason why.

It was still no one's business.

Besides, not even he understood these feelings he had for June.

He was about to head upstairs to wash the travel dirt off himself when Angus scurried back inside, wide-eyed and grinning like a hyena. "Laddie, come with me. Ye won't believe this."

Augustus frowned. "Give it up, ye old—"

"She's here."

His heart leaped into his throat. "Who's here?"

"I'm going to club ye over the head if ye dinna stop being dense. Yer Miss Farthingale, of course. Who else would I be talking about? The lassies dinna go to London. The innkeeper mentioned something about their aunt throwing out her back."

Angus was still going on about June, but Augustus paid him no attention as they strode to the inn's garden where the revelers were gathered. He had yet to see her, and already fire coursed through his blood. All he could think of was to hold June in his arms again. Was it true? How could she still be here?

He had no idea what to do about her or this inexplicable grip she had on his heart. But for now, all he needed was to see her. Talk to her.

Feast his eyes on her.

Breathe in the lavender scent of her skin.

Kiss her.

His heart beat like a war drum in his chest as he made his way through the crowd of revelers in search of her. His gaze passed over the musicians and forty or so guests who were all wearing masks; some had donned costumes.

The Ashcotts had transformed their garden into a magical faerie glen. The place looked enchanted even to his own jaded eyes. Torchlight surrounded the flower beds, and smaller lamps had been placed amid the flowers, while others were hanging off tree branches, bathing the garden in soft, golden light.

Adding to the effect was the abundance of flowers in bloom, particularly the roses. Their gentle scent carried in the air along with the scent of smoke from the burning torches.

Musicians had set themselves up in a corner of the garden.

Bowls of punch and stiffer drinks were set out on tables at the opposite corner.

Guests danced in the center, skipping and spinning in time to the lively music.

He scanned the couples merrily dancing on the patch of grass that served as a dance floor. They twirled and glided in time to the jaunty tune and appeared to be having a jolly good time. June and her sisters had to be among them, for he had not spotted them among those standing on the edges. Of course, he would have to kill the man who dared to dance with June.

He laughed at himself.

Perhaps his reaction was a bit extreme.

He had no right to feel possessive of the girl, and yet he did.

A familiar trill of laughter caught his attention.

A young woman spun briefly into his view, a beauty in a whirl of vibrant silk the liquid hues of the ocean. She had long, dark tresses that undulated like waves against her body. He'd barely caught sight of her before she spun out of view again.

But he had seen his splendid faerie.

It was June, he was certain of it. She could be covered in burlap from head to toe, and he would still know her instantly, sense it in his blood and in his bones.

Where was she now?

He spotted her sisters in their masks, and…were they wearing faerie wings? He grinned. They looked like enchanted creatures, both of them wearing their hair down. Cammy was a lilac faerie and had purple flowers threaded through her hair.

Willow was a rose faerie and had pearls threaded through her fiery tresses.

June could not be far from them.

Suddenly, he saw her again.

His breath caught.

His heart forgot how to beat, suddenly frozen in time as the crowd began to part for him, as though he willed everyone to melt away and leave him alone with the Barnstaple lass who had stolen his heart.

Of course, no one had disappeared.

No one had vanished.

Dancers were still dancing, and musicians were still playing, but the melody seemed muffled and distant, for he could hear little of it above the pounding roar of his heart.

June had been twirling with her sisters, her movements as light as a gently rippling wave upon the water.

She stopped the moment she noticed him approaching.

Then, nothing existed on this earth but the two of them.

All he could see was June, his beautiful faerie queen, and the smile she held just for him. She seemed to float toward him, her feet barely touching the ground as she approached him.

She was draped in a gown of gossamer that hugged the exquisite curves of her body. Her faerie wings softly billowed behind her with her every graceful step. Her face was partially hidden beneath an emerald mask, but all he saw was the beckoning beauty of her lips and the starlight glow in her eyes.

Mercy.

He was almost afraid to touch her, afraid he would wake up and find she had been merely a dream.

She laughed again, and he knew this was real.

Real, and yet not.

He almost believed she was an elfin spirit caught in golden firelight. She'd wound sparkling threads through her hair. They glistened against her dark curls. Gone was the elegant, upswept twist. Her hair tumbled down her back in a dark cascade, the silken ends caressing her hips and spectacular derriere.

His hands itched to do the same.

She was the loveliest thing he had ever beheld.

She held out her hand to him. "Dance with me, Augustus."

Only dance?

He wanted to bury his hands in her hair and bring his mouth grinding down on hers. He wanted to kiss her into eternity, touch and caress her body, explore her every soft curve and claim her for his own. "You look beautiful, *Tallulah*."

Her smile was as bright as the silver moonlight shining down on them. "So do you."

He shook his head and chuckled. "I am caked in dust and must reek of horse sweat and saddle leather."

She moved into his arms as the musicians struck up a waltz. He'd opened them to her as though it was the most natural thing in the world to do. "No, Augustus. You smell wonderful." She reached up on tiptoes and inhaled him, her lips a mere hair's breadth from his neck. "A hint of musk and clean, male skin. It is delightful. Quite manly."

"A man's body after a long day's ride in the heat of the sun is not delightful at all."

"Yes, it is. I was never partial to perfumed fops."

He twirled her around the garden, his gaze fixed on her as though needing to absorb her, needing to keep her etched in his memory, into his heart and soul for all time. Lord, what was happening to him? They were not the only couple dancing, but they may as well have been for all the attention he paid anyone else. He could not lift his gaze from her entrancing face. "I'm glad you're still here, June."

She nodded. "So am I."

"What happened? Why are you not in London?"

"Aunt Charlotte."

"I'm sorry, I should have asked sooner. How is she faring?"

"In truth, I believe she is fine. I suspect she is purposely making up excuses to keep us from leaving Taunton. She did it for my sake, I am certain. I made such an obvious cake of myself over you. She knew I was desperate to see you again."

She grimaced and continued before he had the chance to respond, although it spared him the need to admit he had felt the same. "Oh, that sounds quite pathetic, doesn't it? I wanted to see you again and feared I never would. But here you are."

"Well, it is a pleasant surprise for me, too." He did not know how he managed to keep his voice calm when his body was on fire, and his heart had wild horses stampeding upon it.

"Merely pleasant?"

He chuckled. "A very delightful surprise."

"Thank you, Augustus." She was light on her feet and graceful, unaware of the torment she was causing him as he held her in his arms and guided her in time to the flow of the music. He tried not to think beyond this dance or make too much of these powerful sensations coursing through him, especially knowing he had been assigned back to the Continent and would not remain long in England.

However, no matter how hard he tried to dismiss this attraction between them as something ephemeral, he simply could not. He had held other women in his arms before, but he could not recall any whose body ever felt as soft and warm or perfect as hers.

They needed to talk.

Not tonight.

He needed to clear his head and think logically about her. He could not do it while charmed by this exquisite faerie whose eyes sparkled as blue diamonds and lips beckoned with temptation.

Tomorrow.

They would talk by the bright light of day when their hearts were no longer bewitched by moonlight or pulled by the magic of

Midsummer's Eve.

"You are frowning at me, Augustus."

"No, June. I am merely thinking."

"About us?" She groaned lightly and missed a step, but he had her in his steady grip and easily set them back in time to the music. "I'm sorry. I should not have asked that. You don't owe me anything. I have no expectations nor will I ever make any demands of you."

"Lass," he said with agonizing ache. "You wear your heart on your sleeve."

She nodded. "I know. I am hopeless, it seems. I cannot stop feeling the way I do about you. I've read and reread *The Book of Love*, each time hoping to prove myself wrong. My feelings for you make no sense, and yet I cannot change them. I am so sorry if I make you uncomfortable. I will try my best to keep my heart hidden and simply enjoy the moment."

"You don't make me uncomfortable, June."

"I suppose you are used to young women throwing themselves in your path. Being the consummate diplomat, you've learned how to fend us all off politely."

There was nothing polite about his feelings for her. "I will have some time tomorrow. I would like to talk to you."

She winced. "By talk, do you mean lecture me again about my behavior around men? Truly Augustus, you are the only one I am having these misbehaving thoughts about. As I said, none of this makes sense to me. We have no connection to each other beyond a low-brain one, and I am the one who is in the low-brain frenzy described in the book, not you. You are the man and should be the one feeling this way. It is all so confusing."

She took a deep breath and continued. "I would love to talk to you. I need to understand why I feel the way I do."

"What is it you think you are feeling?" He should not have asked the question since he knew the answer and was not about to declare his love in return. First of all, he wasn't in love with June. How could he be after knowing her less than a day?

What he felt was an overwhelmingly powerful lust for her. But not in any lascivious way. It was a respectful lust, if such a thing existed. One that encompassed desiring her mind as well as her body.

It was not love.

It could not be.

Nor did he want it to be.

"My problem is," she said after a moment, "I don't understand what has come over me. I dare not call it anything more than infatuation. To consider it something more would be quite ridiculous, would it not?"

He nodded.

"We hardly know each other beyond a conversation or two. So, why do I feel so connected to you when we have nothing in common? I keep straining to find the reason why a young Englishwoman from Barnstaple, who has never stepped foot in an elegant ballroom, should believe she has found the man of her dreams in a Scottish highlander who has survived war, risen in rank to heights few men could ever dream of attaining, and is intimately acquainted with kings and emperors in the most powerful royal courts. You've probably attended hundreds of elegant balls and danced with dozens of princesses."

"I've never danced with a faerie princess before." He meant it, too. Despite being a man of reason and logic, he was drawn by the magic of the night and this enchanted garden. Most of all, he was drawn by June's beguiling beauty and physically ached to have more of her.

"Is it true, Augustus? You have never shared a dance with a faerie before? Not even at one of the famous masque balls held at the Austrian court? Surely the costumes found there would be exquisitely elaborate and the women quite stunning in them."

"No, June. That is, the costumes may have dazzled, but that is all. Sophisticated beauties do not hold wonder in their eyes or magic in their smiles as you do." He should have lied to her and pretended these elegant women outclassed her in every way. He should have kept his distance and pretended he was not fascinated by her.

He should have, but he did not.

He could not, even though both of them felt the danger of this attraction and did not know what to do with it. In truth, June did not seem to find it dangerous so much as confusing.

Perhaps this is how he felt as well.

"June, I have a favor to ask of you."

She cast him a gentle smile that had him fixing his gaze on her lips again and wanting to kiss her as they waltzed. "Of course. What is it you wish?"

He took a deep breath. "I'd like to read that book of yours. Would you let me borrow it?"

She bit her fleshy lower lip in thought and then gave a reluctant nod. "I'll bring it to you first thing tomorrow. But you must promise to give it back to me and not damage it in any way."

"You have my word of honor."

She cleared her throat. "I would like to make a small amendment. Would you object to reading it with me? Us. Together. It would help me tremendously."

"I would rather not. I have no wish to be your test frog. I—"

"And you have my word of honor that I shall not use you in that way. I would like you to be my tutor. You have the experience and can explain much of the feelings discussed in this book. Please, Augustus. Say you will."

He gave a curt nod.

This decision was likely one of the worst he had ever made in his life.

Or it could be the very best.

June was right, they needed to learn more about each other, and there was little time in which to do it.

She smiled at him again, and he was certain the garden had suddenly come ablaze with the brilliance of a thousand stars. Perhaps there was a logical explanation, the innkeeper lighting more torches or the moon bursting out from behind a cloud.

But he suspected no such thing had happened, that these rays of light in the darkness were all June's doing. Worse, he knew she would still cast this magical spell over him come morning.

The waltz ended, leaving him with no more reason to hold June in his arms. He had just escorted her back to her sisters, fully intending to remain by her side to discourage any fools who thought to request a dance from her, when the magistrate walked in.

He caught Augustus's eye and immediately strode toward him. "Thank you for returning, General MacLauren. The judge will be arriving tomorrow evening. Too late to hold his sessions then, of course. His hearings will commence first thing the day after tomorrow. I hope that does not put you out too badly."

"No, it is fine." He glanced at June. "I have other commitments to keep me busy tomorrow. It is little inconvenience to me."

Magistrate Brayden appeared genuinely grateful. "I'll ask the judge to hear your matter and take your testimony first. You will be able to leave immediately afterward. I appreciate your coming back for this nasty bit of nonsense."

"I hope it helps you contain those three wretches."

The magistrate cast him a wry smile. "So do I, but I doubt those pampered lords will ever change their ways. We may be able to rein them in for a while, but it won't last. Such men care nothing about the hurt they cause others. Whatever frustrations or rage they feel is never their fault. They are always quick to place blame elsewhere." He glanced at the sisters. "Well, I had better resume my patrol. Enjoy the rest of your evening, General MacLauren. Ladies."

He marched out with a purposeful stride.

Augustus had no intention of retiring yet. His companions were still with him at the party. Not that he needed to watch over them, but even disciplined soldiers could make boors of themselves after a few drinks, especially around women as beautiful as these Farthingales.

Most of the other men attending this party were married, having come here with their wives and some with children, too. There were also several men passing through on business and some unattached, single gentlemen who merited closer scrutiny.

None of them were to his liking.

He understood the hungry look in their eyes when they gazed at the Farthingale sisters.

Did he not feel this same ravenous craving for June?

Even though he prided himself on behaving like a gentleman, he intended to chase away any man who dared approach her. It was a surprisingly territorial thing for him to do, like a lion chasing away the other males who ventured too close to the females of his pride.

Of course, the only female he wanted was standing beside him and putting his heart in palpitations with her every smile. But her sisters needed to be taken under his protection, too. In a brotherly way.

The only one he desired was this raven-haired beauty.

If the sisters wished to dance, then he and his soldiers would oblige.

As it turned out, his absurdly possessive need to chase away all comers was unnecessary. June and her sisters retired to their chamber soon after their waltz had ended.

Augustus kept an eye on them while they climbed the stairs. He waited for them to safely enter their room before he turned back to his friends. "Angus, I'll have you demoted to dung mucker if you dinna stop grinning at me."

"Laddie, will ye come into town with us, or are ye going up to yer room to overly think yer feelings for the lass?"

"I am not overly thinking anything because there is nothing to think about," he grumbled. "You know what Lord Ballinger commanded of me. One more day in the company of Miss Farthingale won't change anything."

Jock nodded in sympathy. "Too bad. Yer grandda would have liked her."

He snorted. "Aye, he would. Come on, let's walk into town."

The streets were crowded, and the taverns filled. Women came up to them, but Augustus once again found none of them appealing. He sat drinking with Jock and Angus while the younger lads, Hamish, Alex, and Duncan, went off with some of the local lasses.

Several fights broke out, but the magistrate's men were quickly on the scene to break them up. He, Jock, and Angus helped them out a time or two. But as the hour passed, Augustus grew restless and decided to return to the inn. "I'm going back."

"We'll come with ye, laddie," Angus said, motioning to Jock.

He had not wanted to interfere with their revels, but the pair insisted he wasn't and strolled back with him.

As it turned out, he was glad they did. Otherwise, they would not have been there to help him back to the inn when he spotted Lord Belfy and his accomplice cousins lurking behind some bushes. The idiots were standing under a torchlight, clearly visible to him.

Did they think a few mere shrubs would hide them?

An instant later, a shot rang out, and a searing pain tore through his head.

Momentarily stunned, he lost his balance and began to reel.

"Laddie, ye're hit!" Angus cried, catching him as he was about to fall. "Och! Jock, help me. He's badly hurt. We need to get him to safety."

Jock had started after the culprits but stopped and hurried back upon hearing the fear in Angus's voice. "Bastards," he muttered and reluctantly placed the pistol he had withdrawn back in the lip of his boot where he'd always kept it hidden. He quickly tucked a shoulder under Augustus's arm to steady him. "They've run off like the cowards they are. How bad is it, Augustus?"

His legs felt as though they were about to collapse under him. "A graze, I think. Maybe worse. Shot went clean through. My head feels cut open. It was Lord Belfy. Did you see him lurking in the bushes with his damn cousins?"

"Aye, but I never imagined they'd shoot." Jock emitted a string of curses and ended with a groan of obvious frustration. "I'm going after the Sassenach scum as soon as we carry ye safely back to the inn."

"No," Augustus said firmly. "Get me back, then doctor first. Send one of the innkeeper's lads in search of him. Then go find the magistrate and tell him what happened. No argument, Jock. You do not go after those men alone."

"But Augustus—"

"That's an order." He winced in pain, each hurried step jostling his head, but he did not want them slowing down. "Tell the magistrate what happened, and let him and his men find those arses. Dinna be a reckless fool. We know who they are and where they live. Och, I'm gushing blood."

Angus groaned. "Augustus, are ye sure nothing lodged in that thick skull of yers?"

"Not sure. I hope not. I'm still talking, aren't I? But I'm bleeding like a stuck pig."

"Bollocks, ye are." Jock was fuming angry as he and Angus reached the inn. "I'll do as ye ask, but what if they're long gone by the time Brayden and his men start searching for them? They've already scurried off to hide like the rats they are."

The door was locked at this time of night, but one of the innkeeper's sons was manning it and quickly let them in. "Go fetch the doctor, lad," Angus said to the fretting boy.

He turned ashen. "I cannot leave my post. Da will flay my hide if I do."

Jock scowled at him. "Then summon your father. Now!"

Augustus was worried that Jock and Angus were going to dump him on his bed and take off after those men, so he commanded them once again not to give chase. "The Earl of Monkton is not going to protect them from this. He'll know where they've gone, even if they do try to run. He will turn them over to Brayden without shots fired."

Angus emitted another anguished groan. "Damn it, I—"

"Enough, both of you." He took a deep breath and then another to keep himself from casting up his accounts. Whoever had shot him only managed to graze his brow, or so he hoped. But he would have a blistering headache by morning. Hopefully, nothing worse.

He wasn't angry with his friends, for he would have done no less if the situations were reversed.

His head was pounding with the force of a hammer blow as they started up the stairs. He was unsteady and nauseated, barely making it up three steps on his own before stumbling.

"Damn it, Augustus. Ye're even more stubborn than we are," Jock muttered as the pair grabbed hold of him again. "No argument, we're going to carry you up."

Perhaps it had been more than a graze, although he did not think it was much worse than that. Surely, he would be dead by now if anything had lodged in his head. But he was a bloody mess for certain, blood pouring down his cheek and neck and seeping into his shirt to thoroughly soak it.

He'd meant to return quietly to his room.

He'd hoped for the doctor to quietly attend him.

And the magistrate to quietly question him and his companions.

But it was not to be.

A few of the innkeeper's staff who were cleaning up after their Midsummer's Eve party saw the trail of blood and began to scream. Jock shouted for them to summon Magistrate Brayden and the doctor. "What's taking the damn innkeeper so long?"

He shouted again for another of the lads to haul the innkeeper out of bed.

Augustus did not have the strength to remind him he had already been summoned. Nor did he have the strength to tell Jock and Angus to shut up and stop cursing like pirates as they lugged him up the stairs.

Mr. Ashcott and his wife soon came running out and began to shriek when they saw his condition. All the noise woke the inn's other guests.

Doors flew open.

He'd barely made it into his room and collapsed atop his bed before soft hands were touching his face, and an angel's voice began issuing orders. "We need bandages, clean cloths, fresh water, and brandy. General MacLauren, please lie still. We have to staunch the bleeding."

June.

He wanted to caress her cheek, but his hands were full of blood.

"Sergeant MacKay, what happened?" she asked Angus. "Oh, never mind. Let's take care of him first. Mr. Ashcott, is the water in his ewer fresh?"

"Yes, Miss Farthingale."

"Good. Here, take my handkerchief and dip it in, then wring it out and bring it back to me. Has the doctor been summoned?"

"Aye," Angus told her.

"And the magistrate?"

"Aye, lassie," Jock said. "We took care of both."

She released a shaky breath, the only sign of her turmoil, for she was otherwise calm and completely in control of the situation. "Thank you. Where's that brandy? We need to cleanse the wound as best as we can and then apply pressure to it to stanch the bleeding until the doctor arrives."

Mrs. Ashcott returned a moment later with it and handed the bottle to June.

"This will sting quite a bit," she warned Augustus as she applied what felt like fire to his head.

Had she poured the entire contents of the brandy bottle to his wound? "Bloody blazes!" He felt like retching, but he was already enough of a mess; thankfully the jolt of pain passed quickly. June continued her efficient ministrations, ordering Angus to hold the damp cloth firmly to the source of the bleed and issuing orders to the others in the room with the authority of a commanding general.

After that, she began to clean his hands, face, and neck.

"I must look like a bloody mess," he grumbled.

"You look wonderful. You're alive and talking, and that's all that matters." She turned away a moment, no doubt to fight back her tears. "Where is that doctor?"

When she turned back to look at him, Augustus reached up and ran a finger lightly along the delicate line of her jaw. "Dinna worry, June. He'll be here soon enough. Between the brawls and drunks tumbling over their own two feet, I'm sure he's been kept busy tonight."

She sniffled. "You need stitches. I don't know how to do that."

"Keeping the cloth pressed to my head is enough for now."

"What if it isn't? Augustus, promise me you'll hold on until he arrives. Promise me you won't slip away."

"I canno' promise ye that, lass." Augustus closed his eyes, realizing he'd slipped back into his brogue. Well, he was a Scot and proud of it. He was a Highlander from Caithness and proud of that, too.

She took his hand and held it to her heart. "Then I'll make you a promise, you stubborn Scot. I promise that I won't let you go. The devil will have to fight me for you, and he will lose."

He chuckled. "I haven't a doubt, lass."

This girl was wonderful.

But he had already been ordered back to the Continent, given time only to ride to Caithness, kiss his grandda, and then ride straight to Dover to cross the channel back to continental Europe. He had been assigned back to Vienna, for now, to temporarily take over Lord Castlereagh's responsibilities.

But the politics of power would now furiously start behind the scenes, and who knew where his orders would take him once a permanent replacement was found for Castlereagh? He knew his name was under consideration, but he was not a politician at heart and was not going to play their games. If they wanted him, he would accept the assignment.

If they chose someone else, where would the powers-that-be send him next?

This is what troubled him most. Did he have the right to court June or make her promises when they would see each other perhaps a few days over the next two or three years? Even if he wound up in Vienna, he had no intention of taking her with him.

How would she ever navigate her way around Vienna society on her own? Those in its elevated ranks were more brutal than the London *ton*.

Of course, she could only accompany him if she were his wife. But how could he protect her when most of his days and possibly his nights would be taken up in negotiations? Left on her own, she was too innocent and would quickly be ground up as fodder by those who lived and breathed treachery and backstabbing as a way of life in their royal courts.

No, he had to leave June in England.

But what then? What if his duties kept him away for more than a few years? What if that time stretched to five or six years?

Did he have the right to deny her a proper husband who would remain by her side and protect her? Not that this beautiful lass needed protecting. She was strong and spirited.

He ought to tell her that he loved her.

He should at least do that, shouldn't he?

No.

She would wait for him forever if she knew he had feelings for her beyond merely wishing to ravage her body.

She would wait for him and possibly lose the chance to bear children if he stayed away too long.

She did not deserve such a life.

Perhaps if she were someone less loving, less devoted to family.

He could not condemn her to such emptiness.

Of course, all of this worry over her assumed he would survive the night.

It was quite possible he would be dead by tomorrow, and

June would never be his.

He lay quietly and allowed her to take care of him, loving her gentleness and the soothing lilt of her voice. He took a deep breath, mostly inhaling the scent of his blood. But he also breathed in her scent, that of a delicate lavender flower, reminding him of those heavenly Highland summers and everything beautiful the world held. "This is getting to be a habit with us."

"You injured and me tending to you?" She released a shaky breath. "A very bad habit, I would say. Do you know who shot you? Those miscreants, I suppose. Oh, Augustus, they came so close to blowing your head off."

He placed his lips to the palm of her trembling hand and gave it a light kiss. "But they dinna manage it, lass."

"I'm not so sure. You ought to see yourself," she whispered, her voice tinged with anguish. "The ugly gash won't stop bleeding. Does it hurt terribly?"

He tried to respond, but the effort suddenly felt insurmountable.

"Augustus?"

He blinked his eyes, trying to focus them on June, but he could hardly make out her features now. "Who blew out the candles?"

June inhaled sharply. "Why? Is the room suddenly dark to you? Oh, my heavens. No one did, Augustus. Can you not see me? How about the fingers I am waving before your eyes? Can you see them?"

"You're waving fingers?"

CHAPTER SIX

June knew she would arrive in London a ruined debutante if she did not leave Augustus's bedchamber, but she could not bring herself to abandon him. He was stretched out quietly atop the mattress, so quiet now she worried he was unconscious. However, he was still clinging to her hand, surely a hopeful sign.

Perhaps she was the one holding fiercely onto him.

It did not matter.

She was not going to leave his side nor would she let him die. In truth, his skin was still warm, and he was breathing evenly. Still, that shot to his head was quite severe, even if merely a graze.

Jock, Angus, and now the doctor were in the room with her.

Their other companions, the three younger soldiers, had returned to the inn and were standing sentry outside his door. Fuming and angry, they all felt helpless and on edge.

"I'm going to shoot those bastards," Jock muttered for what had to be the fiftieth time this evening.

"No, I'll do it," Angus insisted. "Ye're young and have yer life ahead of ye, whelp. Better they hang me."

The doctor looked up and growled at both of them. "Leave it to the magistrate. He is more than capable of bringing those scoundrels to heel. They'll be properly tried and punished."

Angus raked a hand through his hair. "Aye, but ye can rest assured we'll see to their punishment if they somehow avoid the noose."

"Hanging's too good for them," Jock grumbled. "We'll see them drawn and quartered and their bloody guts tossed to the pigs for supper."

June hoped most of their chatter was just men venting their anger and obvious frustration. Augustus, before he had passed out, had ordered them to leave the matter to the magistrate. He knew what his soldiers would do otherwise, and his only thought was to protect them, even as he lay bleeding.

"Sergeant MacKay," June said, noticing the man begin to pace, "I am certain they will be properly dealt with. It is obvious they went after General MacLauren to silence him. This is not merely an instance of uncouth louts getting drunk and out of hand. They purposely targeted him. This, I would argue, rises to an act of treason against the Crown. No one in their family will protect them. They'll be turned over to Magistrate Brayden on a silver platter, stuffed, tied, and trussed. I would not be surprised if the Earl of Monkton delivered them personally."

Angus cast her a wry grin. "Let's hope ye're right, lass. Still, it does no' stop us from wanting to claim vengeance by our own hands. It is fitting and proper that General MacLauren's men take care of those arses. We canno' let the Sassenachs hang them for us."

She frowned at him. "Ignoring the process of English law would make a mockery of all General MacLauren and Lord Castlereagh have worked for since Napoleon was defeated at Waterloo, do you not think?"

"Och, dinna speak reasonably to us, lass," Jock said. "There can be no peace until those cowards are dead."

"They will be," Augustus murmured, surprising all of them when he blinked his eyes and tried to sit up.

June held him down. "Are you deranged? Don't move. The bleeding has finally slowed to a trickle. You'll rupture something vital if you attempt to get out of bed."

"Where's the doctor? Is he here? Have him put stitches in me and—"

"I'll hit you over the head myself if you insist on fighting me." June knew she could never restrain him under normal circumstances, but he was weak as a newborn lamb right now and was no match for her determination. "Behave, Augustus. You are not out of danger yet."

"General MacLauren," the doctor said, "I am Dr. Stratton. I'm glad to see you alert once again, but I dare not put stitches in you yet. The swelling in your head needs to subside a little more before I try."

Augustus emitted a heavy breath and stopped resisting. "How long before I am on my feet again?"

The doctor gave his wound a closer inspection. "A week, I would say. You are fortunate the shot merely grazed you."

"A week," June repeated in a whisper. If he was staying, then so would she. Since Aunt Charlotte had been fabricating ailments to keep them here, she doubted there would a problem convincing her that they should remain a bit longer.

"Three days and no more," Augustus insisted. "Then we ride to Caithness."

The doctor frowned. "Caithness? No, it is too long a journey to attempt after a mere three days. You'll need to rest here at least another week before it is safe to do so."

Augustus scowled. "And I say three days."

June kept her mouth shut while the men bickered.

Augustus had not risen to the rank of general by being an idiot, even though he was behaving like one just now. She hoped he would heal quickly, but if he did not, she would talk sense into him.

In any event, she had three days to make him fall in love with her. Well, not just fall in love but choose to marry her. She knew they were meant for each other. He was the one who needed convincing.

If he was riding to Caithness, she wanted to go with him. However, she would not go unless they were married. To do otherwise would bring ruin to her sisters, and she was not that reckless.

"June, you ought to return to your chamber," Augustus said quietly. "This is no place for you, lass."

She knew he was right.

While unconscious, Jock and Angus had removed his blood-stained jacket and shirt, then carefully removed his boots. He wore nothing but his breeches. His chest was a thing of beauty, broad and muscled, and scandalously exposed to her view. "Don't make me go. Please don't. I'm afraid you'll slip away if I release your hand. I made you a promise to fight the devil if he tried to claim you."

"I'm not holding you to that promise. June, you needn't be stubborn."

"I am not stubborn. I am shaken to my bones. Being overset is not at all the same thing."

He smiled at her. "Scots are far too thickheaded to be taken down by a puny shot to the skull. Dinna be afraid, lass. I will recover."

"Will you promise me? Because I won't leave your side unless you promise me you won't die."

"June—"

She squeezed his hand lightly. "Give me your solemn vow, Augustus."

He glanced at his men.

"Och, do it, laddie," Angus said. "We all need assurance ye'll open yer eyes tomorrow."

Augustus brought her hand to his lips and kissed it. "I give you my sacred oath, June. I will not die tonight."

"Thank you." She cast him a trembling smile and walked out without looking back, for she would never have the strength to leave him if she dared glance back.

Her sisters were still awake and rushed to her side as soon as she walked into their chamber. To her surprise, her aunt was there, too. "Aunt Charlotte, I expected you to be asleep by now."

"How could I possibly close my eyes after all that excitement? Mrs. Ashcott's shrieks had me hopping out of bed so fast, I thought the inn was about to collapse about our heads. And now I've really thrown my back out."

June hurried to her. "Oh, dear. Are you in pain?"

"I will survive it, child. I'm quite strong, you know. When have you ever known me to be ill?"

"Other than all these days we've been stuck here while you've contrived one ailment after another?" June frowned at her. "You've been faking all this time? Why?"

They'd all suspected it, for their aunt had never been a sickly person, as she had just admitted. However, she had never been a good traveler, and she was getting on in years. For this reason, they had remained in doubt and believed her when she complained of aches and pains. Who was to say this wasn't the start of a serious decline?

"Forgive my ruse, girls. I did it for you, June."

Her eyes widened. "Me? Why?"

"To see your General MacLauren again, of course. My dear, your expressive face hides nothing. I knew the moment you set eyes on him that you had fallen in love. Of course, were he a bounder, I would have tossed you all in our carriage so fast your rumps would still be aching from the jarring force of landing on the seat."

"You did this for me?" She gave her aunt a quick hug. "But I don't know if he can ever love me. We were going to read *The Book of Love* together. That is out of the question now."

Charlotte smiled and sank onto one of the beds, patting the mattress beside her for June to sit beside her. "Reading it with him does not matter."

"Why not?" Cammy asked, settling onto the other bed and curling her legs under her.

Willow did the same. "Yes, Aunt Charlotte. How can they understand what they are feeling if they don't read the book?"

Charlotte released a sigh. "My dears, it is just a book. Couples have been entering into love matches throughout time without its help." She held up a hand when all three of them began to toss more questions at her. "The fact that he was willing to read it with June tells me all I need to know. Not to mention the scorching looks he casts her way when he believes no one is watching."

June smiled. "He does?"

She patted her hand. "Yes, dearest. Falling in love with you is not the obstacle."

"Then what is?" Cammy asked.

"His life. His duties. His travels."

Willow shook her head and laughed. "You are quite discerning for a woman supposedly laid up in bed most of this past week."

"I merely peered out my window. That's all it took. Also, maids love to chatter about what they've seen and heard. Believe me, they see and hear everything."

June held her breath. "What have they heard General MacLauren say about me?"

"In truth, very little."

She let it out in a deflated sigh. "Oh."

"He isn't one to convey his feelings in words. Oh, perhaps he is an able speaker when on his diplomatic missions. I have no doubt he is. But for himself? He'll never express his love with flowery prose. At heart he is a man of action. Therefore, one must look for clues in what he does."

Cammy leaned forward. "What actions gave him away?"

Charlotte shrugged. "A lingering look. A touch that holds for the littlest bit too long. A glower at any man who dares approach June. It doesn't take much for a man to give himself away. But as I said, having him desire her is not the problem."

"It's taking the next step and marrying her," Willow acknowledged with a nod. "How do we get him to do that, Aunt Charlotte?"

She pursed her lips. "We cannot do anything. This part is up to June. You must somehow convince him he cannot exist another day without you. In this, your book should be most helpful."

"About appealing to his senses?" Cammy asked. "Sight, touch, taste, hearing, and scent?"

"Oh, I think he's already reached a favorable conclusion about those when it comes to June. No, what she needs to do is change his outlook, tear down his expectations and build their connections. There are several chapters on those topics, are there not?"

June nodded. "Aunt Charlotte, have you read the book? Did you sneak it out of my travel bag while we were out?"

She cleared her throat. "I may have, but that is entirely off the point. Your General MacLauren will be trapped here for the next few days. Read those chapters to him. He must stop thinking of what he'll deprive you of if you were to marry him and start thinking of all that is to be gained by your union."

June glanced at her sisters, knowing they were all wondering the same thing. Being the eldest, she spoke up for the three of them. "Aunt Charlotte, you obviously know much about love. Were you ever in love? Why have you never married?"

She suddenly turned wistful. "Yes, I have been in love. This same sort of deep, aching love that you are feeling for General MacLauren. My young man loved me, too. But he died in battle before we could marry. Some people have second chances. I did not. My Samuel was the only man for me. We'd known each other since childhood and loved each other all the while. Indeed, there was not a time when we did not love each other."

June's heart tightened. "Oh, Aunt Charlotte. We are so very sorry. Why did you never tell us this before?"

She shook her head to dismiss June's concern. "I did not want anyone's pity. Not then, nor do I want it now. Samuel and I shared two decades together, an entire childhood and several years of adulthood. We were to marry when he returned from battle. He never did. But I do not despair. This is more time than many couples are given. We shared more happiness in those years than most married couples are ever blessed with in a lifetime. We weren't merely two hearts uniting. We were one heart, one soul. Once that heart was broken by his death, there was no putting it back together again."

June and her sisters sat in silence, absorbing what Charlotte had just told them.

Charlotte patted her hand. "You can do this, June. You are a Farthingale and will not be daunted."

She laughed and shook her head. "I won't give up on him. Indeed, now I don't mind so much that I made an utter fool of myself when we first met. Being a Farthingale, I could not respond in any other way. I loved him at first sight. I had to let him know."

Willow gasped. "You've told him that you love him?"

June squirmed. "Well, no. Not in so many words. But I am terrible at hiding my feelings. He would have to be dumb as a rock not to understand."

Charlotte laughed. "Oh, June. When it comes to love, this is what men are."

Willow and Cammy were now laughing as well.

After a moment, Charlotte rose. "Girls, I suggest we get to bed. June will have her work cut out for her these next few days. She will need to look her best and keep her wits sharp."

"Goodnight, Aunt Charlotte. Thank you." June turned out their lamps and settled beneath the sheets. She wanted so desperately to lie beside Augustus and hold him close. He would never allow it, of course.

Even half-dead, he meant to protect her from ruin.

Perhaps he only meant to protect himself from having to marry her, assuming her presence in his quarters somehow became twisted into an ugly rumor of something more.

"Nothing to be done about it now," she muttered, closing her eyes and wishing for morning to arrive quickly.

June awoke shortly before dawn but dared not get out of bed

before the sun peeked over the horizon. Only then did she quietly wash and dress. Since her sisters were not yet stirring, she crept out of her room and tiptoed down the hall to Augustus's room.

His three younger companions were asleep just outside his door.

She expected Jock and Angus were stretched out on makeshift pallets inside his room.

Young Hamish awoke when she accidentally bumped his leg while trying to reach over him to knock at the door. "Miss Farthingale, you're up early."

She nodded. "I need to see him, Hamish. How is he faring? Any trouble last night?"

"Nothing more than his usual grumbling." He rubbed his eyes to chase the sleep out of them. "Truly, I think he passed a good night. Jock and Angus are with him now. Angus is an irksome mother hen to us all. We would have heard if anything was wrong."

"Would you please ask if I may come in and sit beside him?"

"No, dinna let her in. I look like dog piss," she heard Augustus call out the moment Hamish poked his head in.

Thank goodness, he was still alive.

He must have heard her and was obviously surly this morning.

Well, she did not care what he looked like or whether or not he was disposed to see her. The mere fact that he had the strength to grumble was a very good sign.

She marched in and dragged an empty chair to his bedside. "Good morning, General MacLauren. I am not leaving your side today, so you may as well get used to me."

"Good morning to you, too." He cast her a lopsided grin, looking impossibly handsome with that sensual, sleepy droop to his eyes and an overnight growth of beard that made him appear quite rugged. "Suit yourself, lass. I know better than to engage in a battle I'm never going to win."

"Smart man." She smiled at him.

He groaned and glanced at his companions. "I don't suppose you would remove Miss Farthingale if I ordered it?"

Angus guffawed. "No, laddie. I dinna suppose we would."

Augustus turned back to her. "Looks like you'll have your way. They won't kick you out, and I am in no condition to do it just now."

She smiled at Jock and Angus. "They are very wise men."

She turned back to him with her brow furrowed and so many questions whirling in her head.

He arched an eyebrow. "You are frowning at me."

"I am worried about you. How are you feeling?" She inspected the stitches along his forehead. "The doctor did a nice job. How is your head? Still pounding?"

"Yes."

"May I hold your hand?"

He chuckled. "Yes, June. No medicine could be better."

His hands were warm and his grip much firmer than it had been last night. His touch was still gentle, but he was no longer weak as a lamb. Indeed, she felt his strength sizzle through her. He cast her another knowing grin.

She cleared her throat. "I suppose you find my concern most amusing."

"No, June. It feels odd, that's all. I am not used to anyone as pretty as you fussing over me." He looked like a dangerous lion with his dark hair in handsome disarray and his skin the lovely shade of gold, no doubt gained by toiling under the sun.

His eyes were dark and held an emerald gleam, a predatory glint that warned she'd be easy prey if he sought to do more than lie quietly in bed and hold her hand. "Where's your book?"

June opened her mouth in surprise. "I left it tucked in my travel bag. I did not think you would be in any condition to read it with me this morning. But would you like to? I'll fetch it now."

"Yes, I will go out of my mind if I am left with nothing to do but stare at Angus's ugly face. Jock's is no prize either."

Angus snorted. "Ye're one to talk. Ye look like a cow's backside, with all due respect, General MacLauren."

"Ye'd better put some clothes on while Miss Farthingale fetches that book," Jock suggested.

June blinked her eyes. "What?"

She stared at Augustus stretched out in his bed. His shirt and jacket had been taken for cleaning, although who knew if the bloodstains would ever wash out of his shirt? They could be boiled out of his jacket, however. His boots were also gone, no doubt to be polished.

His breeches.

Was he still wearing them?

The wicked glint in his eye and grin on his face warned he was not.

She gasped, realizing she had been sitting beside a naked general and was now gaping at him. Still naked. A naked man. His rank did not matter. He was…

Naked.

Oh, the blanket covered him up to his chest. But every bit of his hard, muscled, big ox of a divine body was under there without a stitch of clothing.

She tipped her head up in indignation. "You ought to have warned me."

"I did. I told you not to come in."

She felt herself blush to the tips of her ears. "I thought it was because you did not want to see me."

He chuckled. "No, lass. It was because I did not want *you* to see too much of *me*."

"Send one of your men to knock at my door when you are decent." She darted up from her chair, knocking it over as she scurried out with her face in flames.

Augustus and his companions all had stupid grins on their faces and were chortling.

Her sisters were awake and already dressing when she hurried in and forcefully shut the door behind her.

Willow took one look at her, and her eyes widened. "June,

what happened? You look undone. Is it General MacLauren? Is he more badly hurt than we realized?"

"No," she said, her voice ragged.

"Why do you look…I don't know…shaken?"

She moaned in agony. "I've made such a fool of myself. He wasn't wearing any clothes."

Willow laughed. "Oh, what fun!"

"How much of him did you see?" Cammy tried to sound appalled, but she was soon laughing, too.

She buried her face in her hands and moaned. "Most of him was covered up. But he knew he had nothing on underneath. All of his men did, too. And there I was, prattling at him like an idiot."

"I'm sure he was delighted to see you," Willow assured. "But out with it, tell us about the parts of him that weren't covered up."

She dropped her hands to her sides and stared at her sister aghast. "Willow!"

"Oh, June, she's only teasing. Come help me with my laces." Cammy set her hair aside to reveal they were as yet undone. "But seriously, is he as handsome without his uniform as he is with it on?"

Sighing, she walked over to Cammy and began to assist her. "More so. Oddly, I've never seen him so unkempt. His face was bruised and unshaven. His hair was tousled. Obviously, no comb had been run through it. He must have roughly brushed it back by running his fingers through it. I didn't see *all* of him, of course. Only his arms and shoulders were visible. The rest of his torso was hidden under the covers."

She tried not to think of the divine parts she could see.

His arms and shoulders were big and broad, bulging with muscles.

Cammy turned to her when she finished lacing her up. "Is it bad that he looked so rumpled?"

June emitted a pained laugh. "No. I'm still quite taken with him. He said he would like to read the book with me."

Willow clapped her hands. "That is excellent. But do you think he is up to it?"

"He claims he is." She crossed to her travel bag and took out the faded red leather tome. "We'll see how far we get before he tires. I don't want to push him too hard. He'll need to eat to regain his strength. Most important, he'll need plenty of rest."

"The magistrate will want to question him," Willow added. "I wonder if he's caught those fiends yet. You must let us know what he reports to General MacLauren."

"I doubt I'll hear anything. He will chase me out before he reveals any information."

Cammy picked up a brush and began to slowly run it through her long, blonde strands. "And there's the hearing before the judge tomorrow. Do you think the general is in any shape to testify?"

"He'll be there even if he has to crawl on his knees," June muttered. "He's deferring to the legal process, for now. Indeed, making certain his men don't interfere with the magistrate in any way. But these soldiers are Royal Scots Greys, not puffed-up dandies. They are not going to let those boors go unpunished."

Willow agreed. "Let's hope those wretches are not let off lightly for what they've done. What is wrong with these men that they could not have left well enough alone? A taproom brawl is nothing. They would have risked merely a hefty fine and a stern warning. But to attempt to murder General MacLauren…that could be a death sentence for them, even if he does survive his wounds."

"I know. This is why I hesitate to read this book with him. It feels so insignificant now." June glanced at the book she was holding in her hands, wondering if Augustus would take in any of it while his head was filled with matters deemed far more important.

"If he asked you to read it, then do so with him," Willow said. "It will do you both good to take your mind off those fiends. As for us, let's stay close to the inn today. Those men are desperate. Who's to say they won't come after one of us since they've failed to silence their prime target?"

"Do you think they will?" Cammy asked. "To use us as hostages while they bargain for their release? They are despicable. Let's hope they are not so stupid. They'll be shot dead if they try."

June nodded. "Are we agreed then? No venturing from the inn."

Someone knocked at their door before her sisters had a chance to reply. June went to answer it, expecting it to be one of the soldiers. To her surprise, it was Magistrate Brayden in the doorway. "Oh, Mr. Brayden. Do come in."

He shook his head. "Not necessary. I just wanted to check on you ladies and ask you to remain at the inn today."

June glanced at her sisters. "We were discussing this very thing when you knocked. We'll be here. You needn't worry about us."

"Thank you, Miss Farthingale. I appreciate your cooperation. I'm going to post two of my men to guard you these next few days."

"Is there a need?" Willow asked.

"Yes."

Willow frowned. "Care to elaborate?"

"No."

June sighed. "We hadn't planned on leaving. But I do wish you would explain the reason why we are to be placed under guard. Ignorance does not protect us. We don't mind that your men will be watching over us, but we are also capable of defending ourselves. Is it not more sensible to keep us informed rather than have us blindly walk into a trap?"

He took her admonishment surprisingly well. "You are right. Forgive me if I came across as highhanded. I would tell you if I had more information. For now, it is merely a matter of taking general precautions."

"Does this mean you have still not found the men who shot

General MacLauren?" Willow asked.

"Not yet."

Cammy clasped her hands, a sure sign she was fretting. Of the three, she was the youngest and also the most sensitive. "Did they not return to the Earl of Monkton's estate?"

"Not to the manor house. Likely they are hiding somewhere on or near the property. My brother and some of my men are hunting them down as we speak. Lorcan is a trained tracker. Among the very best. He does this sort of thing all the time in his service to the Crown."

Cammy still looked apprehensive. "What will he do when he finds them?"

The magistrate cast her a wry smile. "We may look like brutes, but we are not. My brother and I are determined to uphold the law. He will do his best to bring them in unharmed."

"I'm sure…I did not mean…forgive me if it sounded as though…" Cammy allowed her voice to trail off. "Your brother looks particularly frightening. That's all. That's why…" Her voice trailed off again.

"He is an honorable man. But you would not ever want to cross him." He turned to pin Willow with a stare. "Or me, for that matter."

June glanced at her sister.

She had been so caught up in thoughts of General MacLauren, she hadn't noticed much of what else was going on around her. Had something passed between Willow and the magistrate? She definitely sensed tension.

In truth, she would not be surprised if Willow had said something to him the other night, probably tossed an irreverent remark when he had ignored her and Cammy after the first incident when those fiends had attacked her and Augustus.

The three of them had been gently raised, but they were not delicate damsels. They were often dismissed because men thought them too young and pretty to be capable of handling anything important. It rankled all of them. Willow, in particular, bridled whenever they were treated this way.

The magistrate may have put them off that night when they had tried to tell him what they saw. But he had come by the following morning to take their information and had not been condescending at all.

In truth, he had listened quite attentively.

"We are not going to do anything to put tomorrow's hearing in jeopardy," June assured him.

"Thank you, Miss Farthingale. Would you mind coming downstairs now, and I'll introduce you to my deputies?" He turned to her sisters. "You as well."

Cammy nodded. "We were going downstairs in a few minutes, anyway, to have our breakfast."

"I will also make sure Mrs. Ashcott sends up a hearty meal for General MacLauren," June said. "He's awake now, by the way. I looked in on him a few minutes ago. He looks awful, stitches across his brow and bruises all along the side of his face."

The magistrate frowned. "He's a very fortunate man. An inch to the left, and he'd be dead."

"I know." She tried to hide her shudder but doubted she had fooled anyone.

Willow put an arm around her. "He's alive and on the mend, that's what matters."

After introducing them to his men, the magistrate returned upstairs to report to Augustus. She and her sisters sat around one of the breakfast tables, but none of them had much of an appetite.

June had taken a moment to see about a meal for Augustus and was assured by Mrs. Ashcott that she had just sent up a tray for him. "His men will take turns coming down here for their meals, that's what Sergeant MacKay informed me. They're not going to take their eyes off him. As for yer aunt, we'll attend to her as well. She's left us her instructions."

June thanked her. "Please let us know if we can help in any way."

"Oh, my dear. You are our guests." She glanced upstairs and

shook her head. "Terrible goings-on these past few days. We knew it was only a matter of time before those lords went too far. They'll get their comeuppance now. Attacking our guests. Attempted murder of General MacLauren. We'll see those fools hanged for what they've done, and no one will be the sadder for it."

An hour passed before the magistrate left the inn.

He did not stop in the common room to bid them good day, but June understood his preoccupation. Those scoundrels were still on the loose, and he now had to be worried they might do harm to the judge if they weren't caught before he arrived this evening.

She glanced upstairs in the direction of Augustus's room and frowned. They had come so close to killing him. Now desperate, would they sneak in and try to finish the job?

Chapter Seven

WILLOW AND CAMMY stopped in to visit their aunt, while June retrieved *The Book of Love* and headed to Augustus's chamber, hoping he would be dressed and fed by now.

She cleared her throat when she reached his open door.

All of his men were in the room with him, laughing at something he had said they obviously thought was hilarious. They did not seem at all concerned three desperate lords were still on the loose. Well, they had been through years of war, under constant threat of death, and probably did not consider these pampered oafs much of a danger to them even though one of them had come close to blowing Augustus's head off.

Augustus smiled up at her. "Come in, Miss Farthingale."

He was lying in bed, surrounded by his men. He had washed and shaved and was now clad in shirt and breeches. His hands were casually propped behind his bandaged head.

She stifled a sigh.

He looked simply glorious.

"You appear to be occupied with other matters. I can come back another time."

"Nonsense. My men were just leaving. They're going to assist the magistrate in his search."

"Oh, I see."

She smiled at Jock and Angus as they led the younger soldiers out. To her relief, they left the door wide open. "My sisters will pop in here from time to time," she said, taking the chair beside his bed. "I am sure the doctor will also come by to check on you again. Not to mention the innkeeper and his wife."

He took her hand. "June, you needn't stay if it makes you uncomfortable. In truth, you should not be in here alone with me. Let's do this downstairs. We can sit in the garden."

"Are you well enough to get out of bed?"

He laughed and slowly sat up. "We'll soon find out, won't we? If I tumble down the stairs, then the answer is obviously no. Come on, *Tallulah*. I'm dying to know what's in this book."

She inhaled sharply.

He groaned. "What's got your hackles up? That I called you Tallulah or that I said I was dying to know about the book?"

"My hackles are not up. You almost died last night. I cannot help but be worried about you."

"Ah, the mention of death. Poor choice of words on my part. I am fine, June. I will heal."

"Promise me."

"Did I not already promise this yesterday?"

"Yes, but only about surviving last night. You have to promise me about today."

His smile turned tender, and he gave her hand a light squeeze. "I promise I will not die today."

"Thank you, Augustus."

He cast her a steamy look that shot tingles through her body. "I know how worried you are about me, lass. I won't jest about my injury. I came close to meeting my maker last night. Facing death has a way of sorting out what's important in one's life."

She nibbled her lip. "Am I important to you, Augustus?"

"More than I ever expected. If you want the truth, I'm not sure how I feel about that." He donned his boots and jacket as he spoke, then led her to the inn's charming garden where the party had been held last night.

To her relief, he had no trouble making his way down the stairs or through the inn's now empty dining room, which opened onto a terrace and the flowers and greenery beyond. All had been cleaned up from last night's revelry, leaving only the abundant flower beds, spotless green grass, lovely shade trees, and a few strategically placed benches.

There was also a large gazebo in a distant corner that contained a small table and chairs for those who chose to have their tea and cakes outdoors. Perhaps they would share a meal here later if they were progressing nicely with the book and did not wish to be disturbed.

Augustus pointed to a bench beside one of the willow trees. "Shall we sit there?"

"Would you mind if we sat on the grass instead? I think you would be able to stretch out more comfortably there." She pointed to a shaded patch beside a beautiful rose arbor. The flowers themselves were in full sun, and their lovely petals already open and sweetening the air around them.

"Very well, I like the idea." He removed his jacket, set it out on the grass under one of the shade trees, and motioned for her to sit. "Wouldn't want you dirtying your pretty gown."

It happened to be a pale blue muslin with delicate white lace trim at the collar and around the cuffs of its three-quarter length sleeves. She was grateful for the offer since the fabric would stain easily upon the slightly damp grass, something she ought to have thought of herself. "Thank you."

The spot they had chosen was perfect for their needs.

The hour was still early, and the sun had yet to beat down on the garden with its full, midday strength. A light breeze wafted through the leaves, carrying with it the fragrant scent of roses and morning dew.

He settled beside her, propping his back against the sturdy trunk of the shade tree and casting her a wickedly appealing smirk. "You have my full attention, Miss Farthingale. Are you ready to teach me all about love?"

She tipped her head up with pride, in fact, prepared to do just that. It mattered not that he was the one with all the experience, and she was the naïve peahen. His experiences had more to do with sex, which had little to do with commitment leading to marriage. "Yes, I believe I am."

"Where do we start?"

"At the first chapter, which I mentioned briefly when we first met. But I would like to add that we must always be honest with each other in our discussions." She could tell by his continued smirk that he thought he was far more clever than any book about love and did not believe it could teach him anything he did not already know. He would soon learn otherwise. "Honesty is the strength of the book. Honesty is the foundation of any solid marriage."

"Ah, so we are leaping straight to the topic of marriage, are we?"

"I am not surprised you uttered that remark," she shot back, irritated that he did not understand how intertwined love and honesty were. "What is the point of falling in love if one of the parties seeks to avoid a more permanent commitment? How can there ever be true love if the parties are not truthful with each other? How can there ever be trust?"

He arched an eyebrow to mark his surprise by her rebuke.

Well, she wasn't going to let him make light of this book. Finding true love and building a life with the one person who made your heart sing was no small matter. Indeed, these binding relations were the pillar of civilization. "You are obviously squeamish about love, which is not surprising since you are over thirty and have not yet committed to any woman."

"Who says I haven't?"

June blinked, then blinked again as she tried to quell the sudden roil of her stomach. The uneasiness spread upward in a painful coil and turned into an ache to her heart. "I…forgive me, Augustus. I just… I'm so sorry. Have you proposed marriage to anyone? I did not…but you…"

She clamped her mouth shut, knowing she made no sense. How could she not have considered this possibility? Had he asked someone and been spurned?

No, who would ever spurn such a man?

Perhaps he had been married, and his wife had died.

He must have noticed her distress, for he sat up suddenly and leaned closer. "No, June. No proposal. No marriage. Nor have I ever been in love. It was a thoughtless remark on my part. I am the one who owes you the apology."

She nodded her acceptance, her relief probably evident in the breath she released. "Do you wish to be in love?"

"Yes, with the right person. It is not something I ever sought to avoid. I don't know. The years just slipped past me. First the war and then my time afterward in Vienna with Lord Castlereagh."

The earnestness of his words gave her hope. But three days was not a long time to open his eyes to see what was before him. Namely, herself. "This book," she said, returning her gaze to the worn pages, "shows us how to think clearly and understand the truth of what is right in front of us."

"What do you mean?" His smirk was gone, and he appeared to be listening attentively and with an open heart.

"We often lie to ourselves without realizing it. Too often, we see what we want to believe is there and refuse to acknowledge what is truly staring us in the face. The biggest mistake people make is ignoring the faults in another that would make him or her not a good match for them. Physical attraction is one thing, and it is important. But that alone cannot sustain love. This book teaches us how to be honest with ourselves, how to understand and appreciate true love when we find it, and how to successfully make a lasting commitment to the one who has claimed our heart."

Of course, she knew she had found true love for herself.

She had felt this way about Augustus within minutes of their first meeting.

But what of him? He had to come around to admitting he loved her and make his declaration first. If she simply blurted that she loved him, she would only scare him off. He probably knew how she felt since she had absolutely no ability to hide her feelings. But to tell him straight out was too much of a confrontation.

He was not ready to say it back to her.

"This first chapter is about the workings of the male brain. I think you ought to read it on your own. I fear it is too scandalous for me to read aloud to you."

"Why, June? We are adults here, are we not? What does it say?" He settled comfortably against the tree once more and closed his eyes. "Go on."

She cast him an uncertain look which went unnoticed because his eyes were now closed. Then a horrible thought struck her. "Is your vision blurred?"

His response was to crack one eye open and frown at her.

The stubborn dolt.

Exceedingly handsome, but still a dolt.

He was scowling at her but had not denied it.

She frowned back. "Does the doctor know this? Did you tell your men? Of course not. You haven't mentioned it to anyone." She rose to return inside and have the doctor summoned, but he caught her hand and nudged her down beside him.

"Dr. Stratton will stop by again this morning to examine me. We are wasting precious time. I want you to read the blasted book to me."

"Fine. But answer me one thing, and I want the truth, not some platitude you think will assuage me. Is your vision worse than it was last night?"

"No, much better. It is improving. I would have said something if it was worsening. I may be stubborn, but I am not an idiot. All right?"

"Yes." She settled back down beside him, her body tingling because they were so close to each other she could feel the heat and strength of him as their shoulders grazed. She took a deep breath, accidentally inhaling his intoxicating musk scent along with that of the flowers and morning dew, and began to read. "Love does not come from the heart but from the brain. It is the brain that sends signals throughout the body, telling you what to feel. Therefore, to stimulate a man's arousal—"

Augustus burst out laughing. "Blessed saints! June, what in heaven's name is this book teaching you?"

"I warned you this part was scandalous. But it is necessary to lay a foundation in order to understand the divergent functions of a man's brain, the low and the high. It is also necessary to understand the differences between the male and female brains. This chapter explains the compelling urge a man has to mate with any female he deems fertile. He does this in order to spread his seed far and wide. This low-brain response is necessary for the survival of mankind."

Augustus shook his head and groaned. "This is what you were spouting at me the other night."

She nodded. "It would be helpful to see your low-brain function at work. I mean, I saw it at work on the night we met."

He groaned again. "Don't remind me."

"But I haven't noticed you staring at my..." She glanced down at her chest. "Um, my attributes the way you did that first night, and I am curious as to what it means. Have you ruled me out as a potential mating partner? Or have you simply gotten better at leering at—"

"I do not leer at you. And I am not going to answer that question."

"Very well." She had expected him to be stubborn, but she would wear him down as they read further into the book. "From what the book says, that mating urge is always 'on' in men. Like a lamp that's always lit. It's just there, in the background, waiting to be turned up or down. Waiting to burn hotter or turn colder. I suppose this is where the expression 'flames of desire' sprang from. You are turning red in the face, Augustus. May we at least talk about it? You don't have to show me anything yet."

"Show you? Yet? Are you mad, lass? I..." He gaped at her.

"Just what do ye think I ought to be showing ye? And ye had better not have asked this of any other man. Ye haven't, have ye?"

"Of course not." She sighed. "Your brogue is back, a sure sign you are irritated with me. I rather like it, not that you have asked for my opinion. Do all Scottish highlanders sound as delicious as you do? Oh, I can see I've upset you. It wasn't my intention at all, so please stop frowning at me. You are misunderstanding my request. I am not asking you to expose yourself."

"June!" He cast her a genuinely perplexed look. "Oh, lord. What sort of man do ye think I am?"

"The best sort, Augustus." However, should he consider stripping off his clothes, she would not be nearly as scandalized as she ought to be. Indeed, he could probably convince her to remove hers as well. Then, whatever would happen—

No, they would have to be married first.

Marriage was never going to happen if he believed her to be daft.

She cleared her throat and continued. "Women have urges of their own, the book claims. The male urge is to sow his seed far and wide. However, not just any woman will do. His low brain must make a quick assessment of every woman he encounters. Those deemed too old, too young, too sickly, are quickly dismissed. Those deemed fertile become the desired object of his attention."

She cleared her throat again and pressed on while he remained staring at her with his mouth agape. "The female urge is to find the mate who will protect her and her children. She must choose a partner who will stay close to their home and fight off predators. Because if he abandons her and their children, they will be left defenseless and eaten by wolves."

She glanced up at him. "Not real wolves, of course. The point is, a woman is at her most vulnerable when she has just given birth to her children. And how is she to feed and care for those children without the strong male to protect her?"

"Are ye done yet?"

She cleared her throat again. "No, just a little more. Jumping back to the man's low brain for a moment. While many women will satisfy a male's low-brain need, very few will meet the standard required by the male's high brain. That's your selective brain, the one that enables you to fall in love and protect your mate and offspring, thereby enhancing their chances of survival. It is the same for any animal in the wild. The female seeks to—"

"Got it. You seek out the strongest to protect you."

She nodded. "Yes, exactly. Just as you seek out the most desirable females for purposes of breeding your offspring. And now we can move on to the chapters about the senses because in choosing the mate we find most desirable, we all have different preferences and opinions on the qualities we seek. Our mate—"

"Will you kindly stop using that word."

"What word? Mate? Very well. I'm just trying to discuss this scientifically."

"Well, ye're not."

She smiled at him. "You are still red in the face. Are you aroused?"

"June!'

"Fine," she said with a sigh. "No more discussion of chapter one. Let us concentrate on the five senses now, sight, touch, taste, scent, and hearing. The importance of these chapters is to teach us how to open ourselves to the truth of what we are seeing, or hearing, and so on. We can use each other as mutual test frogs."

"I am not going to be anyone's test frog."

"Fine, if you wish to be stubborn about it. Then I shall be your test frog. You make it sound as though it is something odious and frightening when it is not at all. I'll prove it to you. What do you see when you look at me?" She shifted closer to him and turned her body toward his so that she faced him.

He studied her for a long moment, then lolled his head back against the tree and groaned. He was doing an awful lot of that.

"Do you need another moment to gather your thoughts before responding? I completely understand. Your brain must be quite scrambled after being shot."

"My brain is just fine."

"I'm sure it usually is." She held back her laughter because he sounded quite peevish. Obviously, this big Scot had an abundance of pride, especially when it came to his intelligence. However, if he was too dense to realize she was perfect for him, then he was not nearly as clever as he prided himself on being.

"Augustus, I expect you are one of the most accomplished men in all England. But your intelligence in business or politics or military matters does not mean you know what you are doing when it comes to matters of love. I should think the Duke of Wellington is a prime example of that. I would not like you to make the same mistake as he has done and spend the rest of your days miserable."

She waited a moment for him to answer, then prodded him again when he remained silent. "Truly, Augustus. This should not be a difficult question. What do you see when you look at me?"

After a moment, his lips quirked upward in the hint of a smile.

He looked so handsome when he smiled.

In truth, he looked handsome all the time.

His eyes were now on her, and she could see the depth of brilliance and keen assessment behind their glint. "The truth then," he muttered softly. "I see a beautiful young woman."

"That's it? More information, please. What leads you to the conclusion that I am beautiful?"

"Soft, rosy lips. Peach-soft cheeks. Vivid blue eyes. Lustrous dark hair. Tempting body. Exquisite body, if I am to be honest about it."

She laughed again. "Yes, I recall your response on the night we met. I was quite delighted to have passed your low-brain assessment. I'm pleased I still do. Tell me more."

He casually bent one leg and rested his arm upon his knee. "Such as?"

"Am I only a pretty face and body to you?"

"No, June. You know you are much more than that." He kept his gaze on her face and groaned lightly.

More groaning, was that a good sign?

"You are intelligent. Brave. Compassionate. Graceful. Genuine. There is no artifice about you. When you smile, it is a warm, beautiful smile. You are wicked with a hearth iron. You looked magnificent as you wielded it against those scoundrels. Have I given you enough?"

"We are only getting started."

"Blessed saints, how much more is there?"

"Plenty. We are only on chapter two. What did you notice about me first?"

He reached out and brushed a stray curl off her brow as it caught on the gentle breeze. "I don't know that I can say I noticed one specific thing first. It felt more like everything about you hit me all at once. The three of you were whispering outside my door, your backs to me as you looked down on the wedding celebration. Perhaps it was your voice that caught my attention first, its lovely lilt. Then I noticed your body. When you glanced up, I saw your face."

"What did you think of it?"

He grinned as he brushed that same windblown curl off her brow again. "I thought you were spectacular. I even dubbed you *Spectacular June* when you came downstairs to sit beside me. I knew you would try to approach me because I'd heard your plan. I was hoping you would."

She laughed and shook her head. "I was scared to death. I had never done anything like that before."

"It was obvious. But you needn't have worried. You were charming."

"I made a fool of myself."

"Not in the least. I had set out to teach you a lesson because I did not like the idea that a rustic from Barnstaple would use me as her test frog. But I quickly saw that I had underestimated you in every way. Until those miscreants came along, I was enjoying your company immensely. What did I think when I saw you up close? Face of an angel. Soft, melodic laugh. Intelligence, wit, and charm. Not to mention a body so exquisite, it put my heart in palpitations."

"It did?"

"Yes, June. It did. Let's get back to reading the book, shall we?"

She cast him a beaming smile. "So I passed your low-brain test?"

"With top honors, Miss Farthingale. Move on to the next part."

"All right. These chapters on the senses are really about training us to judge clearly and see beyond a pretty face or charming voice. Any partner we choose ought to be pleasing to our senses. However, it is important not to be carried away by them. Finding the person who pleases us in all those ways is merely one part of our journey. Sometimes we are so overcome with joy in finding that person, we purposely overlook their faults because we have convinced ourselves the object of our physical desire must also be the perfect partner for us."

"I think I see. A man may be physically pleasing, but he may also drink excessively or gamble. Perhaps he is lazy. Or may be unfaithful."

She nodded. "Exactly. It does not even have to be something sinful. Perhaps one of them enjoys quiet nights at home while the other loves to entertain. One loves the city while the other loves country life. One may be too controlling or nagging while the other one desires more liberty or more of a partnership within the marriage."

Augustus regarded her steadily. "Perhaps one knows that his life will require extensive travel that will necessitate his being apart from his wife for long stretches of time."

"Why could he not take his wife with him?"

"It could be he is traveling to a dangerous area unsuitable for his family's safety. It could be that his wife would feel isolated and miserable to be apart from her family for so long if he did take her with him."

So, this was his concern, just as Aunt Charlotte had warned.

He was worried about taking her away from her family if he were posted to Vienna or elsewhere in the world. He was afraid she would be lonely and out of her element in an unfamiliar city where she did not speak the language. "Other wives must be in the same position. This cannot be an unusual thing. Can they not befriend each other? I am sure this is what commonly happens, the wives forming a circle of friends while the husbands are busy at work."

"It isn't only that. There will be times when a wife will be called upon to entertain. A bachelor is rarely called upon to do this, but once he is married, it will be expected of him. It would be nothing were it merely a matter of entertaining a small circle of compatriots. But his wife would be expected to entertain royalty or high-ranking government ministers and do it effortlessly and without mistake."

"Such as seating her guests in proper order of rank? Or having the proper place settings, the correct order of silverware and glassware? The best wines? Knowing what foods one of those important personages adores and those he cannot abide?" She could not feel insulted by his remarks because he truly did not know her.

In truth, she had never entertained other than merely assisting her mother when necessary. But she had learned enough, for their house had a constant stream of guests through it. Of course, her parents had never entertained personages more elevated than their local magistrate, but common hospitality and consideration were applicable to all guests regardless of their status, weren't they? "Do you think a young woman who is little traveled and has not yet made her debut would be overwhelmed by the responsibility?"

He regarded her steadily. "June, oftentimes truces are reached at the dining table. Alliances are formed. Deals are made. It is not merely a matter of the right dinner plates. It is understanding the subtleties and nuances in every word and gesture. It is about having the right connections. It is—"

"And you think an ignorant girl from Barnstaple will hold you back? That is what this discussion is truly about. You are not interested in falling in love. You wanted to know about this book because you do *not* wish to fall in love with someone unsophisticated and are trying to figure out how to avoid it."

"June, that is not so. I am not resistant to falling in love."

His words only made her heart ache more. "You are right. You have said *would* like to fall in love, and I know you are not a liar. I ought to have been more specific. What you really wish to do is *not* fall in love with me."

"June…"

"This is the disaster you seek to avoid. Is this not so?"

Chapter Eight

Blessed saints!

Augustus felt tension coil throughout his body. A muscle twitched in his jaw. How had his discussion gone from a casual one about the general properties of love to an intensely personal one about them? And now June was tossing daggers at him with her beautiful, glittering eyes.

They were still the most exquisite blue he had ever beheld, and he could not stop looking at them…or at her, because she was a bundle of radiance as she scowled at him with all the passion of her convictions.

What had he said that was so wrong?

Weren't these issues important for a man in his position to consider when he took himself a wife? Isn't this what she had been reading to him? "All right, June. I've obviously upset you."

She sighed. "It isn't what you've said."

"Yes, it is. Honesty is best, is this not what you told me at the outset? Perhaps I have been a little too honest with you." He did not like to see her hurt, especially knowing he was the cause of her pain.

"No," she said with evident frustration. "What you are doing is not being honest with yourself. This is precisely what the book is warning us not to do. You have come up with all these questions about the suitability of your future wife. Obviously, you have given it thought."

"Is this a bad thing?"

"Not at all. It is right that you should raise these concerns. But what you have done wrong is form your own conclusion and are now twisting the facts to support your conclusion. Have you even contemplated asking for my opinion?"

He hadn't, as both of them well knew.

"Augustus, why would you make such an important decision affecting both our lives without discussing it with me? Would you not consult with Lord Castlereagh on a diplomatic matter or your fellow generals on military matters?"

"This assumes these questions I am raising about a suitable wife are specifically about you." Which they were, but he was behaving like a dolt because he had never felt so strongly about any woman before, and it frightened him.

He could stand fearless, weaponless, and outnumbered amid an enemy cavalry charge, cannons bursting all around him and a dozen bayonets pointed at his gut. That was easy. Facing his feelings for June was infinitely more daunting.

"Are those questions not about me?"

Of course, they were. But how could he admit it to June without giving her false hope?

"Oh, I see," she said, unable to hide her disappointment in the face of his continued silence. "Yes, I thought…because you kissed me, and you agreed to read *The Book of Love* with me. I'm sorry. This is mortifying. You claimed there was no one else, but perhaps there was, and you simply did not wish to admit it to me."

He groaned.

He was making things worse by his continued silence, but he did not know what to say to her without giving her false hope.

How could he admit to feeling more than a passing attraction?

One did not upend one's life, one's future, on to a girl one had known hardly longer than a day.

"I did not realize there was someone else who held your

heart. I accused you of twisting facts to reach the conclusion you wished to reach when this is exactly what I have done."

She appeared ready to burst into tears.

He was an idiot for giving her a hard time about it. "June, there is no one else. It is about you. Surely, it is obvious. Ignore my stupid comments. And you are right. These matters concern both of us. It was not fair of me to shut you out. I can only say that I have been on my own for so long, I was not even aware of how efficient I had become at shutting everyone out."

He reached out and touched her cheek. "But if you were to become a part of my life, then I had better get used to sharing my thoughts with you, shouldn't I?"

"Yes." She arched an eyebrow. "Not just sharing yours but listening to mine as well."

He nodded. "When it comes to personal matters, you seem to have more sense than I do."

"Oh, I doubt it. But I do have this book, and I cannot tell you how many times I have rushed back to refer to it since I've met you." She smiled, now seemingly mollified by his explanation. "I cannot say whether I would be the capable hostess you require, but I know I would not be afraid of trying."

Indeed, she was a fearless little thing.

She had gone after his attackers that first night and laid them low with admirable brilliance. What she lacked in brute force, she more than made up for in cleverness. It was his mistake in dismissing her abilities.

He had been so caught up in worrying about her being eaten alive by others in the Vienna social circles, he did not consider that she, with her beautiful smile and quick wit, might be the one to vanquish them.

"Augustus, I am not afraid of traveling to Vienna or wherever your posts may take you. It is the first thing that crossed my mind. Would I want to leave England? What would I be losing if I went with you? Would it be worth giving up so much to be with you?"

"These are not questions with easy answers, June."

"I know. But I would like the opportunity to talk about these concerns with you. I've never been outside of England. I would miss my family, of course. But when all the choices are weighed—and I've done nothing but make lists in my head of the advantages and disadvantages—the decision is simple for me. Having met you, I cannot imagine my life without you."

He marveled at her certainty.

She saw her choices with such clarity.

If only he could be so certain. But this was not him. He did not leap to judgment. He methodically considered all possible outcomes.

He also had the benefit of experience, while June was making her decisions based on hopes and dreams.

"Augustus, building a life with you would be more important to me than anything I might ever have to give up." She cast him a wry smile. "But I do not think you have come to any decisions about me. I don't know that I am as important to you as you are to me."

"Don't say that, June. You are obviously someone I care about, or I would not be sitting here with you and that book. There is nowhere I would rather be than right here with you, making a thoughtless arse out of myself."

She laughed. "You are brilliant and wonderful. I am enjoying every moment spent with you."

"As I do with you, but this is one of my concerns. There will come a time, and likely very soon, when I cannot take you with me on my travels. How would you feel about this?"

A hint of sadness cast a shadow over the vibrance of her eyes. "I thought about this possibility, too. I knew there had to come a time when we might feel safest by my staying behind in England to raise our children while you are sent elsewhere in the world."

Children?

He hadn't even wrapped his head around taking a wife, and she was already leaping forward to starting a family.

And yet, he could not imagine anyone other than June in that role. He had never felt so strongly about any other woman, and he had met some of the most beautiful women in Europe. Not only beautiful but intelligent, as well. He had even met a few with every attribute a man could possibly desire. Wealth, beauty, intelligence…not to mention talents in bed.

None of them came close to stirring his heart the way June had. "Tell me truly, June. How would you feel about the necessity of long stretches apart?"

"That is an easy question for me. However, I would pose it slightly differently."

"What do you mean?"

"The question I would ask is, how would I feel about keeping my loved ones safe? It would always be my first consideration. I would never insist on joining you if my presence would put us in danger, and especially if we had children. I would always do my best to keep them safe. If that meant our remaining apart, then this is how it would be."

"But not all wives…or husbands, for that matter…handle the separation well. It is a fact. Not all marriages can survive this."

June set aside the book and clasped her hands on her lap. "For me, this is where family becomes so important. I would have the support and comfort of my Farthingale relatives during your absences. This is exactly my cousin Violet's situation. Her husband, Romulus Brayden, is a captain in the Royal Navy and in command of one of its fighting ships. He is away for months at a time. It is not easy for either of them, but she has the family to keep her busy and can always turn to them for help whenever Romulus is on duty. It would be no different for me."

She picked up the book again. "This book isn't merely about finding true love, but about knowing how to build a life together. Whose life is ever perfect? Everyone faces challenges. I think the question to ask is, will we accept these challenges? Will we accept each other for who we are and what we must do? This also goes back to the question of our faults. What faults can we tolerate in a marriage? What faults would absolutely destroy a marriage? The answer is not the same for everyone."

"I see what you are saying. It has to do with compromise and expectations."

He must have finally said something right because June cast him a beaming smile. Truly, she had such a beautiful smile. How could he not wish to wake to it every day? "Why are you grinning at me, June?"

"A large part of the book is devoted to discussion about our expectations and also about our connections. I am glad you mentioned it. I was hoping we would have time to get to this topic."

"Haven't we been speaking of just this thing for the past hour?"

"It has hardly been half an hour, although it must feel excruciatingly long for you." She was smiling at him and spoke in apparent jest, so he merely smiled along with her and listened as she continued. "Yes, we have been speaking of it, but the book explains it so much better than I ever could."

"Then let's leap ahead, shall we? We can always return to the five senses afterward."

She nodded. "I would like that."

"Go ahead, tell me about expectations and connections."

"Well, I am not sure what connects us, since I am not sure we have anything in common."

He had his back propped against the bark of the tree once again and was feeling quite comfortable seated on the grass with this lovely lass by his side. "June, even a little thing such as you and me sitting here is a connection. Another young lady might have refused to sit outdoors. Another might have preferred to sit on the bench rather than settle on the grass. And certainly, on that first night, any other young lady would not have picked up a fire iron and taken down two of those drunken oafs."

She tipped her head in obvious confusion. "How does this connect us?"

"That first night revealed you are spirited, clever, and brave. Of course, I also found you strikingly beautiful, but those qualities of cleverness, spirit, and bravery are those of a Highlander. You may have been born and bred in England, but you have the heart of a Scot. Being one myself, I admired this in you."

"Thank you, Augustus. I am honored."

"Here's another way we are connected," he said, finding himself quite enjoying this discussion. He could not recall ever speaking at length to a woman like this, never so openly and honestly, and never so interested in hearing her opinion.

Which showed what an idiot he had been to avoid this discussion with her until now. "Choosing to sit on the grass reveals your love of the countryside. You feel at home hiking through hills or stretching out upon a patch of meadow grass and enjoying the sun and air. It is possible you will also enjoy the London season, but I do not think your heart will ever be in a city. Nor is mine. Caithness is my home, no matter how many years duty calls me away."

"My sisters and I were so reluctant to go to London. Perhaps we will enjoy the balls and theaters, shops and museums, but I doubt we will ever think of ourselves as Londoners even if we end up living there for most of our lives."

He liked watching June, loved the way her pretty mouth pursed when she was thinking, or how her eyes gleamed when exchanging opinions with him. She was easy to talk to and never felt out of her depth. "Tell me about the chapter on expectations. What does your book say about that?"

"Oh, plenty." Her hair caught the sunlight as she shook her head and laughed gently. "It is quite simple, really, and yet something so many of us stumble over. I still do, even after reading it time and again. Boiled to its essence, it is saying that our expectations must be reasonable and realistic. If we demand too much of our partner, we are asking for strife. But our partner must also be reasonable in his expectations. We cannot demand perfection in each other. Nor can we agree to a marriage thinking we are going to change one thing or another about each other."

She shifted closer, her eyes bright as she imparted her knowledge. "For example, if I were the sort to require your devoted attention and you were the sort who wanted to be left alone most of the time, we would have a problem. I would be constantly demanding of your time, and you would constantly feel frustrated and confined. But if I understood your desire to be left to yourself, perhaps we could compromise, and I would have your attention at supper every evening or for certain events or other times during the week. It would be a troubled marriage if you refused this compromise, unless I was willing to accept your terms and forge my own friends and activities without you."

"Assuming ours is a love match. Most people marry for reasons other than love. If a woman married a man for his wealth and title, then she might be quite happy to leave him to himself so long as he provided a roof over her head and ample pin money."

"Oh, that is true. Many *ton* marriages are like this, and the parties are well satisfied not to see each other too often, especially after the required offspring are produced. Yes, it is all about what one expects in their union. This is why love matches sometimes do not work out. We want so much of each other, and it hurts that much more when we do not obtain it."

He nodded. "True, the pain is always far greater when you care for someone."

"This is why so many families scoff at these love matches." She cleared her throat and glanced away as though suddenly shy. "But Farthingales do not. We only marry for love."

Well, he'd known it. June did not hide her feelings. It seemed she had fallen in love with him practically at first sight. It ought to have scared him, perhaps troubled him. In truth, he merely felt elated.

He had felt this same attraction toward her. Only he refused to leap to the conclusion that he had fallen in love. This was his nature, to be deliberate. Never to take a step forward without considering all the possibilities. Also, a stumbling block he could not get over was the fact they had known each other for so little time. Should it not take months to come to a decision on an important matter such as marriage? How could they ever trust each other well enough to leap into a lifetime commitment?

Yet, June was so sure.

Perhaps it was different for women.

He was not going to tell her that, however. She would punch him in the nose if he did. Fortunately, there was no need to say anything. Dr. Stratton found them and put an end to their conversation. "Ah, there you are, General MacLauren. Good morning, Miss Farthingale. How is our patient today?"

"In excellent health," Augustus responded immediately. He rose and offered a hand to June to help her up as well.

"Check his vision, Dr. Stratton." She bent and picked his jacket up off the ground, giving it a little shake before returning it to him. "Do not let him talk you out of it. He cannot read, which is why I was reading to him this morning."

The doctor did not bother to glance at the book but immediately turned his attention to Augustus. "Is this true?"

If ever a stubborn, prideful Scot existed, Augustus supposed he was it. Since he had no inclination to respond to the question, June decided to answer for him. "Yes, it is true. And I had better come with you while you examine him because I do not want him denying any other aches or pains."

"Miss Farthingale," the doctor said, sounding quite appalled, "I hardly think it is appropriate."

She tipped her head up in indignation. "Dear me, I know it is not appropriate. But he will not admit to any discomfort unless he is called out on it. Is it not more important to know how he is truly feeling?"

"General MacLauren, will you allow this?"

Augustus grinned at her. "I do not think I have a choice in the matter, Dr. Stratton. Clearly, a Farthingale outranks an army general in such matters. But we need not return to my bedchamber." He motioned toward the gazebo. "Would you have any objection to examining me over there?"

Dr. Stratton arched an eyebrow. "I suppose it will be all right. I'm here to look at your stitches and the area of the wound. But I also need to check your muscular coordination, and as Miss Farthingale pointed out, your vision."

June gave a nod of approval.

Not that anyone had asked her for it, but Augustus did not mind her interference. In truth, he liked June's concern for him. He and his brother had not had much experience with a woman's soft touch since his mother and Thad's had died too young.

June was kind and compassionate and would make a good mother to their children. *Blessed saints!* Had he just allowed that thought to cross his mind?

But creating those little heathen offspring with June was something he would quite enjoy. Had he not spent the last few days fighting the urge to bed her? To sink himself deep inside her? Had his dreams not been filled with unmentionably erotic fantasies about her?

He ran a hand along the nape of his neck, suddenly feeling hot.

Scorching.

Inconveniently consumed by the blazing fires flowing through his blood, if he wished to be honest about…which he did not.

He held out a chair for June to sit when they reached the gazebo, but she shook her head. "I'll stand out of the way. Let Dr. Stratton look at you."

He did not argue, merely sat down and tried not to wince when the doctor lightly touched the area of his stitches. It was tender, and the man's touch was nowhere near as pleasant as June's. He dutifully responded when asked how many fingers the doctor held out and had little trouble with the range of tests put to him.

He felt only the slightest bit dizzy when the doctor moved his hand in a wide arc from left to right and had him follow the motion with his eyeballs only. "That's it, General MacLauren. Keep your head straight. Move your eyes only."

Apparently, the doctor was satisfied with his progress.

He then checked Augustus's neck, carefully turning it to the left and then the right.

He had Augustus move his fingers and then raise his arms.

Next, he had him hold out his hand and then bring a finger to the tip of his nose, which he did quite easily.

"Now, General MacLauren. Please stand up, count to three, and then sit down again."

He did as the doctor asked.

"Again, General MacLauren."

He repeated the motion.

June, he noted all the while, had her lips pursed and was absently nibbling her lusciously plump, lower lip as she listened to the doctor's requests and watched him comply. He knew his vision was clearing because he noticed the fleshy quiver of her lip, noted the way it turned a deep pink each time she lightly bit down on it.

He desperately wanted to kiss her.

June was going to tip him over the edge if she did not stop that sweet nibble.

He looked away before he made a fool of himself.

"Well done," Dr. Stratton said, looking quite pleased as he finished the examination. "You seem to be healing nicely. This does not mean you have my permission to overdo it. I want you to get plenty of rest, and do not exert yourself over the next few days. You may feel fit at the moment, but your head is still in delicate shape. A brain bleed is no laughing matter. Keep the area of the wound clean, as I showed you yesterday. I'll take those stitches out in a week's time, assuming all continues to improve. Do you have any questions for me?"

"No, Doctor." He glanced at June and arched an eyebrow. "June?"

She blushed. "No."

The doctor grinned. "I will look in on you tomorrow."

Augustus gave a grateful nod. "Thank you."

He did not bother to mention that he intended to ride off with his men once the assizes judge held his hearing tomorrow and took his testimony. He would discuss it with the doctor another time and outside of June's hearing.

He stood beside her in silence as they watched the man stride away.

Once they were alone again, Augustus glanced toward the shade tree. "Care to resume reading the book?"

His jacket was slung over the back of his chair. It was made of a delicate, wrought iron that hardly held his size and brawn. It matched the equally delicate table and the other chairs surrounding it. Since he had not bothered to don his jacket while he was being examined, he did not bother to put it on now.

His question surprised her, but she seemed pleased by it. "I would love to continue reading, but not if you are tired. As the doctor said, you must not overdo it."

He laughed. "Sitting in the shade on a warm summer's day with a pretty girl who will read to me is hardly overdoing it. But we can stop if you wish."

She shook her head. "I intend to steal every minute I can with you. Is it not embarrassingly obvious? I have no wish to end our time together."

He took her arm and led her out of the gazebo. "Nor do I, June."

They went back to their spot under the shade tree, which had the added advantage of privacy. There was no clear view of them from anywhere inside the inn. One would have to walk out into the garden and along the rows of flower beds and boxwood to notice them seated on the grass. They were also partially hidden by a small willow tree with weeping leaves that were healthy and in full bloom.

He spread out his jacket and waited for her to sit down on it before he once again stretched casually beside her and settled his back against the tree trunk.

"We left off speaking of expectations and connections," she said, now nestled by his side and looking as beautiful as the roses in the garden. "But I hate to take this discussion out of order. There is a natural progression to these topics. First, the author teaches us about the differences in the male and female brain and what we each look for in a suitable mate. Then moving on to how our senses respond to that desirable mate. Once we understand these physical responses, only then does the author move on to the questions important in actually building a happy marriage."

"We did hop ahead," he agreed, propping his hands behind his head and watching June as she turned the pages of the book. "But I thought we made good progress. It does not matter to me in which order we take things. If your preference is to return to the five senses, then so be it."

Not that he felt the need to explore these five senses.

His had been going off like a fireworks display ever since meeting June.

There was no question she pleased him in every way, but if she wanted to be methodical about it, then he would not give her a hard time. He had nowhere else to be and nothing else to do.

Even if he had, he would have found a reason to seek her out and spend time with her.

He simply enjoyed her company.

Looking upon her was sheer delight.

They could sit together without talking, and he would never grow bored. Even in silence, she had the most expressive face, and he was constantly fascinated by it.

She also had beautiful breasts. Yes, utterly low-brain. But should he not have these feelings for her?

The wind picked up slightly so that June now had to hold the pages of the book down to keep them from blowing back and forth. The heightened gusts also blew her curls loose. A few fell over her forehead and whipped in her eyes so that she frowned and struggled to push them back.

"If you turn to face me," he suggested, "the breeze will go against you and keep the hair out of your eyes."

"An excellent suggestion." She shifted her spectacular derriere and tucked her legs under it, contentedly settling into this new position facing him.

Her smile simply dazzled him.

Everything about her dazzled him.

She noticed he was staring at her and blushed. "Um…" She licked her lips. "We left off at the sense of sight. Shall I pick it up from there?"

"If you like."

"Um…well, it isn't only my choice. What would you like me to do?"

Something very naughty that involved removing her gown and allowing him to lick places on her body that would make her coo and purr.

But that did not bear comment.

He cleared his throat. "Just read, June. Isn't this what we are out here to do?"

"Well, yes. But these chapters are about the senses."

"And?"

"Having a test frog would be most helpful at this point. Have you changed your mind about being mine?"

"No. I am nobody's test frog."

"But that means I must be yours then. I am not sure it will work out as well. I should be the one testing things out on you and seeing how you respond."

He cast her a lazy smile. "Oh, I think it will work better if I test them out on you."

"Do you think so?"

"Yes, June. Because I know just how to make you respond."

Her eyes widened, and the little pulse at the base of her throat began to throb against her lightly flushed skin. "Um…all right…I think…"

She took a deep breath that drew his eyes once more to her magnificent breasts.

They heaved lightly as her breaths quickened.

Lord in heaven, he was going to devour this girl.

She licked her lips again. "What do you propose to do to me?"

CHAPTER NINE

JUNE WANTED SO badly to run her hands along Augustus's body. His shirt of white lawn enhanced the size of his muscles and made his shoulders appear quite broad. He was lean and sinewed, nothing soft about him, not even his expression as he looked at her.

A shiver of delight ran through her.

Did he want to touch her?

She cleared her throat which was now impossibly dry. "We've discussed sight. Next is the sense of touch. Um…this is the point where you touch me and see how I respond."

Why did he suddenly look so pained?

But he edged closer, apparently willing to continue. "Is there anywhere, in particular, you would like me to touch you?"

Oh, please. Everywhere.

She stared down at the book because she was going to make a fool of herself if she continued to look at him. "Nowhere impolite, of course. Not that such thoughts crossed your mind. You are a gentleman."

He laughed.

"Are you not?"

"No, June. I am not. I would caution you to keep that in mind."

Sweet mother.

Is this why her body felt deliciously on fire?

She held out her hand. "Let's start with something simple like the touch of our hands."

Of course, she would love to do more. His muscled arms and those gloriously big shoulders of his were definitely beckoning to her.

"All right, but never mistake this touch for something simple. It is not. It is a deceptively potent sensation."

"Thank you for the warning. I shall keep it in mind while we explore this sense." Her hand was still held out to him, but he had not moved to take it yet.

Breathe, June.

She glanced up and found herself staring into his fiery gaze. Well, she thought it was fiery. Perhaps it was just the sun beating down on him, although they were in the shade.

She could do with a lemonade.

Or a bucket of cold water thrown over her head.

His gaze was still hot enough to melt her insides.

"Why are you frowning, June?"

Because she could not explain any of what she was feeling. He should not be looking at her in that I'm-going-to-set-your-body-on-fire way. *Hah!* She was already in flames.

Besides, they had already discussed the sense of sight and were moving on to the next sensation, which was touch.

Her hand was still out.

Why had he not taken it yet? "I find this chapter quite difficult to understand."

He regarded her earnestly, no trace of mockery or condescension. "Why?"

She should not have suggested they continue reading this book. She should not have brought them back to the beginning chapters on the senses.

She took a deep breath as he now took her hand in his, and tingles shot up her spine. "Whenever you touch me, I respond from somewhere deep within my soul. This feeling does not spring from any logical place. I cannot control it, Augustus. It is just there. How can anyone understand a feeling such as this? How can anyone tame it or put logic to it?"

"One cannot. As I said, it is a powerful sensation."

She nodded, trying to ignore the soft swirl of his thumb over the top of her hand. "I tingled when you held me as we danced last night. I felt as though I belonged with you and to you. I'm sorry. I do not mean to embarrass you with my honesty. Well, I suppose I am embarrassing myself. Was it the same for you, Augustus? What did you feel when I was in your arms?"

He grinned. "Do you think I had the capacity to hold a logical thought once I had my arms around you?"

Her eyes widened. "Did you tingle as well?"

"No. Men do not tingle. Let us just say I enjoyed it very much."

"You are being polite. You've held many women in your arms, those of the highest ranks in society. Elegant. Beautiful. Sophisticated women. I must be quite ordinary compared to them."

He appeared surprised by her remark. "Why would you say such a thing? These others were nothing compared to you. I've never enjoyed myself more than I have with you. Did I not give you glowing compliments earlier?"

She squelched her amusement. *Glowing?* This big Scot did not exactly toss love sonnets at her and declare himself in raptures. He had said she was pretty, and he liked her body. "You said very nice things indeed. But you've probably said the same to those beautiful, sophisticated women you met in Vienna."

"I hate that word."

"What word?"

"Sophisticated."

"Why?"

"Because *sophisticated* people take on other lovers and do not make a scene when the affair is over. *Sophisticated* people do not care if their spouses are unfaithful or if they are unfaithful to their spouses. *Sophisticated* people put fashion and elegance over honor and morality. Scots are not sophisticated people."

"But you move around effortlessly in those elevated circles."

He emitted a mirthless laugh. "This is exactly why I am determined to return to Caithness, because it has become effortless for me. But that man who made his way through the Vienna courts and palaces is not truly me. That man is a mere facade I am adept at showing to the world."

"And who are you truly?"

He shook his head and laughed. "You are a little snoop, aren't you?"

She grinned. "Yes, I will not deny it. All Farthingales are snoopy. It is in our blood. But we are not gossips. Well, we do enjoy a good gossip, but that is something altogether different. We do not blab secrets told to us in confidence."

"But is this not the point of gossip?"

"We are not malicious about it, and we never betray friends or family. Anything you tell me in confidence will remain between you and me. I promise, Augustus. I like talking to you. Very much. Please tell me about yourself. I am eager to know more of you."

He tucked a finger under her chin and gave it a little tweak. "As I am curious about you."

She rolled her eyes. "There is very little about me that you do not already know. I haven't had anywhere near your life experiences. But tell me, who do you feel you are at heart?"

He shrugged. "Who am I really? I am that boy who used to climb the soaring crags along with his little brother and look out for him, so he did not scrape his knee. I am the young man who drank ale, tossed ridiculously heavy cabers at our Highland games to impress the lasses, and swapped exaggerated stories with his granduncle and MacLauren kinsmen at our clan gatherings. I am the soldier who went off to fight Napoleon because it was the right thing to do. And I am the man who stayed behind to work tirelessly with Lord Castlereagh to try to keep the fragile peace on the Continent. We all need hope for a better future for ourselves and our loved ones."

He ran a hand through his hair and sighed. "But there will never be peace. There will always be men such as Napoleon who want to grab power for themselves and rule with an iron fist. Even among our allies, there is always dissension. Over borders. Over spoils of war. Over dominance in the region. Over perceived insults and other petty, stupid things."

"And yet, if you are not there to help Lord Castlereagh control them, then who will do it?"

He shrugged again. "There are others."

"As capable as you?"

He seemed amused by the remark. "I like to think not, but I am sure there are. The Duke of Wellington's brother, for one."

"He is only one man. Would he not want you with him to help out?"

"It is likely." He stared at her with pursed lips and an intensely thoughtful look. "We've gotten off the topic. Should we not be speaking of the book? I believe we meant to discuss the sense of touch."

He stroked his thumb over the meaty part of her palm and then casually swept it over her wrist.

Dear heaven.

Did he realize what he was doing to her?

He lightly entwined his fingers in hers, his flesh rough against the softness of her own. That roughness added to her pleasure, for his hands were big and warm, his fingers elegant and sensuous.

"How does my hand feel in yours, Augustus?"

"You would not care to hear it."

"Yes, I would. You can tell me anything." But she was worried, for their discussion about his diplomatic role only served to illustrate how important he was to the fate of England and how insignificant she was with her complete lack of experience. "Honesty in all things," she reminded him. "Tell me what is going through your mind."

"Honesty," he murmured, returning his gaze to hers with a seductive heat she found immensely appealing. How could a girl's heart not take flame when he cast her that smoldering look? "No, I think not yet. You are my test frog. You go first."

She slipped her hand out of his grasp. "I see. I suppose that makes it clear."

He shook his head as though perplexed. "What have I just made clear?"

"You have decided I am unsuitable for you."

"What?" He caught her hand again. "What makes you think this is what I have on my mind?"

"I am not suggesting you detest me. Indeed, I think you rather do like me, but not enough to ever consider including me in your life."

"Now, who is forming opinions without bothering to ask for mine?"

She tried to slip her hand out of his grasp again, but this time he would not let her. "Let us move on with the rest of it, June. But perhaps we can skip over the other senses."

"Why?"

"I expect they are only part of the story. One may find that special person to be beautiful, to have a soft, lovely voice. To have skin as delicate as a peach and lips that taste just as sweet. Perhaps her scent is that of roses…or lavender…we Highlanders are particularly fond of that scent because it reminds us of home."

She blushed. "That is my scent."

"I know. But there are reasons beyond one's senses that may make one person wrong for another."

"Or perhaps that person is absolutely right for the other, but that other is a stubborn Scot who is too thickheaded to admit it."

He laughed. "You are berating me again, June."

She shook her head in denial. "No, I am trying to make you open your eyes and fall in love with me. But you have a way of pulling back whenever you feel you are letting me in too close."

"June, what am I to say to that?"

"You needn't say anything. The last thing I wish to do is push you in a direction you do not wish to go. The point of us reading the book and exploring these sensations is to teach us how to recognize true love and not fall into the trap of a doomed infatuation. It is not about forcing you to feel something you do not feel for me. Truly."

He drew her closer so that she somehow ended up on his lap, his arms around her and her body pressed to his. The book had fallen aside and was now spread open on the ground.

She gave it not another glance, for her was attention now riveted to Augustus, to his mouth and dark eyes, to the handsome angles of his face. But her senses were shockingly aware of their body positions. Her breasts were pressed against his broad chest, and her bottom was resting between his legs and—

She meant to scramble off him, but he chose that moment to crush his mouth to hers, and she was swept up in a whirlpool of sensations, drowning in them, to be sure. His lips were warm and splendid, moving against hers with possessive prowess. Grinding and teasing, probing along the seam of her pursed mouth to nudge it open, to lick it lightly and stroke it with his tongue.

When she opened to him, he dipped his tongue between her teeth in gentle exploration.

Oh, sweet heaven!

His delicious invasion was not too much and not too little.

Indeed, it was exceedingly perfect.

Was she the only one he had ever kissed this way?

How could she be?

She wound her hands around his neck and pressed closer, loving the heat and strength of his body. Loving his scent, male heat, and musk. He gave a soft, rumbling growl, feral and demanding, but also exquisitely protective.

Every one of her senses exploded. Touch…oh, his hands felt so good upon her body, seeming to burn through the layers of muslin and the linen of her chemise.

Taste…she caught the hint of coffee and marmalade from his

earlier breakfast while he plundered her lips. Was there ever a better kiss?

As for hearing…that growl, low at the back of his throat, so primal and territorial. It was quite thrilling to think that he, a man of distinction and poise, could revert to a feral, prowling beast who marked what was his and defended it against all rivals. Not that he had a worry on that score, for no one else had shown interest in her while in Taunton. Those wretched, cowardly curs who had attacked them the other night did not count.

She took a deep breath, hoping to clear her senses and stop returning his kiss with shameful abandon. She wanted to lick his skin, but what they were doing was already outside the bounds of propriety.

Heaven help her if others thought to stroll into the garden. They would certainly catch an unexpected eyeful. But if they were caught in this outrageous position, then Augustus would be forced to marry her in order to save her from ruin.

Of course, she wanted to marry him.

But not this way.

He ended the kiss abruptly and stared at her.

She opened her eyes and stared back.

He appeared horrified by what they had just done.

She wasn't bothered by it in the least. He was the handsomest man she had ever beheld, and she had thoroughly enjoyed this unexpected kiss.

He eased her off his lap and set her back down on his jacket. "I had better go," he mumbled and hastily rose, grabbing onto the tree trunk to steady himself since he had gotten to his feet too fast, and his head was obviously spinning.

She could have told him this would happen when he leaped to his feet as though just bitten by a snake. If the kiss was not to his liking, then why had he drawn her onto his lap and kissed her with wild abandon?

She stood beside him and placed a hand on his arm. "Don't you dare run away, Augustus. You cannot swallow me whole with that kiss and then pretend it did not happen."

"You don't understand."

"Oh, I understand perfectly. Why do you think I am determined to read *The Book of Love* with you? You've contrived a dozen reasons in your head why you should not marry me. In this, I know exactly what you are thinking. It cannot be love at first sight. Certainly not with this naive chit from Barnstaple. I'm riding off to Caithness as soon as I can stand on my own without toppling."

"June—"

"Am I right so far? But this is mostly about Vienna and how unsuitable you truly believe I am for the task of being your wife amid all those sophisticated people. We spoke about it, but it seems I have not convinced you that your concerns are unwarranted."

She paused to stare at him. "Perhaps you are purposely being dense and want to push me away because you are more comfortable with these *sophisticated* people you supposedly abhor. In truth, I hate that word, too. Sophisticated women do not require any commitment on your part. They will flirt with you, and some will expect you to resume your dalliances. They might be peeved when you refuse but will move on to another lover and not demand anything more of you."

"June, you are wrong."

"It was easy when you could flirt back or take them to your bed. Is this what made you a brilliant diplomat? Selling your body to those princesses and courtesans?"

"June!"

"Oh, do not dare tell me I have gone too far and insulted you. I am trying to get you to open your eyes to the happiness in front of you, but you are still looking at this exercise as a means to avoid it. Being a bachelor in Vienna was easy for you. Returning to Vienna with a wife like me would be quite difficult, or so you think. I am not *sophisticated*. I would expect my husband to be faithful. Or perhaps you are more interested in pursuing power and connections by marrying an Austrian princess, living a life of elegance and ease as her royal consort."

This time his growl held no soft allure, only anger. "Are you through insulting me?"

She buried her face in her hands and nodded.

She could not have done a better job of convincing him of her unsuitability. Her words had been bitter and shrewish, particularly after that magnificent kiss.

She had loved it, and yet it had overset her to think this was his way of kissing her goodbye, and he might never kiss her like this again. But instead of accepting it for whatever he meant it to be, she wanted more and could not bear the thought of his riding off, never to see her again.

Why ever would he want an ignorant harpy such as her for a wife?

To her surprise, he drew her back in his arms. "Don't struggle to escape me. Just let me hold you."

"Why? I am obviously inept and cannot keep my thoughts from spilling out of my big mouth."

"I like your mouth. It is quite beautifully shaped. Stop squirming. I want to talk to you."

"You still wish to talk to me?"

She felt his smile as he said, "Yes, June. I do."

"Even though I just proved myself to be a liability as your wife? I know it is your intelligence that got you where you are, not your male…thing…you know, that body part."

"I am quite aware of that body part. It is a monumental struggle to keep it quiet whenever I am around you."

She glanced up in surprise. "Truly?"

"Yes, June. Truly."

She took a deep breath. "May I start again? What I am trying to say came out all wrong."

He nodded.

"Well, what I clumsily am trying to tell you is that I admire you and believe in you. You are a man of rare quality, and everyone in the highest ranks of English government, as well as those in foreign governments, must appreciate your intellectual talents."

"That is an improvement over telling me I am lazy, and I wish to bed every woman I set eyes on."

She groaned. "That is not how I meant it to come out. My point is, most diplomats and generals are not nearly as handsome as you, and yet treaties are signed, and truces are enacted. In fact, I would venture most of those men are fat and soft and reek of spirits or stale cigars. I've heard Lord Castlereagh is nothing to look at. And most are married, although I do not know how many wives travel with their husbands. Still, they are married, and things get accomplished, and many of those marriages are successful. But I expect those wives who do travel with them know how to keep their mouths shut. Clearly, I do not."

"Are you trying to talk yourself out of the role?"

She shook her head in confusion. "Are you suggesting I have any chance at the role?"

June did not get her answer. Whether he meant to respond or simply meant to avoid the question was something she would never know. Her sisters came running out in search of them, calling out their names excitedly. "June! General MacLauren! Where are you? The magistrate has caught the men who shot you!"

Augustus released her and bent to scoop up his jacket and her book. He shoved it into her hands and then quickly donned his jacket. "Stay at the inn. Remain with your sisters. Keep out of trouble."

"Why? I mean, yes. I will keep out of trouble. But where are you going?"

"Bollocks, you're beautiful," he said, cupping her face in his hands but tilting her head slightly to place a kiss on her cheek. "Do not leave the inn."

He strode off, quickly nodding to her sisters as he passed them.

They cast her questioning looks.

She shook her head and motioned for them to follow her back inside. "Do not make too much out of the kiss you just saw. It was merely a kiss on the cheek. He isn't going to offer for me. But what of those men? Tell me all you know. How were they captured? Did the Earl of Monkton cooperate? Even if he did, I wonder what he is going to do about their situation."

Willow frowned. "Do you think he will insist on their release? Why would he? They've brought shame to the family name. Surely what they've done is a hanging offense."

"I don't know that he will openly insist on their release. How can he without casting himself in a bad light with the Crown? But I am worried about what he might quietly do next."

"Such as what?" Cammy asked.

"Lord Belfy is his brother. Lord Hurst and Lord Mercer are his cousins." June pursed her lips. "If you and Willow were locked up in the magistrate's gaol with the threat of a death sentence hanging over your heads, do you doubt I would help you to escape?"

Chapter Ten

Augustus was not surprised to receive a visit from the Earl of Monkton later that afternoon at the inn. He had seen him at the magistrate's office when he had gone over there earlier with Jock and Angus to find out more details about the capture of his assailants.

The earl had not spoken to him then, for he had been too busy talking to his brother, Lord Belfy, who was as unrepentant a man as Augustus had ever seen.

"The cousins appear more subdued," Augustus had quietly mentioned to the magistrate, Shayne Brayden, when he, Jock, and Angus had stepped into his private office to chat.

The magistrate had nodded. "Those two, Hurst and Mercer, gave themselves up without a struggle. But Lord Belfy…there's something wrong in the head with that one. He has always been a troublemaker. Molesting women, beating up peaceful citizens. The earl coddled him and was quick to pay off those who might press charges. But all his riches won't be enough to pay off everyone he's hurt this time."

Jock cursed softly. "We noticed some of your men had to be treated by Dr. Stratton."

"Yes, Belfy put up a fierce fight. Fortunately, none of the injuries are too serious."

They had all expressed relief these three were safely behind bars and would now remain there until the judge arrived.

"Lorcan and I will personally stand guard over those three tonight," the magistrate had assured him. "They won't escape trial."

Which, Augustus supposed was the reason the earl had now come to pay a call on him. They were seated in the privacy of the gazebo, and he expected the earl was about to plead for mercy for his wayward brother.

"Thank you for allowing me a moment of your time, General MacLauren." The Earl of Monkton was a man in his mid-thirties, tall and slight of build. He had light brown hair and dark eyes that reflected concern and pain over his brother's situation.

Augustus merely nodded. "Shall I have tea brought out? Or would you care for something stronger?"

The earl shook his head. "Nothing for me, thank you. My stomach is in knots. In truth, I feel about ready to cast up my accounts." He tossed Augustus a wry, mirthless smile. "I won't stay long, but I wanted to deliver my personal apology for what my brother has done to you. Oh, I know there is still a trial to take place, but can there be any doubt as to the outcome?"

Augustus took a moment to try to take the measure of the man. "You have been stepping in to protect your brother throughout his life, so I've been told. I should think the proper outcome is quite in doubt unless you step aside and stop protecting him."

"Which I am going to do. It is past time he took responsibility for his actions. My wife, a woman I happen to love dearly, is expecting our first child. She has given me an earful about what she thinks of my brother. In truth, she is deathly afraid of what he might do to her and our child. To me, as well. I never believed he would ever hurt me or my loved ones, but I am no longer certain of it."

"It is obvious he is a man out of control." Augustus sat back and waited for the rest of what the earl had come to say. His brother was a lost cause, but what of the cousins? Was he here to plead for leniency for them?

"I will not dismiss your injury as a harmless accident, for my brother almost killed you," the earl began slowly. "I have spoken to my cousins, Lord Hurst and Lord Mercer. They tried to assure me it was only meant as a prank. They claim my brother intended to shoot into the air merely to scare you, but he tripped in the dark, and his pistol accidentally went off."

"And you believe that hogswallop? I saw them. Your brother did not trip." Augustus tried to keep his anger in check, but he wasn't feeling diplomatic at the moment. The bastard had purposely tried to kill him, and he was not going to allow the Monktons to use 'it was an accident' as a defense.

"No, I don't believe them," the earl admitted. "I pressed further and finally got the truth out of them. They thought to contrive that story to keep them out of the hangman's noose. But now that they have sobered up and realized the enormity of what they have done, they are sorry for all of it. They regret accosting a genteel, young woman and then attacking you at the inn when you attempted to protect her."

"And?"

"They admit they were armed last night, as most gentlemen would be when walking about after dark, especially on a night such as Midsummer's Eve. But they assured me they never drew their weapons. However, they saw my brother draw his pistol."

"And they did nothing to stop him."

The earl nodded. "To their regret. He had convinced them to go in search of you, but only for the purpose of giving you a scare. It was a lark, only meant to be a prank, at least this is what they believed. They never suspected my brother would actually harm you, even when he drew his pistol. He was the one who shot you last night."

He paused to glance once again at Augustus. "Of course, you saw him. You know the shot was his. My point is, they are willing to testify against my brother in return for leniency for themselves."

They were little more than rats deserting a sinking ship, willing to say or do anything to save themselves, but their testimony would add certainty to a conviction for the truly dangerous one among them. "And you will allow this?"

The earl nodded. "My cousins are foolish men, but not evil. My brother, however, is quite another matter. Even as a child, he took pleasure in hurting animals. He was a cruel boy and often punished for it, of course. But I suspect he even took pleasure in his own punishment. I was relieved when he went off to Oxford to start university. But not even that was much of a reprieve. He was sent down almost immediately after the start of the school term and only permitted back when my cousins began their term. I hoped they could keep him in check, but it seems he wound up corrupting them instead."

Augustus spoke calmly, but it was a struggle. "What terms are your cousins asking for themselves?"

"They know it is impossible to avoid punishment and are willing to take what is due them. But do you not think imprisonment? They will accept to be banished from England. I would suggest they be sent to Australia. With hard work and a clean start, they might make something of themselves."

"And your brother?"

Tears formed in the earl's eyes. "I have told my wife she has nothing to fear from him, but it is a lie. I am also afraid of him, of what he is now. There is a sickness in him that has only grown worse over the years. If he ever laid a hand on my beautiful Eliza, it would destroy me. She is my heart. I knew it from the first moment I ever set eyes on her."

He emitted a snort and continued. "My family scoffed at me. A love match. They thought I was mad for choosing love over wealth and advantageous connections. Have you ever been in love, General MacLauren?"

Augustus did not answer the question.

The earl nodded. "Well, I suppose you think me as great a fool as my family does. But I do not regret marrying her, not for a moment. I would have proposed to her the first day we met, but I was worried she would think me mad. As it was, my family believed I was reckless for proposing to her after knowing her merely a month. But I digress. My point is, I shall fight to protect her and the children we shall have together. I shall fight for her until my dying breath. My brother has become too much of a danger, and I can no longer come to his rescue."

He groaned and continued. "His punishment is in your hands and that of the judge. I cannot bring myself to say aloud what I hope he will do. Lord Belfy is my little brother, after all. I was willing to protect him with my life, but not now. No longer."

Augustus felt a tug to his heart and quite a bit of pity for the earl. Was this not exactly how he felt about his own little brother, Thad? As a lad, he had been fiery, smart-mouthed, and prone to mischief. Of course, Thad had turned into a brilliant and valiant man. Augustus was truly proud of the adult he had become.

The earl slapped his hands lightly on the wrought iron table and rose. "I have taken up enough of your time. Give thought to what I have said. My cousins are not bad men. I would hate to see their lives forfeit for my brother's foolish actions."

Augustus rose along with him. "I will give it serious consideration, my lord."

People often believed men in command of armies and seasoned in battle grew hardened. But it was not so. If anything, most military commanders were acutely aware of how precious every life was and tried their best to save as many as possible.

It was no coincidence that most involved in the Vienna peace conferences were high up in the military ranks of the country they represented. But this discussion was about Lord Belfy, and the answer to dealing with him was fairly clear to Augustus. Yes, he would agree to softer terms for the cousins if they would testify against the wretch and assure his conviction.

But he said nothing yet to the earl and would not offer him any indication until he had spoken to Jock, Angus, and the local magistrate, Shayne Brayden.

He considered discussing the matter with June as well, but

this was too grim to talk over with her. How could he even open such a conversation with her? No, he could not. Once assured the cousins were merely young men led astray and did not have these same cruel tendencies, he would accede to the earl's request.

The less June knew of it, the better.

Lord Belfy was going to be punished no matter what the outcome of the trial. His own men would kill him if the judge did not convict him, so it was better to work behind the scenes to assure a sentence of imprisonment for life. He was not about to turn Jock or Angus into murderers, which is what would happen for certain if the verdict was not to their liking.

He sighed.

This nasty business roiled even his stomach, and he had been immersed in war and death for years. He could never have such a frank discussion with June, nor did he want her to see this side of him. She might consider it brutal, but he could only look upon it as practical. Lord Belfy was not going to reform. He had to be stopped before he caused more harm.

He walked the earl out, both of them quiet and lost in their thoughts. The earl was obviously broken up about his brother but determined to do whatever was necessary to protect his wife and any children they would have.

A love match, he'd said.

The earl turned to him and shook his hand. "Until tomorrow, General MacLauren. I am immensely relieved to see you up and about. I was afraid I would have your death on my conscience as well."

"We Scots are too stubborn to be brought down so easily." Augustus nodded. "Until tomorrow, my lord."

"I've heard Scots are impossibly thickheaded." The earl grinned at the remark, but his moment of mirth quickly faded. "Thank goodness for that. I mean it sincerely."

Augustus watched him stride out of the inn.

He turned to walk back to his room, knowing he had overly exerted his body, and it was craving rest. *Bollocks.* He'd done little more than sit in the garden for a few hours and then walk next door to the magistrate's office.

How had doing nothing still managed to fatigue him?

He glanced toward the inn's dining room and spotted June having a light repast with her sisters and aunt. He paused at the foot of the staircase, wanting to ignore her and continue to his quarters.

The Earl of Monkton had spoken about falling in love with his wife.

Love at first sight, he'd said.

Did such a thing truly exist? How could anyone be certain to the depths of their soul that another was meant for them? Was he the only fool who did not believe in such a possibility?

Logically, such a thing could not be.

Any love marriages that worked out were merely a fortunate coincidence. How could they be anything else?

But he could not ignore the intense feelings he had for June. Were he assigned to duties in London or even anywhere in England, he would have pursued her without question. Probably made an arse of himself courting her since he was no glib poet and had no ability to pull flowery love verses out of the air.

Oh, he could sway countries into entering peace treaties.

He could coax just about any woman into his bed.

He could speak with passion and conviction.

But to set aside all barriers and speak from his heart? To lay it bare and risk it being crushed? Was he doomed to follow Wellington's mistake? To propose to the girl and spend the rest of his life ruing his mistake?

"Idiot," he muttered and hastened up the stairs to his room. He shed his boots and jacket and then dropped onto his bed, sinking his large frame into the soft mattress. He had not thought his body was tense, but it must have been, for he remained tossing and turning for a long while. Finally, he felt his taut muscles begin to relax and was just about to drift off to sleep when he thought he heard someone outside his door.

He half expected to hear a knock and June's lilting voice call his name.

But no one knocked.

No one called his name.

It was for the best.

His resistance was dangerously lowered, and he would not behave as a gentleman should, assuming she was so bold as to enter his room. Yet, he hoped she would be so bold. The girl was sparkle and fire.

Everything about her made him burn.

His last thoughts before he fell asleep were of June, of course.

If only they had more time together.

How much was enough time?

Did *The Book of Love* have an answer for this?

CHAPTER ELEVEN

JUNE, HER AUNT Charlotte, and her sisters had just been served tea in the inn's cozy sitting area later that evening when the judge who rode the western circuit of assizes arrived at the inn to great fanfare. "Look, June. He's here," Cammy said in an excited whisper, setting down her cup with a clatter and craning her head for a better view.

They had settled in the very same comfortable seats where she had first chatted with Augustus, and she immediately turned toward the inn's reception area. A distinguished, older gentleman stood there with an entourage that included the magistrate and his brother, Lorcan Brayden, and several other burly men who probably served on the magistrate's night watch.

The inn suddenly buzzed to life despite the lateness of the hour.

The serving staff began to scurry, and others in the parlor began to whisper and point. Several guests cheered. Apparently, Lord Belfy had been a plague on Taunton, and all were eager to see him get the punishment he deserved.

"He looks quite stern and imposing," Willow said, her eyes widening as the judge glanced at them, then turned away to exchange sober words with the magistrate.

"They are taking no chances," June murmured. "One would think the Duke of Wellington himself had come to visit."

Aunt Charlotte was also staring at the men who stood only a

short distance from them. "They are taking precautions, just as they should. This is the magistrate's chance to rid the town of that piece of offal, and he will take nothing for granted. I like that young man, Shayne Brayden. He has a good head on his shoulders."

Willow snorted. "First of all, he must be approaching thirty years of age. Not young at all."

"Positively ancient," June teased her sister. "I'm sure his knees must creak. Do you think he oils them every day?"

"My point," Willow said, ignoring her jest, "is that he is overbearing and arrogant. He does not speak but merely grunts."

Cammy chuckled. "Oh, Willow. That isn't true. He's been very nice to us. If he grunts at you, it is only because you are constantly poking and prodding him as though he were a bear in a pit. Perhaps if you were more polite to him, he—"

"Perhaps if he were not so rude to me, I would be."

June could not contain her grin. "Oh, dear. Did you ever consider that he gets under your skin because you like him?"

Her sister's eyes popped wide. "Believe me, I do not. When I get my chance at *The Book of Love*, I assure you it will lead me to someone other than that oaf."

"We'll see," their aunt murmured before taking a sip of her tea. "Well, girls. Are we done here now? Had our fill of staring at these handsome Brayden boys? Let us head upstairs before the guards they've brought along block the halls."

Cammy sighed. "Oh, dear. I suppose there will be no sneaking down the back stairs for me tonight. If I want my pie and glass of milk, I had better fetch it now."

"Grab a slice for me," Willow called out as Cammy started toward the kitchen. She had barely taken three steps when Lorcan Brayden turned to watch her, frowned, and started after her.

"It appears you are all to be guarded tonight," Charlotte remarked.

"They certainly are being cautious," June said. "I don't understand why now that Lord Belfy is safely behind bars. Magistrate Brayden mentioned my presence might be required in the courtroom tomorrow, but he doubts I will be called to testify. It is General MacLauren's testimony he believes is vital. He seems to think it will be a bad thing if I am called."

"Why?" Willow asked with a huff. "Does he not consider you competent?"

June sighed. "Oh, do stop berating him. He is not concerned about my competence. But Lord Belfy is fighting for his life and will stop at nothing to save himself. The easiest way to do that is to destroy my good name in the hope of also tarnishing General MacLauren. He will make me out to be a bawd who was selling herself to General MacLauren for the evening."

Willow gasped. "The knave!"

"Oh, he is far worse than that. Let us hope the judge will not allow him to speak any of his nonsense. But it is a possibility that I will be called to the stand since a man's life is in the balance. I expect the judge may decide to hear all witnesses, even you and Cammy. You were looking over the railing and saw everything that was going on."

"I am not concerned," Willow said, but she sounded hesitant. "What can Lord Belfy do to me or Cammy?"

June shifted in her chair and stared directly at Willow. "Very well, I will show you how easy it is to destroy a young woman's reputation. Miss Farthingale, what is that book the three of you were toting around the night your sister was allegedly accosted?"

Willow laughed. "June, don't be ridiculous. How can our looking at that—"

"Answer the question, Miss Farthingale. What is the name of that book?"

"*The Book of Love.*" Willow's cheeks turned pink as understanding dawned on her.

"So you see, what do you think every man in the courthouse will think of us? And they will not bother to listen to us explain that it is a book about finding true love. Their brains will immediately sink to believing it is something tawdry and lewd. They will make bawds out of all of us, and Aunt Charlotte will not be our chaperone so much as our…I cannot even bring myself to say what they will call her. Do you understand now? Indeed, I hope we do not have to be in the courtroom at all."

"I see your point. It makes me ill."

June nodded. "However, I am more concerned about the damage to General MacLauren's reputation. I do not care if that madman accuses me of being a harlot, for no one in Taunton will believe him, and if the rumors reach London, I doubt my name will be worthy of mention. But General MacLauren will be ruined if those lies were ever to reach London and the Foreign Office. Everyone knows his name, and it will now be connected to that 'tart' he met at the inn and the brawl he got into over her. All his years of toil and sacrifice will be worth nothing if a lunatic's mad ravings were to bring scandal upon him."

Charlotte reached over to pat June's hand. "Now, dear. Do not get yourself worked up over the matter. The judge is not going to permit Lord Belfy to utter any such nonsense. If he is old guard, as I believe he is, he will not allow the accused to speak at all. The trial will be quick, and the outcome certain. The Earl of Monkton came to see General MacLauren today. Did you not notice them speaking quietly in the garden this afternoon?"

June nodded. "I did, but…what do you think they said to each other? I assumed he was here to beg for leniency for his brother."

"No, dear. I do not think so. Something in the earl's manner and the way General MacLauren responded to him. I think they've struck a deal of some sort."

"What sort of deal?"

"Testimony of Lord Hurst and Lord Mercer leading to a conviction of the earl's brother in exchange for leniency for them. Do you think your General MacLauren is the sort ever to leave anything to chance? No, he and the earl have struck their bargain. The hearing tomorrow will be mainly for show. The outcome is certain."

June wanted to laugh it off as absurd, but was not his thoroughness precisely what made Augustus so effective at the bargaining table? He had fixed the trial.

Well, he could not have done it without the cooperation of the Earl of Monkton or the magistrate. Had they already discussed it with the judge? Would tomorrow's hearing merely be a show for the spectators?

June began to fret as she considered Charlotte's words. "Augustus would not have Lord Belfy's cousins lie to save themselves, would he?"

"Of course not. He is merely ensuring they tell the truth. Do you have any doubt Lord Belfy meant to kill him?"

"No, I have no doubt about it. But what of the cousins. Do you think they are innocent in the attempt on his life?"

Charlotte pursed her lips. "I do not know. I suppose we shall just have to see what happens tomorrow."

Cammy returned with a tin half-filled with pie, bringing a halt to their conversation. Lorcan strode behind her, still frowning. He joined them for a moment but did not sit down, and his purpose soon became clear. He merely meant to lecture them. "Do not wander off on your own tonight, no matter how safe you think it might be."

He arched a dark eyebrow toward Cammy. "Lord Belfy has friends in the area. He and his cousins run with a fast crowd. We may have the three of them contained, but there is no telling who will be stupid enough to come to their rescue."

With that, he turned and strode away.

Cammy sighed. "He followed me to the kitchen and thoroughly boxed my ears when he noticed the hallway was empty. Yes, it was a perfect spot for a bounder to accost me. But no one was there, and no one did."

Aunt Charlotte cast her a look.

Cammy shifted. "He was right, of course. But the man hadn't said two words to me before this, and yet he would not shut up all the way to the kitchen and back."

They left the sitting area and walked upstairs, but June allowed the others to go on ahead while she paused at Augustus's door. She knew Lord Belfy was guilty and a danger to the innocent citizens of Taunton.

She did not doubt he had escaped punishment for crimes he had committed many times before. Were not all those instances a 'fix' in the undeserving wretch's favor? This time, he was not going to weasel out of his responsibility.

She was about to knock on his door but changed her mind. Augustus had been ordered to rest. Instead, he had spent most of the morning with her and then much of the afternoon with the magistrate and the Earl of Monkton.

If he was sleeping now, she did not want to disturb him.

They would talk tomorrow after the trial.

After all, he was in no condition to ride off immediately afterward. Nor would he leave without seeing her first because that would mean he did not care about her.

But he did care, and he had told her so.

Still, this was not just about her.

It was about him, as well.

He refused to believe love at first sight was possible.

"Oh, Augustus," she said in a whisper against his door, "run away from me if you wish. But do you think you can run away from your feelings?"

CHAPTER TWELVE

AUGUSTUS AND HIS men strode over to the administrative building behind the magistrate's office. It housed the courthouse where the trial was about to start, a simple room that held the aura of authority with its cherry wood wainscoting and the imposing bench at the front where Shayne Brayden conducted his weekly hearings, and on occasion, full trials.

As a magistrate, he was in charge of dispensing justice for most crimes that occurred in Taunton. However, the more serious offenses were docketed for the Lenten assizes and were the jurisdiction of the judges appointed to ride the western circuit.

"Ye must be important, laddie," Jock teased him. "They've opened the Midsummer assizes here in Taunton just for ye."

Augustus grinned. "Only because the Crown and the cabinet ministers desperately need me at the moment…or think they do. If Castlereagh were healthy, they wouldn't give a rat's arse about me."

"Lord Belfy should have thought of that before he shot ye," Angus muttered.

Hamish held the door to the courtroom open for him. "The man's a loonie, that's fer certain. I'm keeping my hand on m'pistol and hoping the bastard gives me an excuse to use it."

Augustus frowned at him. "This is Brayden's jurisdiction. Let him handle it, or we'll be caught up in bureaucratic paperwork and never make it to Scotland in time. I had to claw and scratch for even these few weeks before we must return to Vienna."

The lad nodded. "Aye, General MacLauren. But what I wouldn't give to show him our Scottish brand of justice."

Augustus felt the same but would never acknowledge it to his men.

Jock walked in beside him. "Ye're serious then. Ye mean to ride out today after the trial?"

He nodded.

"Och, laddie. Ye're going to break that pretty girl's heart. Does she realize we're leaving today?"

"No, and I forbid any of you to tell her." It was callous of him, he knew. But he had to make a clean, fast break, or he did not think he would ever have the strength to leave her.

He glanced around the courtroom, first to take stock of those in attendance and make note of any who looked suspicious. He would not put it past Lord Belfy's circle of friends to do something foolish to help him escape.

Of course, if they were too stupid to realize aiding the cur would brand them as traitors to the Crown and mark them for death, then they would get what they deserved.

While he did not consider himself particularly important, the Crown did. It came as no surprise that word of the shooting had reached Lord Ballinger in Bath. He was outraged and had immediately sent missives to Lord Liverpool, the War Ministry, and the Foreign Office if the reports he had received were accurate.

Lord Ballinger must have also gotten word to the assizes judge, for this was no longer the trial of a man up on charges for attempted murder. Lord Belfy was on trial for the additional charge of treason. If convicted, his penalty would be death.

Anyone who dared interfere with this proceeding would also be viewed as committing treason against the Crown.

Only after assessing the attendees and passing a remark or two to his men about them did Augustus dare turn his attention to June. She and her sisters were seated in the front row with their Aunt Charlotte watching over them like a mother hen.

His heartbeat quickened.

Of course, it did.

He could not be anywhere near her without his heart responding.

However, he frowned. Why were the ladies even here? And seated in the front row? He posed the question to the magistrate when he came over to greet him.

"The judge insisted on it," he said, running a hand through his hair in obvious consternation. "Don't ask me why. There's no reason for it other than they're beautiful women, and he would rather look at them than at the prisoner. But he has assured me that he will not call them to the stand unless he finds a compelling reason to require it. Your testimony and that of Lord Belfy's cousins are all that should be necessary for a conviction."

Augustus was not at all pleased with this assurance and scanned the crowd once again. He did not know why he was so on edge, but he was not going to take any chances, especially now that June and her sisters were present.

The judge, Lord Burnham, was not here yet, but Augustus knew he would not enter the courtroom before all were ordered to be seated, and he was formally announced with all due pomp and circumstance. In all likelihood, the man was already ensconced in the private judicial chambers, donning his robes. "Do you think I should have a word with him as well? About the young ladies, that is?"

"No. I've made it clear to Lord Burnham that he is not to distress them. He reputedly has a roving eye, but I reminded him of who you are and that His Majesty will ask for a personal account of his conduct of the trial. That put the fear in him."

Augustus hoped so.

He did not want anyone, not even the presiding judge, to upset June or her family. It eased his conscience to know the magistrate and his brother were going to be around to protect them after he rode off.

June noticed him as he took a seat in the pew behind her. She turned to him with a generous smile. "Good morning, General MacLauren. How are you feeling today?"

"Quite well, Miss Farthingale."

Lord, she was lovely.

She had on a demure gown the color of cream and wore a dark blue pelisse over it. Not that he was really looking at her gown other than to notice she filled it out spectacularly. But this was her, *Spectacular June*. He'd thought so from the moment he had set eyes on her.

Her dark hair was drawn back in an elegant twist, the style more severe than she usually wore it. There were no light curls framing her face. Not that any were ever needed. Her face was exquisite and anchored by those big, blue eyes of hers.

She maintained her smile as she spoke to him. "You are dressed in your regimentals. You look quite impressive, especially with all those medals pinned to your chest."

"You look quite impressive yourself." He tried not to glance at her chest. Failed. Because of that damn book. He was keenly aware of his male, low brain. When it came to June, he had utterly no control over it.

Thankfully, she did not appear to notice the direction of his gaze.

It had been brief.

Almost imperceptible.

He hoped.

Although June evoked his low-brain senses with infuriating regularity, she was most certainly in the high-brain category. Indeed, she was the only woman who had ever stirred this depth of feeling in him.

If only they had more time.

He knew he would fall in love with her.

Did he not already wish to protect her to the end of his days?

So why was he running away from her? It was a cowardly

thing to do.

Well, he knew why. He wasn't scared so much as obsessed with the uncertainty of it all. How was it possible to form a lasting attachment in a matter of days?

It was madness to propose to a girl he'd only just met and greater madness to carry her off to the Continent with so many unknowns swirling around them.

He gave it no more thought as the bailiff pounded his walking stick to silence the chattering crowd and then cried, "Oyez! Oyez!"

Lord Burnham strode out clothed in his robe and wig.

Lord Belfy and the two cousins were marched in.

The Earl of Monkton, he'd noticed earlier, was present and had quietly taken a seat at the back of the courtroom. Hamish and Angus were standing behind him with their backs to the wall and close to the door. Lorcan Brayden had done the same, now standing on the other side of the door.

The judge preened as he acknowledged the Farthingale women in the front pew and eyed them a bit too avidly for Augustus's liking.

He wanted to leap over the railing and punch the judge.

Of course, he would do no such thing.

But he wanted to, for the man's gaze lingered on June, and he did not like it one bit. Lorcan Brayden was standing by the door. He would have a word with him on the way out to ensure the judge was never left alone with June. If the pompous arse dared call her into his private chambers after the trial, he wanted one of the Brayden men standing right beside her.

Still, the notion of abandoning June disquieted him.

Shouldn't he be the one to stand beside her and protect her?

The warring thoughts in his head would drive him mad.

He dismissed them and paid close attention as Lord Hurst and then Lord Mercer were called to the stand testify. They each gave the same account, pointing the blame at Lord Belfy and accusing the earl's brother of purposely shooting him. They also admitted to all three making improper advances toward June and accosting him when he sought to intervene on her behalf.

The judge's eyes went to June again and lingered on her overly long, so that even June noticed and began to fidget.

The judge then called Augustus to the stand.

Augustus identified the man who shot him, then showed the wound to his temple and the stitches still freshly sewn in it. He also had a very light purple bruise around the area of his eye and a small scab on his lip where the chair had caught him in the face.

But the two cousins had already connected the purposeful attempt on his life to Lord Belfy, and he had now confirmed it, so there was no more to add about the shooting. He then gave a first-hand account of the brawl on that first night, impressed by the thoroughness of the judge's questions.

Despite his roving eye, there was no doubt the man was an experienced judge who understood the law and held tight rein over his courtroom.

Having laid the groundwork for Lord Belfy's criminal behavior, Lord Burnham now set about closing the noose around his neck. "Obviously, this shooting was not a random act," he intoned. "Lord Belfy knew of your vitally important position in the Foreign Office, did he not?"

"Yes, he knew who I was."

Lord Burnham nodded. "He knew who you were because he had attacked you several days earlier, had he not?"

"Yes, my lord. He had."

"Yes, as you testified just a few minutes ago. Was his attack on you that first time prompted by you in any way?"

"No, it was not."

"Tell the court in detail what happened that night, General MacLauren."

In detail?

Just how much detail did the man expect?

He gave his testimony with due gravity, giving only the specifics he deemed relevant. He was not going to breathe a word of

June and her damn book or of her coming down to purposely strike up a conversation with him.

The statements he did provide, as well as those of the men testifying before him, would be enough for a conviction.

Surprisingly, Lord Burnham pressed on. "Was there not a young lady involved?"

Well, he was an experienced trial judge, so Augustus was not going to openly question the wisdom of adding details. He had wanted June's name kept out of this as much as possible.

"A young lady," he said, and purposely avoided looking in the direction of June, "was quietly seated among other respectable guests in the sitting area of the inn having a lemonade when those three lords, Belfy, Hurst, and Mercer, stumbled out of the common room and attempted to harass her."

"Will you point out the young lady to the court?"

Augustus ground his teeth. "Does it matter who she is, my lord? Is it not enough that she is a young lady of good character who did nothing to deserve their rude behavior?"

"I understand your gentlemanly instincts, General MacLauren. I also understand the young woman's delicacy and wish for discretion. But I must be thorough in the conduct of my trial. Who is the young lady in question?"

He supposed his strangling the judge would not leave the man disposed to cooperating in the conviction of Lord Belfy.

"Miss Farthingale," he said reluctantly, hoping it would put an end to the matter.

"I understand there are several Miss Farthingales seated in the courtroom. Would you point out which one to the court?"

He was going to refuse but then noticed the look of alarm in Shayne Brayden's face as well as in that of the Earl of Monkton and knew he had better do as he was asked, or everything would unravel. He motioned toward June. "But there is nothing the young lady can add to my statements. To ask her to testify would needlessly overset her. I do not think the Crown will be pleased to have you persist in this matter."

He'd thrown down the king card.

He hated to do it, but he was not going to allow anyone to upset June. No, he was the only arse who was allowed that privilege.

Bollocks.

He felt wretched, knowing he would soon ride off and break her heart.

"You are most considerate of her feelings," Lord Burnham said. "I can do no less. Miss Farthingale, I shall take your testimony privately in my judicial chambers."

June leaped to her feet and shot Augustus a cautionary look to stop him from lunging at the judge. "That will not be necessary, my lord. I am quite capable of testifying right here. Although, as General MacLauren stated, I do not know what else I can add that has not already been testified to by the prior witnesses."

Lord Burnham turned to him. "General MacLauren, thank you for your testimony. You may stand down." His stern demeanor vanished a moment later as he turned to June, practically salivating as he bid her to come forward and take the stand.

When she did so and was sworn in, he practically toppled out of his chair to lean closer and begin to ask his questions of her.

Augustus had meant to leave now that his testimony had been given, but he could not while June was on the stand. Not that anyone was stopping him, only his own urge to protect her. He remained standing with his arms tensely folded across his chest, taking a position beside Shayne Brayden, who had not left his post beside the Farthingale women in the front pew.

The judge paid them no attention, his gaze now riveted to June. "My dear, take your time and tell us what happened that evening."

"As General MacLauren and the other witnesses have already stated, Lord Belfy, Lord Hurst, and Lord Mercer saw me seated in the sitting area having my lemonade and approached me. They were drunk and making lewd comments. General MacLauren also happened to be seated nearby and bade me to stand behind him."

"And did you?"

"Yes, of course. I did so immediately. I was scared and quite appalled by their behavior."

"Indeed," the judge intoned, "any young woman of good character would have been sickened by their shocking actions. What happened next?"

"General MacLauren said I was his wife, and they were to leave me alone."

Augustus winced.

Good grief.

Did she have to repeat his exact words?

Angus and Jock would never let him live it down. He'd have to endure their jabs the entire ride to Scotland. Not that they would be teasing him about it, but they would be rebuking him as an idiot when it was obvious he'd felt strongly about June from the first.

He returned his attention to June as she continued.

"Of course, he only claimed I was his wife because he believed those gentlemen would then walk away and stop their unwanted attentions. Instead, Lord Belfy merely laughed and tried to punch the general. His two friends did the same. All three assaulted him at once. Quite cowardly, don't you think, my lord?"

The judge agreed.

"He fended them off and was winning the fight..." She paused and turned once again to the judge, who had not taken his eyes off her the entire time. The roof could have fallen atop his head, and he would not have noticed. "Might I add, General MacLauren was making every effort to avoid the fight. I wish to be clear on this point. But these men were drunk and base in their behavior. They would not stop. Lord Belfy came up to him from behind and hit him over the head with a chair. *With a chair*, my lord. Ambushed him. Is that not outrageous?"

"Indeed, Miss Farthingale."

She nodded and spoke on. "It momentarily dazed him. By this time, Lord Belfy's cousins had recovered somewhat and meant to come after him again. As I said, they were heinous and vicious. They would not stop their attack."

The judge was fascinated by the indignant heave of her chest. "Then what happened?"

June nibbled her lip.

The fleshy lower lip pinkened and swelled.

Lord Burnham nearly toppled out of his seat again.

Good lord! Was June doing this on purpose?

Augustus glanced around.

The magistrate also had his gaze on the onlookers. He then turned to Augustus, arched an eyebrow, and grinned to convey he also had caught on to what June was doing. It seemed every man in the courtroom was staring at her. She had them all entranced if the bulge of their eyes was any indication.

Gad, did she realize…no, how could she when she had no experience with men? Other than him, of course. Not that a mere kiss or two could count as any real experience.

Damn it, that book!

She had turned every man in the courtroom into her test frogs.

He stifled a groan as she bit gently down again on her exquisite lower lip and continued.

"Well, the other guests seemed too stunned to move. When I realized everyone was too frightened to assist him, I knew I had to do it. I could not allow those fiends to hurt him when he had so valiantly come to my rescue. So, I grabbed a nearby fire iron and struck Lord Hurst in the back of the knees with it. My father taught me this trick. It is one of the weak spots on a man and would bring him down effectively without causing too much hurt."

The judge was listening intently. "And General MacLauren had recovered by then?"

"Well, no. Not quite. I had no choice but to hit Lord Mercer with the fire iron when he tried to punch General MacLauren again." She blushed profusely. "My father taught me of another spot on a man that would bring him down efficiently. So I hit him *there*. I hope you understand my meaning. Good manners forbid me from being more precise. I was about to do the same to Lord Belfy, but by that time, General MacLauren had recovered, and the innkeeper and his sons had arrived to hold those men down until the magistrate was summoned. I don't think I can add anything more other than to say General MacLauren was dressed in his uniform and had on all his medals, which, as you can see since he is wearing them today as well, is quite impressive. There is no way these three lords could have mistaken him for anything other than the distinguished commander of the Royal Scots Greys."

She folded her gloved hands atop the stand's railing, obviously waiting for the judge to allow her to stand down.

The man merely stared at her, gaped at her to the point Augustus wanted to smack him in the head and remind him he was conducting a trial…and that he was an old married man who should not be gawking at June.

Well, he was gawking at her as well.

But his behavior did not count because he was in love with her.

No, not *in* love yet.

Potentially in love.

Assuredly on his way to falling in love with her.

Perhaps desperately there already.

Damn it.

Being shot in the head must have addled his senses.

June cleared her throat and reached for her handkerchief to dab her eyes. "This is all most distressing, my lord. May I stand down now?"

"Yes, of course. You have been most helpful and accommodating, despite your ordeal. Magistrate Brayden, would you be so kind as to escort Miss Farthingale back to her seat?"

"Of course, my lord." He strode to the witness stand and extended a hand to assist her down, then offered his arm to lead her back to the front pew.

Augustus tamped down the pang of jealousy. Not that the magistrate had given him any reason to be jealous. The man was all business, and in truth, had been one of the few not ogling June while she was on the stand.

The judge pounded on a gavel at his side. "Are there any more witnesses to be heard from?"

"I wish to speak," Lord Belfy announced, coming to his feet.

Lord Burnham regarded him, appalled. "No, you may not. This is my courtroom, and I will not hear of it."

Lord Belfy angrily rattled his shackles at the judge. "I am an earl's son and brother to the current Earl of Monkton," he shouted. "I shall not be treated like a commoner!"

"Then you ought to have behaved like a gentleman and not attacked one of England's highest-ranking diplomats. The king's own man! As Miss Farthingale just attested to, he was wearing his uniform. You could not have mistaken his position. In attacking him, you attacked the Crown. You compounded your treasonous act by attempting to kill him. If you open your mouth again, I shall order you removed from my courtroom and hanged this very day!"

Lord Belfy finally realized he was not going to escape punishment. No one was treating his behavior as a prank but something far more serious. He was on trial for attempted murder and treason. While he might have escaped death for the charge of attempted murder, it finally sank into his tortured brain that the penalty for treason was death, and he would not escape it. "Whore! Harlot! You did this to me! I'll kill you! I'll kill you!"

He broke free of his bailiffs, who were caught by surprise by his venal outburst and the strength his madness had suddenly given him. He tore across the courtroom in a trice and lunged at June.

Augustus was on him before he got close to her. "Watch the others," he called out to the magistrate, worried that Hurst and Mercer would also do something supremely foolish while they were all distracted by Lord Belfy.

But he needn't have worried.

A glance around showed the magistrate, and two of his men had already placed themselves between the Farthingale women and everyone else in the courtroom. Lorcan had grabbed Hurst and Mercer and had a hand on each of their necks, although neither of them appeared to have moved a muscle.

He did not think they would, but who knew what went on in the minds of those idiots?

Meanwhile, Jock, Angus, and the younger soldiers in his retinue had their eyes on the crowd and were now holding onto two other men.

Lord Burnham was ashen as he scrambled to his feet. "Magistrate Brayden, take the ladies to my private chambers while your bailiffs restore order here."

As soon as June and her family had been safely hustled out, Lord Burnham turned his rage on Lord Belfy. "Do not now ask for mercy, for you are undeserving of it. You are no peer to assert any privilege whatsoever, nor are you deserving of one. Miss Farthingale's composure on the witness stand lulled me into believing you were not the vicious beast she feared you were. But you have shown me to be wrong. His Majesty will have my immediate report, and there is now a roomful of witnesses to support the sentence of hanging I now pronounce on you."

He grunted in disgust and pounded his gavel. "This trial is over. Bailiffs, return this man to his cell and keep him bound in chains until such time as he is hanged."

He stormed out, leaving the courtroom in an uproar while he raced to his private chambers. June and her family were there now. Augustus wanted to follow the judge, but it was more important to make certain Lord Belfy was safely taken away. Lorcan was already leading the cousins, who appeared gray as ghosts, out the door to take them back to their cells.

The Earl of Monkton stood silently in a back corner, seemingly about to burst into tears. He would have felt this same way if his beloved brother, Thad, had turned into a monster. However, he also had to be thinking of his wife and any child they brought into the world. They would be safer with his brother no longer around to harm them.

The courtroom was cleared within minutes, and Lord Belfy and the cousins were returned to their cells. The two men collared by Jock and Angus were handed over to the magistrate for further questioning.

"What are ye going to do now?" Jock asked him.

Chapter Thirteen

"I STILL WISH to ride off today," Augustus said, ignoring the frowns and disapproving stares of his men who were looking at him as though they were ready to mount a mutiny. "None of the ladies were hurt. The magistrate has all firmly in hand."

Angus was still casting him a look of disapproval. "I dinna think we should ride out, yet. The magistrate may want to question me, Jock, and the lads about these other two gentlemen we caught reaching for their pistols."

"And ye canno' just leave Miss Farthingale now, not after that bastard tried to attack her again," Hamish said. "It would be a vile and cowardly thing to do."

Augustus ran a hand through his hair. "I have no intention of leaving without seeing her first and making certain she is truly all right."

Angus patted him on the shoulder. "Then do it now, laddie. Ye owe it to the sweet lassie."

Yes, he did.

But he also needed to be on his way before he spilled his heart to her.

His guts were still in a twist at the thought of what Belfy might have done to her had he been able to grab her. "I will. But you lads go over to the magistrate's office and give him your statement about those two men. Find out who they are and what they were doing in the courtroom. Were they friends of Lord Belfy? Or the cousins? Find out all you can about them."

Because if there was the slightest chance they meant to hurt June, then he had to remain to protect her.

He watched his men leave and then strode to the back of the courtroom. He paused at the door to Lord Burnham's private chamber, took a breath, and marched in. June, her aunt, and sisters were all in there with Lord Burnham. The old goat was seated beside June, patting her hand as though to calm her, although he was obviously more overset than June had been about the entire affair.

"Miss Farthingale," Augustus said with an aching groan, ignoring the others when they all turned to look up at him. "June…are you all right?"

He wanted to take her in his arms and kiss her senseless.

Which was all the more reason he had to be on his way.

She nodded and cast him a delicate smile. "I am. Thank you for coming to my rescue again."

"I'm sorry you had to experience any of it."

She shook her head. "He gave us all quite a fright."

"What do you say we return to the inn?" her Aunt Charlotte suggested. "I think we all need some tea to calm us down. Of course, I expect you gentlemen may wish for something stronger. But I am badly in need of a cup to calm my nerves."

June immediately agreed. She rose, slipping her hand out of Lord Burnham's grip, and walked straight toward Augustus. "Will you escort me back, General MacLauren?"

He cast her a smile and offered his arm. "Yes, of course."

Lord Burnham had no choice but to be a gentleman and offer to escort Charlotte, although it was obvious by the longing gaze he cast June that he wished for her instead.

In a pig's eye.

The man was practically salivating over her. Burnham would have to kill him before he'd ever let him put those pudgy, wrinkled hands on his June again.

Yes, she was his.

His.

And no one else's.

No, she isn't.

He was just being a possessive arse about it.

She was not his, and he had no right to lay claim to her unless he stepped forward and did something about it, such as offer for her hand in marriage, which he was not going to do. Not now, anyway.

Cammy stepped up and took the judge's other arm, so the man was quickly mollified.

Augustus turned to Willow and arched an eyebrow.

She scooted to his side with a grin, wrapping her hand in the crook of his elbow.

The courtroom was not far from the inn.

Cammy began to pepper the judge with questions to keep him talking the entire while. Clever girl. No doubt she wished to allow Augustus time to talk to June. But he said nothing to her. What could he say with Willow listening to his every word?

He could not tell June he would have tea with her and then ride off, perhaps never to see her again. It would only hurt her feelings, and she probably knew he was going to do this anyway. To confirm it would only cause her greater upset.

Hadn't she been through enough this morning?

The Ashcotts ran to them as soon as they entered the inn.

Augustus was not surprised. News traveled fast in a small town, and the courtroom was close by. They must have heard several reports of the theatrics by now. "Oh, my dear Miss Farthingale!" Mrs. Ashcott cried, smothering her in a beefy embrace. "What you must have felt when that madman lunged at you!"

June nodded. "He gave us all a fright, but General MacLauren stopped him before he could do me any harm."

"I, for one, am still trembling," Charlotte said. "Mrs. Ashcott, would you be so kind as to lead us to a table? I think I must have a chamomile tea and some of your lovely pie to calm me down."

"At once," she said and led the way to one of their best tables overlooking the garden and a particularly attractive bed of flowers.

As everyone followed her to the table, Augustus held June back a moment. "June..."

She gazed up at him with her big, trusting eyes. "Yes, Augustus?"

He wanted to tell her that he would be stopping in London for a day or two on his way down from Caithness to Dover. No, that wasn't what he wanted to tell her.

He wanted to tell her that he loved her.

No, that wasn't what he wanted to say either.

The entire point of his leaving immediately after he'd given his testimony was to avoid saying anything to her.

Well, he did not know what he wanted to say to her.

It was ridiculous. He was one of England's most able negotiators. A diplomat. Orator. Army general. And he did not know what to say to June.

Mostly, he wanted to kiss her.

Hold her lovely body in his arms.

Lose himself in her soft perfection.

But he wasn't going to do anything in a dining room full of guests, not with everyone now staring at them. He kept his gaze on her and ignored everyone else. "You had the entire courtroom in your thrall when you gave your testimony."

"Did I?" She cast him an innocent smile that did not fool him for a moment.

"Yes, *Tallulah*. You did. Don't forget, I've read that book with you. I know what you were up to."

She arched a delicate eyebrow. "Did it work?"

He nodded. "Yes. Did you not hear the sound of male eyeballs popping all around you and male tongues flopping to the ground?"

She laughed lightly. "No, I did not. Augustus, I wasn't trying to entice the men in the courtroom. I merely wished to gain their sympathy, especially Lord Burnham's. Why did he call me to the witness stand? Everyone was sure I would not be required to testify. I was afraid something had changed that I was not aware of. I did not mean to play the coquette. But I did hope to come across as weak and simpering if he asked me a question I did not wish to answer. I had to lay the groundwork for that, didn't I?"

"You played it perfectly, June. As for being called to the stand, no it was never intended. I have no idea why it happened, other than to think Lord Burnham was quite taken by your beauty and wanted to see you up close."

She regarded him with some surprise. "That's it?"

"Yes, June. That's it. Did it not cross your mind? You know for a fact all men operate on a low-brain level. It does not shut off with age. Lord Burnham probably spends most of the year riding the circuit, listening to all sorts of sordid tales, and looking upon mostly unwashed and not very pleasant people. He must have thought he'd died and gone to heaven when gazing at you."

She rolled her eyes. "My sisters are much prettier."

"No, June. There is no one more beautiful than you." Well, he hadn't meant to say this either. Nor had he intended to say it with such depth of feeling or to caress her cheek as he'd said it…and with everyone watching. "No one," he repeated because he'd obviously lost brain cells along with getting shot in the head.

He needed to distance himself from her, not encourage these feelings they held for each other.

She touched a hand to his arm.

His blood immediately caught fire.

"Thank you, Augustus. You know this is the way I feel about you, too. But I want your promise…"

"Another promise?"

She nodded.

He arched an eyebrow. "I have already promised I would survive Lord Belfy's shooting me, did I not? Have I not kept my word? I am on the mend now. It was just a graze."

She frowned at him. "It was more of a gouge."

"Fine, it was a gouge. A little deeper than a graze. What do you wish me to promise you next?"

He wanted to kiss away the sudden look of pain in her eyes. "I want you to promise me that you will never forget me."

"I'm sure I have already promised you this. Very well, I shall do so again. I promise you, June. You are an angel. How can you think I would not remember you to my dying breath?"

A tear formed in the corner of her eye. "Then why must you leave today? Oh, I know you are going as soon as we have our tea. Your men gave your intentions away. Not a single one of them would look me in the eye this morning. You are leaving today, and I am in dread fear you will walk out of my life forever. My heart is already breaking into pieces."

He caressed her cheek again. "June…don't…"

But he did not know what he meant by it. *Don't love me? Don't worry, I will be back for you? Don't think of me ever again because I'm going to leave you and never come back?*

She took a deep breath. "I don't think I can sit here calmly having my tea. Would you be so kind as to give my apologies to the others? I cannot do this, Augustus. I would follow you to the ends of the earth if you asked me. I would endure years of separation if I knew you would come back to me. What I cannot endure is a life without you."

"Stop, June. Don't say anything more." He caressed her cheek again, groaning inwardly, for he was the biggest arse imaginable for not getting down on bended knee and proposing to her right here and now. "Go to London with your sisters and Aunt Charlotte. Go to every blasted ball, musicale, and theater. Go shopping and riding and dancing and enjoy your time there. Here's my promise to you…I will stop in London to see you on my way back from Caithness. But that is all the promise I am going to make you. If your feelings for me have not changed, then we shall talk further at that time."

It was a crumb.

He'd given her a crumb, and she had every right to smack him over the head with her reticule and call him a knave for it.

Instead, she merely nodded. "Thank you, Augustus. It is all the promise I need."

She deserved more.

She deserved everything.

"Shall I walk you to the stairs?" he asked, knowing she was still overset and might not have changed her mind about sitting with Lord Burnham and her family.

"No, I'll have tea with the others." She emitted a ragged breath. "Will you be joining us, or will you ride off now?"

"I had better not join you. I want to stop at the magistrate's office and see what else is going on."

She frowned lightly. "Those two men your soldiers carted out of the courtroom. What was that about?"

"Perhaps nothing. Jock and Angus thought those fellows were acting suspiciously. The magistrate has them now and is surely taking down whatever information my men can give him. I'd like to be there when he questions those fellows. After that, we'll ride off."

"I see."

He raised her gloved hand to his lips and kissed it lightly, sorry he could not touch his lips to her warm skin. "Until London."

"Until London," she said in a broken whisper.

He marched off without looking back, forcing his attention to these strangers now in the magistrate's custody. They might have drawn their pistols for several reasons, including merely an innocent precaution on the chance more violence erupted. Or they could have been friends of Lord Belfy and the cousins, there for the purpose of helping them escape.

If their presence was not innocent, then they would know better than to open their mouths and admit to abetting treason. He also doubted the magistrate would learn much about them in one afternoon. More investigation would be necessary. Perhaps the Earl of Monkton would be helpful in identifying them and determining their true purpose.

The magistrate's office was packed with men. In addition to the magistrate and his prisoners, present were the magistrate's brother, several bailiffs, and his own soldiers. He was pleased to note the earl was also there, looking a bit lost and out of his depth.

"My lord, do you know who they are?" Augustus asked him after they exchanged polite greetings.

Monkton grunted in disgust. "Yes, friends of my brother and my cousins. Fools, the lot of them. But they seem to be cooperating with Magistrate Brayden. Singing like birds now that they understand they are dealing with charges more serious than a brawl at the inn. I do not think they realized they were getting themselves involved with a matter of attempted murder and treason."

Augustus thought it was quite guileless of the earl to believe this. "How could they not know? Surely they heard the testimony. Even without hearing a word of it, did they not wonder why the court was opened for a summer assizes? That alone should have given them warning this was no ordinary matter."

The earl cast him a sardonic smile. "You assume these are thinking men. Had they a brain between them, they would not be friends with my brother or cousins."

Augustus grunted in acknowledgment. "I suppose. So will they now be held as well?"

"I hope so. The magistrate and I were just getting to that point in our discussion when you walked in. There are a few other gentlemen—though I hardly dare call them that—who make up their fast circle. These brainless friends of theirs need to be accounted for. There were at least another three at the wedding celebration. They might have left Taunton to return to London, but we will need to make certain of their whereabouts before we can rule anything out."

"What of the bride and groom?"

"The bride is another cousin of mine. But she and her husband are off on their grand tour and had no part in this. Nor did the other relatives who attended their wedding. No, it is this unruly group of my brother's friends upon whom the magistrate needs to focus his attention."

Magistrate Brayden finished his questioning of the two men a few moments later and took a moment to step into his private office with him and the earl. "My lord," he said, addressing the earl and offering him a chair. He then did the same with Augustus, but he preferred to remain standing and declined.

The magistrate settled in the chair behind his desk. "Lorcan and I can take care of these five. Of course, Lord Belfy is our greatest concern. He will be guarded by two of my men at all times until…well, until his sentence is…"

"Carried out?" The earl nodded. "You need not soften the blow, Brayden. It has taken me years to admit what my brother is. Now that I have, I suppose it still hurts. But he's made his choices, and they have always been bad ones throughout his life."

The magistrate nodded. "I'll be calling in another of my brothers to assist me. Donal. He's our middle brother. There's me, Donal, and Lorcan is the youngest," he explained to Augustus since the earl seemed to know these Braydens fairly well. "He is also one of the king's agents. Of course, he is used to dealing with rebel plots against the Crown, foreign assassins, and weapons smugglers, not privileged troublemakers. But I'm sure this fast circle is no match for him. I'll ask him to stay on and help us out."

"I heartily approve," the earl said. "Let Donal know he will have my full cooperation."

"Thank you, my lord."

"When will he arrive in Taunton?"

The magistrate smiled. "He happens to be here now. But he knew Lorcan and I would be busy today, so he took himself off fishing. Had he known there would be quite this much excitement, I'm sure he would have put off his excursion. He'll return tonight."

The earl appeared well satisfied. He slapped his hands to his thighs and rose from his chair. "Well, I think this about covers it. My wife will be eager to hear about the trial and all that happened. Do you think I might hire Donal to guard my wife and her sister for the next few days? Especially if these other friends are still lurking in the vicinity? I think we will all feel more secure at the manor knowing we have one of you Braydens close by."

The magistrate came around his desk to escort the earl out. "Yes, my lord. I'll mention it to him. I don't think he'll have a problem with the arrangement."

Augustus remained in the magistrate's office until he returned. "That man is eating his guts out in fear for his wife," Augustus remarked.

"Can you blame him? He is deeply in love with her, and she is about to give birth to their first child. His brother is as mad as a wounded boar and has collected friends who may not be quite as mad as he is, but they are certainly amoral degenerates certain to be into all manner of ugly business."

"Do you really think these other friends are still lurking in Taunton, intent on freeing Lord Belfy?"

The magistrate snorted. "Freeing him? I don't think so. They are all rats but hardly foolish enough to attempt it and risk swinging along with him. But I would not put it past them to cause some other mischief simply because they are petty and vindictive."

Augustus frowned. "Do you think they will harm June, Willow, or Cammy? I mean…the Farthingale sisters."

He grinned. "I know their names. There isn't a man in town who hasn't noticed them. Their uncle will have to hire Bow Street runners to partition off Chipping Way once those three arrive in London. Every eligible bachelor within a hundred miles will be lining up to court them." He broke into laughter.

"What's so funny?"

The magistrate shook his head. "They've tried to discuss it

with me and Lorcan, but we've avoided the topic. However, seems we are related through marriage. Several of their cousins are married to ours. Actually, four Brayden-Farthingale matches at last count."

Augustus grinned. "Blessed saints, are you not quaking in your boots?"

"Afraid we are doomed, too?" He shook his head and laughed again. "Not likely. They think Lorcan and I are grunting baboons. And by the way, your cousin Robert MacLauren has also just married one of the Farthingale cousins."

Augustus thought he was jesting at first. Yet, how would the magistrate know of Robbie otherwise? "Mr. Brayden, I—"

"Please, call me Shayne. It is a small world, and it seems we are all connected through these beautiful Farthingales. There is nowhere to run to avoid them."

"Call me Augustus." He rubbed a hand across the nape of his neck and gave a wry laugh. "Obviously, I've been more out of touch than I realized. Robbie is married? And to a Farthingale, no less?" He cleared his throat. "He has a reputation with the ladies. Was it a forced match?"

"No, from what I heard, he fell in love with Heather Farthingale and fought heaven and earth to marry her."

"Robbie in love? I'm sure he wrote to me about it, but I must have been on my way back to England and did not receive word. The letter will catch up to me eventually."

They spoke a little longer, their discussion once more concentrating on the prisoners.

Once Augustus was satisfied the magistrate had all the information he needed from Jock and Angus and was well staffed to guard Lord Belfy and his circle of scoundrels, he knew it was time for him and his soldiers to depart.

He held out his hand to the magistrate. "It was a pleasure to meet you, Shayne. Although not under the best of circumstances. We're off for Caithness next."

"Against doctor's orders?" he said as he shook it.

"It's just a graze. I'm fine." More of a gouge, as June had insisted, but he was not going to admit it to anyone else. "I'll have it tended to once I am home. If anything comes up that I ought to be told about, then send word to the Earl of Caithness's townhouse in London. I'll be stopping there for a few days before we ride on to Dover."

"I will."

Augustus strode out and bade his men to follow him back to the inn. However, he did not immediately return inside. Instead, he went to the ostler and asked him to ready their mounts. He had packed most of his belongings, leaving only the matter of changing out of his dress uniform and putting on garb more fitting for a long ride.

He went up the back stairs, purposely hoping to avoid crossing paths with June. Or so he told himself, but he desperately wanted a last look at her.

No, he'd never leave if that happened.

He'd promised to see her in London.

Was this promise not enough?

CHAPTER FOURTEEN

"IS HE STILL here, Mrs. Ashcroft?" June asked later that evening before retiring to bed. She hadn't seen Augustus since they had gone into tea with Lord Burnham in the early afternoon. From the woman's pitying expression, she knew the answer before she had finished asking the question.

Still, she desperately held onto hope.

"No, my dear." The kindly woman shook her head, understanding exactly who she meant. "General MacLauren and his men rode off several hours ago."

She nodded. "Well, goodnight then. We shall be on our way to London in the morning. Thank you for all you've done. We've had a lovely stay."

"If one overlooks Lord Belfy and his horrid friends," Mrs. Ashcroft muttered. "Well, we'll soon be rid of him. Lord Burnham's not one to waste time. He'll have him hanged right quick, gentry or no. The Earl of Monkton won't stand in his way. Not after that coward shot one of England's finest heroes in the head."

She tsked and continued, turning quite chatty now that June was listening attentively. "The earl will do all in his power to see it done right quick. He has to suspect his brother would have come after him next. After all, if his lordship is deceased, then Lord Belfy becomes the earl, don't he? Then who's to stop him from his mischief?"

She paused just long enough to take another breath and continue. "The man's not even his full brother. A younger half-brother. Seeing as how the earl turned out to be a kind and gentle man, I'm thinking that sickness sprang from Lord Belfy's mother."

Mr. Ashcott joined them in time to put in his opinion. "Enough of that, Mrs. Ashcott. We don't need to be upsetting Miss Farthingale now that everything's back to settling down. It was a pleasure having you and your family with us. Enjoy your London season. I expect you'll all catch yourself husbands right quick."

Mrs. Ashcott cuffed him.

Her husband looked at her askance. "What did I say?"

"Can you not see? Miss Farthingale is in love with General MacLauren." She cast June another pitying gaze. "He'll come around in time, my dear. Just be patient."

June forced a smile. "We did get along well, but I would hardly call it love." However, she did not persist in denying her feelings since neither of them believed her anyway. "Well, good night."

She hurried up to her room.

Her sisters and aunt were already there and dressed for bed. Cammy helped her slip out of her gown. Willow took it from her hands as June was about to pack it away. "We'll do it tomorrow. You must be exhausted after today's excitement."

"I wish I were." She sighed and reached for her nightrail. "But my mind is racing. I cannot stop thinking of Augustus. I never believed he would leave me behind. I really didn't." She glanced at *The Book of Love* that was sticking out of her travel bag. "I was so sure he had fallen in love with me. He exhibited all the behaviors mentioned in the book. How could I have been so wrong?"

"You weren't wrong," Cammy said. "He promised to see you when he stopped in London. He wouldn't have given you his word of honor if he did not mean to keep it."

"But what will a few hours in London do? Assuming I'm given even that much. I'm sure he'll be summoned to dine with the king. He'll immediately be invited to the most elite parties, those filled with cabinet ministers and elegant daughters of dukes and earls, perhaps even a princess or two. Will he even have five minutes to spare for me?"

Willow hugged her. "If he doesn't move mountains to see you, then he is an undeserving wretch, and you are better rid of him."

"Thank you, Willow. But that does not help at all. He is not a wretch. He is magnificent in every way." She donned her nightrail, brushed out her hair, and then climbed into bed.

Aunt Charlotte's door had been open, and she must have heard their chatter. She walked in and sat at the foot of June's bed. "My dear, do not be unhappy. Love has a way of working out. If it is any consolation, I know he has deep feelings for you. But a man like Augustus cannot be rushed. Indeed, would you feel as you do for him if he were a brash fellow who declared his love within a day of meeting you? I think not."

She leaned over and placed a kiss on June's cheek. "Sleep well. Who knows what the morning will bring?"

"I love you, Aunt Charlotte. Thank you."

"Oh, my angels. I wish only for your happiness. Now I had better return to my bed before another ailment overcomes me, and we shall be forced to remain here another week."

Cammy and Willow laughingly groaned.

But they all fell asleep with smiles on their faces because their aunt knew just what to say to keep up their spirits.

June awoke early the next morning. Her sisters and aunt began to stir soon afterward. But she was the first one up and the first one to be washed, dressed, and packed for their journey. "June, do be a dear and let Mr. Geoffries know to prepare our carriage," her aunt said, a little slow to move this early in the day.

Cammy and Willow, both of them eager to be on their way, went in to help their aunt dress and do up her hair.

June greeted the inn's staff as she walked through the inn and out the door. She paused a moment to take a deep breath and enjoy the morning sun and the sweetness of the air. It promised to be another beautiful day. "The ostler," she muttered, heading to the stable in search of him.

Within the hour, this courtyard would be bustling with activity as carriages were brought around for the departing guests. Perhaps people were a little slow to get started today, for it seemed a little too quiet.

She gave it little thought, for darkness fell late at this time of the year, and coachmen could count on sunlight 'til almost ten o'clock in the evening.

The doors to the stable were open, and several grooms were busily at work inside the dank, hay-strewn building. She darted out of the way as one ran by, leading a pair of fine-looking bays out to the trough for water. "Have you seen Mr. Geoffries?" she called out to the young man.

"Not lately, Miss Farthingale. But he's around here somewhere. I was in the back stalls with these fine lads." He patted one of the horses affectionately on the neck. "Shall I look for him for you? Perhaps he is in the tack room."

"I'll look there myself." She made her way past the stalls through a small door that led into the ostler's work and storage area. "Mr. Geoffries?"

He wasn't there either.

She called for him again, even louder this time.

Another of the young grooms suggested she look for him in the carriage house which stood next door to the stable. "Thank you. I will."

She walked over, avoiding more grooms who were bringing out horses to hitch to the various conveyances stored within the carriage house. If she did not find Mr. Geoffries there, she would simply go in search of their driver, Mr. Pierson, and leave instructions with him.

She raised her gown slightly to skip over some muddy spots

on the ground.

It hadn't rained much over the past few days, and the lanes were mostly dry. But horses had to be watered, so she imagined some of the water in those buckets had slopped on the dirt and muddied it.

Her travel boots were now soiled. After talking to the ostler, she would return to the inn through the kitchen and see if someone could hand her a rag to clean them off.

The carriage house was oddly quiet as she approached. Not everyone was chipper in the morning, and men especially did not enjoy conversation at this early hour of the day. Her father never did and often buried his head in his newspaper while her mother, Aunt Charlotte, and she and her sisters chattered away.

She laughed and shook her head, thinking of her poor father. But he never complained about his daughters nor did he ever show disappointment that none of them were sons.

As she entered the carriage house, it took a moment for her eyes to adjust from the brightness of the outdoors to the darkness of the wooden beamed expanse. The scent of hay, coach leather, and polish assaulted her senses.

She stepped further inside. "Mr. Geoffries. Mr. Pierson. Are you in here?"

Someone was moving about. She could hear their faint, fast breaths, as though having just exerted themselves or excited about something. But what was so exciting about a carriage house? "Mr. Geoffries, is that you?"

She took another step in and stumbled over something.

It felt like a man's leg.

The door suddenly closed behind her, pitching the place in darkness. "Wait! I'm in here!"

She turned to run for the door and pull it open but was grabbed from behind. A man's hand suddenly covered her mouth, and he began to drag her behind one of the carriages. "Lord Belfy asked us to give you a present from him," the man, who spoke in a cultured voice, said with a vicious laugh.

Us?

Was there more than one of these fiends here?

What did they mean to do to her?

She wasn't going to wait to find out. She bit his hand and then smashed her head against his chin, hoping he would loosen his grip enough for her to break free. But she was also worried about Mr. Geoffries and Mr. Pierson. She had stumbled over a man's leg. What had these fiends done to them?

Dear heaven.

She hoped they were still alive.

She punched her assailant in the stomach with her elbow and ran for the door, but a second man caught her and put a hand to her throat to muffle her scream. "That's it, struggle away. You won't escape us."

She smashed her fist into his throat and once again tried to run, but she hadn't landed a solid enough punch. All she had managed to do was anger him. He threw her to the ground and cursed when she managed to land a hard kick to his knee. "Damn it! He didn't tell us she was this much of a spitfire."

The first man was nursing a bloodied nose. She could see the blood on his elegant, white handkerchief. "Forget the rest of our plan," he said, sounding pained and nasal. "Just cut her face, and let's go."

These monsters were going to leave her scarred. She felt around for anything to use as a weapon. There had to be something in here. Something close by. She grabbed what felt like a pitchfork and rolled to her feet, swinging it with all her might. "Take that you low-brain scum!"

She aimed for the tender spot between the second man's thighs, then whirled and slammed the hilt of it into the first man's privates, as well. She was about to swing it again and slam it into their eyes or throats when the doors suddenly opened, and light shone in.

She blinked, now blinded by the sudden glare. But she was fighting for her life and would not stop fighting until they drained the life out of her.

Were more accomplices coming to their aid?

No, she realized with sobbing relief when she saw someone punch the second man with enough force to break his nose. She heard the crack of bone and his agonized moan as he fell to the ground in a heap and did not get up again.

June silently cheered, realizing he was unconscious. She wanted to speak, but her throat still hurt from where one of those men had grabbed her and squeezed hard.

Her rescuer now turned to the first man, hauled him up, and slammed his fist into the man's face. He also fell in a sprawl on the ground, but he had not been knocked out cold.

June saw the glint of something metal in his hand and realized he was holding a knife. Her rescuer had noticed it as well and now crushed his booted foot atop the prone man's hand. "Drop the knife, ye bastard."

"Augustus?"

"Blessed saints! Are ye all right, June? Did they hurt ye?"

"No, I'm just a little bruised. Nothing more," she managed to croak.

More men came through door.

"Jock, take her back to the inn. Angus, ye and the lads see to these savages. If they give ye any trouble, kill them. I mean it. Grab the knife I kicked under that carriage. Search the other man. This one had it in hand and meant to use it on June."

"The bloody bastards," she heard Hamish mutter in disgust. "We'll search them for weapons. They're bound to have more."

"Alex," Augustus continued calmly, "see to Mr. Geoffries. They've knocked him out. Duncan, run next door to the magistrate and summon him here. If Lorcan is with him, tell him to search the grounds for more of Lord Belfy's friends."

Jock put a gentle arm around her to lead her out, but she resisted. "They might have also hurt our driver, Mr. Pierson. Please, look for him."

Augustus was breathing hard as he stared at her. "June…we

will, lass. Ye're trembling. Och, are ye sure they dinna hurt ye?"

"I promise, they didn't."

"That's good, lass. Go back to the inn with Jock. Ask Mr. Ashcott to summon the doctor. I'll come to see ye as soon as I am through here."

"You do realize your brogue is back," she said, still unable to believe he stood before her.

"I know. I'm unsettled."

"Why did you come back? Thank goodness you did, but why?"

He cast her the gentlest smile. "I'm looking at the reason."

"Me?"

He nodded. "Let me finish up here, and we'll talk."

That sounded quite promising.

She wanted to run into his arms but did not think her legs would hold up even for the short distance between them. The realization she was safe now struck her with stunning force. She had taken no more than two steps out, gently led away by Jock, when her knees buckled.

She cried out.

Jock caught her. "Och, lass!"

She felt herself being lifted, but it wasn't Jock's arms that came around her. "Augustus." She wrapped her arms around his neck and buried her head against his shoulder.

"Jock, take over for me. You know what to tell the magistrate when he arrives."

He gave her a light kiss on the forehead and carried her back to the inn. "I shouldn't have left ye. Forgive me, lass. I'll never leave ye again."

He was still overset, and the sweet, deep resonance of his brogue revealed it.

"Is that a promise, Augustus?"

He did not have time to answer before Mrs. Ashcott once more began to shriek. "Mr. Ashcott! Mr. Ashcott! Come quickly!"

"I'm taking her up to her guest chamber," Augustus said,

starting for the stairs. "Where are her sisters and aunt? Still there? Or in the breakfast room?"

"Still upstairs, General MacLauren."

"Thank you, Mrs. Aschott. We've summoned the magistrate. Let him know where we are. And bring up tea and honey for Miss Farthingale."

"I'll be fine in a moment. You shouldn't be carrying me up the stairs. It cannot be good for your stitches."

"I'm not letting go of you." He kissed her again on the forehead.

"Fine, be that way."

He chuckled. "What way? Possessive and moronic?"

"I was thinking along the lines of wonderfully romantic." She would have said more, but she sounded hoarse and raspy, and that could not possibly be romantic. The sound of love was not that of a croaking bullfrog.

The door to her guest chamber was open. She could see her sisters gathering their reticules and the small travel pouch that held *The Book of Love*. But they stopped what they were doing and gaped as Augustus carried her in and deposited her gently on one of the beds. "I don't think you'll be leaving Taunton today," he told them as he propped several pillows under her back and quickly dabbed his handkerchief in the ewer, wrung it out, and pressed it lightly to her throat.

He then drew up the small chair tucked under the vanity, placed it by her side, and settled his big, brawny and breathtaking frame on it.

Her sisters giggled as he took hold of her hand. "I told ye, I'm not letting go of ye."

Willow cast her a ridiculously wide grin. "June, does this mean you are ready to turn the book over to me now?"

Her eyes widened in horror. "Willow!"

"Yes," Augustus said, his gaze never leaving hers.

June gasped.

So did her sisters.

So did her Aunt Charlotte, who had just walked in and likely heard most of the conversation. "Girls," she clucked, scooting toward Willow and Cammy with surprising agility, "come downstairs with me now."

Cammy's eyes widened. "But they'll be alone. How is this proper?"

Charlotte gave her a light pat on her backside. "Child, have you learned nothing from that book?"

She hauled Cammy out.

Willow lagged behind a moment. "I've always wanted a brother. Our father will be pleased not to be the only man in the house." She cast Augustus a mirthful wink as she closed the door behind her on the way out.

June blushed furiously. "They presume too much."

"No, love. They know exactly what I am feeling, and it is time I told you." He entwined his fingers in hers, his grip warm and encompassing. "I love you, June. I think I fell in love with you the moment you tipped your impertinent chin up in the air and told me your name was Tallulah Monkton-Kidd."

He looked exceedingly handsome with his sloppy grin and the emerald fire in his eyes. "You will always be my *Tallulah*. More important, you will always be my one and only. The only woman I shall ever want. The only woman I shall ever love."

She worried that she had been hit over the head and was now having scrambled dreams. But his touch felt real. So did his smile as he stared at her.

"We'd barely made it out of Taunton yesterday when my big gray, Titan, stopped cantering and refused to budge. Even my horse sensed I was in love with you and thought I was behaving like a bloody idiot."

She laughed. "I believe this is how the expression 'having horse sense' came about."

"My men agreed with Titan." He raked a hand through his hair. "I'm sorry I put you through my idiocy. I would have returned last night to tell you, but I wanted to make another stop first."

"Where?"

He patted his breast pocket. "To obtain the special license. That is, if you will have me. And just to be clear what I am asking..." He leaned forward and kissed her lightly on the lips. "Will you marry me?"

"You said the M-word."

"And I'm not taking it back."

She eased the damp handkerchief off her throat and sat up. "Oh, Augustus. Is there a doubt this is what I've hoped for since I set eyes on you?"

He shook his head. "You certainly have been expressive about your feelings. But I want you to know that I have no doubts either. I never did, June. I simply refused to believe that after all my years of experience, all my cynicism and jaded outlook, it could happen so easily and feel so immeasurably right."

She threw her arms around him and hugged him fiercely. "I love you so much, and I was so afraid I had lost you. I knew you were the one for me even before I had ever spoken to you. We saw you and your men stride into the inn and request rooms for the night. I gasped because I thought you were the handsomest man I had ever seen in my life."

"Obviously, you are in need of spectacles," he teased.

"My eyesight is perfect. When you drew me behind you and told that horrid Lord Belfy I was your wife...*yes*, I thought right then and there. Yes, I am hopelessly in love with this man, and I wish to be his wife."

"We can be married today."

She eased back to stare into the emerald depths of his eyes. "You're serious?"

He nodded.

"You don't waste time once your mind is made up, do you?"

She expected a teasing remark and was surprised by the sudden seriousness in his expression. "Had we ridden into the inn's courtyard even a minute later, I would not have seen you walk to the carriage house or notice the door suddenly close behind you. I am shaken to my bones that I might not have been there to save you. I know you did most of the work fighting off those men. But there were two of them, and they had knives drawn."

He took a deep breath and stared at her with pain in his expression. "Can you ever forgive me?"

"There is nothing to forgive, Augustus. You came back. Even if you hadn't, there would still be nothing to forgive. What we are doing, what we are feeling, defies logic. I know how these feelings upended you because you are probably one of the most logical men in all of England. You pride yourself on it. You are the great man you've become because of it."

He drew her into his arms and onto his lap.

"Then this must be the logical next step," he said, dipping his head to hers and capturing her lips in an exquisitely gentle and yet deeply intense kiss that set her heart thrumming and her pulse fluttering.

This is how she dreamed it would be with Augustus. Those big, muscled arms of his holding her protectively as he went about the business of kissing her and putting a curl to her tingling toes.

Well, all of her was tingling now, not just her toes.

She sighed into his mouth and ran her hands along his hard, taut body. His hands were roaming all over her now. Along her back, her waist. Her hips.

He cupped one hand to her breast, seeming to like the way the soft mound filled his palm. She liked it, too.

Exceedingly.

"June, I can't get enough of you." He licked his tongue lightly along the seam of her lips, teasing and nudging them open so he could enter and explore her mouth, taste her on his tongue, and lose himself in the sensation of her.

His hand, a soldier's rough hand, was still planted on her breast. This came as no surprise to her. Low-brain male. Female breast. The innate need was obvious. He ran his thumb lightly over its budded tip, and she almost fell off his lap with the surprising pleasure of it.

What was this sensation?

It was the most powerful thing she had ever experienced.

All manner of thoughts sped through her brain, none of them proper. She wanted to shed her clothes and have him shed his because she had to touch his skin. She wanted to put her mouth to his body and lick it. How would he taste? Hot? Salty?

A knock at the door put an end to her wanton reverie.

Augustus groaned and drew his mouth off hers. Wordlessly, he settled her back on the bed and rose to open the door.

She took the damp handkerchief and put it to her throat again, not that the bruises pained her, but her body was a fiery torch after that kiss, and she needed something to cool herself down.

"Oh, my dear! Have you been crying?" Mrs. Ashcott scurried in, set down the tea tray, and rushed to her side.

No, she hadn't been crying.

She was flushed because she had been kissing the incredibly handsome general who was standing behind the woman and arrogantly grinning, no doubt quite pleased with himself.

"We are going to be married," she blurted, not knowing quite what else to say since Mrs. Ashcott would realize in another moment that her flame-red cheeks had nothing to do with tears but with Augustus kissing the daylights out of her.

The woman shrieked in delight. "I knew it!"

"In fact, we would like to be married here at the inn," Augustus said.

"Today," June added, then glanced in alarm at Augustus. Had she overstepped? Well, he was the one who'd told her that he did not want to ever leave her side again. And what was the point in kissing her the way he had if they were going to wait to do something more about it?

But he merely nodded to confirm the request. "Let me fetch your aunt and sisters so you may tell them the news."

"General MacLauren, you stay right here with the lovely lass while I get her family. The magistrate is here now, too. He'll want to speak to both of you. Good thing you stopped them curs when you did. Those beasts wanting to cut up your beautiful face, Miss Farthingale. They deserve to burn in hell, the lot of those vermin."

Augustus's expression turned to ice. She'd never seen an expression of such cold fury. "Cut your face? Is this what they meant to do with their knives? Mrs. Ashcroft, stay with June. Do not leave her side."

He stormed out of her chamber, and she could hear him striding down the hall and leaping the stairs. The inn's door slammed as he stormed out.

She hadn't thought to mention it once he'd taken her in his arms, the horror having fled and been replaced with joy at his return.

She had expected to tell her entire story once the magistrate questioned her.

But Augustus looked angry enough to kill those men.

Oh, dear heaven.

Is this what he intended to do?

Chapter Fifteen

Within the hour, the Ashcotts had closed off a portion of their elegant dining room to accommodate all those now gathered around June. The doctor had already come and gone, determining her to be fit. She had suffered no more than some bruising to her neck, which would disappear within a day or two, he'd assured her.

Her aunt and sisters were seated beside her, too overset to leave her alone for a moment.

Augustus and his companions were seated across from them. At the head of the table sat the magistrate while his brother, Lorcan, the one Cammy had taken to calling a grunting boar, stood with his back to the wall, his expression stony and his eyes silvery and lethal.

This was not the wedding gathering, but the magistrate's attempt to question her in order to determine how to charge these friends of Lord Belfy. He had wanted to speak to her in private, but her sisters and Aunt Charlotte insisted on hearing what she had to say. Augustus insisted on staying now that she was his betrothed.

Jock, Angus, and the other Scots Greys stayed on the magistrate's orders because he was afraid they would go to his office while he was here and kill those men who had tried to harm her. It did not make a bit of difference that the privileged lords had failed in their attempt.

"Ye're General MacLauren's wife now," Angus had explained. "It is our duty to avenge ye."

"We're not married yet," she reminded him.

But none of Augustus's men seemed to acknowledge this fact. They considered the two of them wed because Augustus had held her hand and said he loved her in front of his men, and she had unwittingly repeated the same to him, also in front of them, also still holding hands.

Apparently, this was considered a handfasting.

The Scots had been witness to it, and even though they were not in Scotland where such a thing was recognized, they may as well have been as far as all of them were concerned. The handfasting was equivalent to a betrothal. If the couple consummated their betrothal within a year, they were then considered married.

Augustus was nursing his swollen knuckles and staring at her with the steamiest, smoldering eyes, so she knew he wanted that consummation to happen tonight, whether or not they stood before an English minister and exchanged vows.

He was not going to force her, of course. He was far too honorable for that. But she did not think she could resist him, or even wanted to, should he make the overture. Fortunately, he had already arranged for the minister to perform a properly recognized English ceremony in order for them to wed shortly before supper.

The ceremony was scheduled to take place in a matter of hours, assuming the magistrate did not lock up Augustus for…she did not know what he had done to these friends of Lord Belfy's, but it was no gentle rebuke if his swollen knuckles were any indication.

June cast Augustus a frown of disapproval.

"I did not kill them, June."

"You broke their jaws. Did you think I would not understand what the magistrate meant when he said they would not talk at present? It did not mean they would not give a statement. It meant they *could* not talk because of what you did to them." She sighed and shook her head. "You did not have to do anything to them. The magistrate was about to haul them away."

Lorcan Brayden cleared his throat. "They attempted to escape, and General MacLauren stopped them."

"Aye," the Scottish contingent said in unison.

So, this was going to be their story?

The magistrate said nothing. "Miss Farthingale, tell us what happened this morning."

She related the tale, knowing she had to confirm that these men had indeed planned to wood carve her face, and then winced as every male seated around the table took on baboonish, warlike expressions. She was seriously worried they would rise up in outrage and hang those lords on the spot. In truth, these latest friends of Lord Belfy did deserve punishment.

She was not an utter nodcock, and her gut did churn with worry that those beasts might yet escape punishment because of their status in society.

They had frightened the wits out of her.

They had meant to turn her into a hideous, scarred creature, and would have succeeded had she not been able to fend them off long enough for Augustus to come to her rescue.

They might have stabbed Augustus, too. Gutted him and laughed about it, had he not taken them down first. These men cared not a whit for whom they hurt.

When her questioning was over, June began to nibble her lip with worry.

Augustus came to her side and knelt beside her. "What is it, June?"

"Do you still wish to marry me?"

He seemed surprised by her remark. "Why wouldn't I? Not to mention that my men consider us married already."

"But what do you say, Augustus? You are a man of peace, and I've turned you into a retribution-seeking avenger in the span of a day."

He took her hand in his. "I am not a bloody saint who preaches piety and turns the other cheek. I have spent too much of my life on a battlefield, trying my best to save as many of my brothers-in-arms as possible. Yes, these Vienna conferences are organized for the purpose of bringing about peaceful solutions. But that is not, and has never been, the nature of man. So what Castlereagh and all who work with him are really hoping to do is contain all parties, and where possible, keep the fighting to a minimum so that we do not descend to savagery and warfare."

"But you honor the rule of law."

"I do. I will never harm an innocent and will always strive to protect those who are helpless and vulnerable. But men such as Lord Belfy and his friends are monsters in the making. I've seen enough of their sort to know they have to be stopped before they gain enough power to be untouchable. They consider themselves above the law and hold no respect for it. There is only one thing men such as these will ever understand."

"A bigger fist?"

"I showed them mercy in merely punching them. I wanted to kill them because they tried to hurt you. I will kill them if they so much as glance your way again. Any man would do the same to protect those he loves. You did not turn me into anything I am not. You did not make me do something I would not otherwise have done."

"Then you still wish to marry me?"

He nodded. "More than ever. You are brilliant and courageous. I am amazed by your heart and bravery. I shudder to think what they might have done to you had you not fought them off as valiantly as you did."

She blushed at the compliment. "We never discussed what will happen after the ceremony. Will you take me up to Caithness with you?"

"My men like you more than they like me," he said with a grin. "I'll have a rebellion on my hands if I dare leave you behind. In truth, I hope you are willing. I would never force you to go, but I would be honored to have you meet my grandda and have him meet you."

Her heart melted. "I would love that. Will you take me to Vienna, too?"

He frowned. "I'll take you with me anywhere and everywhere, so long as it does not place your life in danger. I was a fool to worry about your being unable to handle the intrigue rife in these elite, political circles. You are a natural. You will have everyone tamed and eating out of your hand within a week of your arrival. Most of the men there will fall in love with you."

She put a hand to his cheek. "I only care about you loving me."

He kissed her palm. "That I do."

He rose and turned to the magistrate and his brother. "June and I are getting married. You are invited to the ceremony and a wedding supper afterward."

Shayne Brayden grinned. "It will be our pleasure. I'll never refuse a good meal."

"What about those odious men?" Willow asked. "What's to become of them? Do you think their families will insist on their release? Would you not be obligated to grant it?"

Shayne leaned back casually in his chair. "Within a matter of hours, your sister will be Mrs. MacLauren, wife of the king's Continental military commander. If their families want those men released, they will first have to crawl to the king and explain why they attacked the general's bride on her wedding day. I will not release them on any authority less than a royal command."

Then his expression hardened. "I can assure you, His Majesty will bankrupt them with his stiff fines if they dare ask for clemency. No, the only discussions their families will have is with me. They will do all in their power to keep the news from reaching the king's ears."

"And what will you tell them?" Willow asked, obviously still fretting.

"I do not take bribes, Miss Farthingale."

Willow gasped. "No, of course not. The thought never crossed my mind. I was just curious as to what you have the authority to do if pressured by these powerful families?"

"I have the authority to leave them rotting in a prison cell until the Lenten assizes held next year." He turned to June. "I will need you back here to testify against them at that time, unless they will admit their wrongdoing and accept the terms of their sentence."

She glanced at Augustus.

He nodded. "We will return if you need us."

"Thank you. I will send word if it proves unnecessary. If the trial must go forth, it is likely Lord Burnham will preside again. Do you think he will soon forget Lord Belfy or his cohorts? If these other two are fortunate, he will sentence them to nothing worse than being shipped off to some remote part of the world under threat of death if they ever dare return to English shores."

June listened attentively. "You mentioned the Lenten assizes. Will they remain confined here in Taunton until then?"

He pursed his lips. "I may have to move them to the magistrate's gaol in Exeter. It is a far sturdier prison. Also, their trial might be moved up if it is decided to try them there."

"Then they would be in that magistrate's jurisdiction," Cammy commented. "What if he decides to be more lenient?"

"He won't," Lorcan said.

June and her sisters looked up at him.

"How can you be so sure he won't?" June asked, glad he was on their side, for he seemed made of stone, and she could not imagine any man surviving his boulder of a fist coming at him with full force.

Lorcan cracked a smile, perhaps the first she had ever seen out of this stoic man. "He's our cousin."

Aunt Charlotte's eyes perked. "Another Brayden?"

"No." That was the extent of Lorcan's conversation. He folded his arms across his chest and resumed his position with his back against the wall.

The magistrate was more forthcoming. "He's related on our mother's side. But the point is, thanks to you, this band of rowdies will no longer remain free to menace the citizens of Taunton. They've run roughshod over Exeter, as well, so there is no one in the area who will shed a tear as these men get the punishment long overdue them. Eight lords in all. We've now got five of them in custody, thanks to you."

He turned to his brother. "If the last three are so foolish as to remain close by, Lorcan will track them down."

Charlotte smiled at him. "Thank you, Mr. Brayden. It eases my mind to know these brigands will be brought to heel." She now turned to June and her sisters. "Come, my dears. We must prepare for the wedding. Of course, this means we will remain in Taunton at least another day to see you safely off with your new husband, June."

Cammy's eyes began to tear, and she emitted a shattered breath, "I had not thought of any of us parted so soon. It will just be me and Willow now. Oh, Aunt Charlotte, must we go on? Is it not enough that one of us is so happily settled? Please, may we go home now?"

Charlotte regarded her with motherly affection. "It must be on to London for the three of us. Look upon it as a visit to your cousins. Your Uncle John and Aunt Sophie are eager to have us spend time with them. It will be great fun. You'll see."

June was not so certain. Yes, Cammy would enjoy being with all their cousins, but she would not enjoy the grand balls and elegant soirees to which they would be invited. Willow would manage it because she was made of sterner stuff and could handle anything. But Cammy was their little sister and painfully shy, especially around men.

Of course, because she was so beautiful—men could not resist—they all sought her out. These were just the Barnstaple men, decent and hardworking, who knew their family and would never do anything to dishonor her. Cammy had to be frightened out of her wits at the thought of meeting the sharper, more arrogant London rakes, who would flock to her like rams to a ewe in heat. They were not likely to be as vicious as Lord Belfy and his rabble, but demanding and oppressive just the same.

The ladies excused themselves and went upstairs to prepare for the wedding.

June considered offering to take Cammy with her, but Charlotte would never allow it. Even if she did, that would mean Willow would be facing the marriage mart on her own. That was not fair to her.

"Don't worry about me," Cammy said once they were back in their guest chamber and sorting through June's gowns. "I know Uncle John and Aunt Sophie will look out for me. If I wish to beg out of an affair, they won't force me. Who knows? I may decide I like the London whirl after all."

June did not believe Cammy would ever enjoy London but appreciated her putting on a brave face.

"What will you wear for the ceremony?" Charlotte also began to search through June's neatly packed trunk. "The blue silk, I should think. It will be perfect. Let Willow style your hair and coil those shining threads you wore on Midsummer Eve through it."

She nodded, but a thought suddenly struck her, and she began to nibble her lip. "I'll never be able to bring all these clothes with me. Augustus is in a mad rush to get to Caithness. He only has a month to get up there and back down again to Dover for the crossing to France. Then he's off to Vienna from there. We'll never manage it if I bring along more than a simple travel pouch. Oh, dear. This is already getting complicated."

Her aunt took her by the shoulders. "June, these little problems will sort themselves out. If General MacLauren has come to this realization, then so must you. My dear, do not get caught up in the unimportant. We'll take your gowns with us and make arrangements for you to collect them when you return south. You and he being together is what matters. It is *all* that matters. You will get over not having a fancy dress. You will never get over missing out on precious time together."

She hugged her aunt, remembering what Charlotte had told them about her own true love. How devastating for her to be parted from him so early on. But Charlotte's memories of their time together are what allowed her to move beyond the sadness and hurt. "Thank you, Aunt Charlotte. I will always keep that in mind."

They next chose gowns for Willow and Cammy to wear.

In truth, the hour flew by.

Before June knew it, she was standing beside Augustus in the garden gazebo, the minister before them, and the warm summer air gently surrounding them. Her family, his soldiers, the Braydens, and the Ashcotts stood behind them. All of them, especially Angus, were sniffling and dabbing away joyful tears. Well, she did not think either Shayne or Lorcan Brayden were shedding a tear. Likely, they were breathing sighs of relief that their party would soon be leaving Taunton.

She thought Augustus might hesitate when exchanging vows, but his voice rang true and strong as he pledged his heart to her. "I promise to honor and protect you…" Yes, this was him, strong, honorable, and protective.

She pledged her heart to him with equal confidence.

"I love you," she whispered once the minister had ended the ceremony and pronounced them man and wife.

Everyone cheered.

He kissed her softly on the lips.

"Congratulations," Angus said, clapping Augustus on the back and then turning to embrace her in an enormous bear hug. "Ye're something special, lass. I began to despair our laddie would ever marry. A good sort like him deserves happiness. Ye'll give him that by the buckets." He cleared his throat as his eyes misted again. "I'm starved. Let's eat!"

They walked inside to the dining room and enjoyed the sumptuous repast Mrs. Ashcott had her staff prepare for them. She had outdone herself, and June went out of her way to compliment her on what seemed to be a never-ending stream of courses, from the elegant white soup, to the lamb pie and honey-glazed ham, to the *couronnes* and *peches melba* brought out for dessert.

But as darkness fell, the men finished their after-dinner drinks and rose. It was time for the celebration to end. She and Augustus thanked the Ashcotts profusely. While his soldiers went to the inn's taproom for another round of drinks, Charlotte bustled her sisters upstairs to their rooms.

June watched them climb the stairs, feeling so odd not to be with them.

"What do you say, June? Shall we retire, too?" She turned to Augustus, suddenly realizing she was meant to sleep with him tonight…and all the nights to follow.

She did not resist when he took her hand and led her upstairs. But she hesitated when they reached his door. "I…"

She hadn't brought any of her things to his room.

He gave her hand a light squeeze. "What is it, love?"

"I didn't think to move my belongings in here before the ceremony."

He smiled. "You may not have thought beyond the ceremony, but your aunt is a very wise woman. I think you will find all you need waiting for you in my room. Ours now."

"Oh." She looked around as he led her in and closed the door behind them. She noticed her brush and soaps, as well as a travel gown and other attire appropriate for riding out tomorrow. Her sturdy travel boots. Her robe. "Oh, dear."

"What's wrong?"

"My nightgown is missing."

He chuckled softly and wrapped his arms around her. "Och, lass," he said, his brogue husky and tantalizing. "Ye won't be needing that tonight."

CHAPTER SIXTEEN

AUGUSTUS STRUGGLED TO contain his grin when June's eyes widened at his remark. "I won't be needing my nightgown?"

"No, love. You won't." But he would not force her to do anything she was not ready to do. He'd waited this long to find happiness and certainly could wait however long it took for June to feel comfortable around him. Well, he hoped the wait would not be too long, but he was not going to rush her or demand things from her that she was not yet willing to give. "Leave your chemise on if this makes you feel more comfortable. Or I can give you one of my shirts if you'd prefer something more sturdy."

He sighed and ran a hand through his hair. "June, I won't force you. I'll do nothing more than hold you in my arms if this is all you wish to do."

She bit down lightly on that fleshy lower lip of hers, the one he was aching to kiss and taste. "Do we not have to consummate our union? Is this not expected?"

He sat on the bed and drew her onto his lap. "It is expected. Desperately hoped for, on my part. But I know all of this happened very quickly for you." He laughed and shook his head. "Quite unexpected for both of us. I never thought to acquire a wife on the journey."

"Would you prefer not to…"

He laughed again. "Would I rather wait to make you my wife in this way? No, June. I am ready to explode with wanting you."

She wrapped her arms around his neck and nestled against him. "I've spent every night since I met you cuddling my pillow and pretending it was you. I am looking forward to the real thing. But I have no experience. I don't know what to do."

It swelled his heart to know he would be the first and only man to touch her.

That her lips would know only his.

That her body would respond to his touch alone, and he would be the one to see the wonder in her eyes.

He had been around enough women to know those who would keep to their vows and those who would stray. June had given him the promise of her love and would hold to it always.

It humbled him and also shamed him, knowing how casually he'd accepted married women into his bed. Safe, uncomplicated. Easily disentangled.

But the promise he'd made to June was also a lifetime promise, one he would keep to her until his dying breath.

He cupped his palm to her cheek. "Do you trust me, June?"

"Yes, Augustus, with my heart and my life."

"Good, then trust me with your body as well. I can assure you, I will worship it." He laughed lightly. "I think I have done nothing but that in my mind since the day we met. Low brain, humming at full speed."

"You hide it well."

His smiled slipped a little. "Years of experience at bluffing, whether at cards or around a negotiation table. I had gotten quite good at this. Suppressing all feelings. Stowing away any inconvenient ones. But I want you to know, I'd never felt love until you came along. That was a wave swell I could not ignore, no matter how hard I tried."

He ran a hand lightly up and down her back as he spoke, sensing the moment she eased in his arms. He tipped her head up slightly and planted a soft kiss on her lips.

She tasted like one of the sweets put out for their wedding feast, sugary and delicious.

He deepened the kiss, loving the feel of her giving mouth on his, especially her fleshy lower lip that drove him wild simply watching her nibble it. Her arms tightened around his neck, and she pressed against him, seeming to melt into his body.

She wanted him but did not yet understand what it was she wanted. Nor did she have any notion of the pleasure they would both receive when she gave herself to him.

He would show her now.

While he kept his kiss gentle, he slowly increased its urgency so that she would feel the intensity build. At the same time, he began to undo her gown, easily slipping it off one shoulder. He felt the quickening of her heart against his as he began to trail soft kisses down her throat to the base, where the little pulse beat with anticipatory excitement.

He suckled that little beating pulse lightly, afraid to do more for the bruises around her neck. However, he stifled his rage, knowing it would frighten her. Tonight was for them alone. All he wanted to do was pleasure her.

His tension eased when he evoked a whispered moan out of her. He then began to trail kisses along the delicate curve of her shoulder.

He smiled, feeling her skin warm against his lips.

He dipped his head lower, now having no barrier to the swell of her breast. Blessed saints, he'd been dreaming of tasting her there for what felt like an eternity. He tugged the gown a little lower to get at the soft, creamy flesh.

She gasped as his tongue swirled over it and squirmed against him when he took its rosy peak into his mouth. "Augustus," she whispered in surrender and clutched his head to her breast.

Then she remembered his stitched head and quickly let go, muttering an apology.

"Love, I'm not delicate. You won't hurt me." He held her securely in his arms and had no intention of stopping unless she asked him to. This was the nature of men in lust, and he was indeed that with his wife. He did not care if every one of his stitches popped, which they wouldn't. Even if they did, it was only a graze…gouge…not life-threatening.

He slid the gown off her other shoulder and took the same pleasure with that beautiful peak.

She tasted so good.

Roses and cream.

Her skin warmed to his touch as he kissed and teased her. She was like a beautiful rose blossoming under his touch. "June, you are so lovely."

"So are you." She worked his buttons, wanting him to remove his jacket and every layer beneath it. So did he. Blessed saints, he wanted so badly to feel her skin against his, to see all of her. Hold her. Explore that glorious body of hers.

He set her on the bed and stood to rid himself of his clothing.

She watched in fascination while he shed each layer, her eyes wide and as vibrant blue as the ocean.

He was eager to have her shed her layers, as well. But she did no more than kick off her slippers and continue to watch him. However, the gown was still off her shoulders. Out of modesty, she had drawn her chemise up to cover her breasts.

But the gown remained loose and easy to slip off.

He would tend to that chore once he'd removed all but his trousers, which he managed quickly, and returned to her side. He stood her up while he finished undressing her, first removing her stockings for her. His hands lightly grazed along her thighs as he drew them down and followed with his lips trailing kisses down her shapely legs and then up again to the inside of her thighs.

He knew she was excited.

He felt the heat of her skin and her soft, shallow breaths as he now rose to unpin the lush mass of her hair. Waves of dark silk tumbled down around her shoulders and over her breasts. More dark silk fell down her back to curl at her waist.

"June," he groaned, tucking her hair over one shoulder to keep it from getting trapped beneath her when he set her on the bed. He wanted to play with it, run his fingers through her magnificent curls.

He eased her flat atop the mattress.

Every pulse he possessed was hot and throbbing as he stretched out beside her.

He soaked her in, smiled as he gazed at her perfectly proportioned body. Well, she was perfect for him. He'd known it from the first, for his low brain had danced a jig the moment he had laid eyes on her. She was even more perfect without her clothes on, although she still wore her chemise. But it was sheer and arousing, for his eyes sought to complete what he could not yet clearly see.

He still saw plenty, for the dusky rose circles at her breasts and the darker patch between her slender thighs was temptingly visible.

He wound his fingers through her hair and settled himself over her body, propping on his elbows so as not to crush her beneath his weight. She began to squirm like a pup under him, the innocent movements threatening to set him off like fireworks. "June, what are you doing?"

"Trying to take off my chemise."

"Are you sure?" He wanted her to feel comfortable with him and was pleased when she nodded. He helped her out of the garment and then quickly unbuttoned the falls of his trousers, slipping them off as well.

There was nothing between them now.

He saw the look of trepidation in her eyes as she gazed down at him.

He chuckled. "We will fit. I promise you."

She nodded. "And I'm sure it will be wondrous."

He might have believed her if she hadn't sounded so hesitant. "It will be, love. Do you trust me?"

"Oh, yes, Augustus. I do." She reached for him and drew him to her so that her soft skin and resplendent curves molded to his body, and her breasts pillowed against his chest.

It was all the encouragement he needed to taste her, kiss her, suckle, and lick her. He watched her respond to the stroke of his finger at her most intimate spot and knew the moment she had tipped over the precipice, her shudders surrounding him, quivering against his finger, and her breathy moans ready to take him over the precipice as well.

He positioned himself over her and eased his way into her wetness.

This was her first time, and he wanted to be gentle, but he took his cues from her, allowed her to take the lead in moving against him, driving him deeper inside her. Driving him wild with her pouty lips and body that was more perfect than he'd ever imagined.

He wrapped his arms around her as they began their mating dance in earnest, now taking over their coupling. Kissing her. Tasting her. Embedding himself in her.

Moving inside her.

She was tight and beautiful.

Her breasts were a thing of splendor.

He could not get enough of her, wanted to devour her, bury himself deep inside her.

He felt himself ready to explode, but he held back his own release when he realized she was responding again. She looked so lovely with her head tipped back and her body arched in splendor.

He suckled and thrust, wanting her wild and crying out for him.

When she did, he let himself follow.

The world spun out of control as he gave a final thrust. Fireworks tore through him. Explosions rocked him. These were no gentle wave swells coming to shore, for those were too tame for what he was experiencing. These fiery bursts, enhanced by her own wild and writhing response, tore through him with relentless force.

He poured himself into her, hot and liquid as the flow of lava.

She wrapped her arms around him, entwined her legs around his waist, held him until he was drained and completely spent.

He collapsed like a big, sweaty lump atop her, still connected and throbbing his last inside her. After a moment, he eased out of her, propping on his side to hold her close and caress the delicate line of her jaw. "How do you feel, June?"

She laughed softly. "Is it not obvious? I never knew such a thing existed before tonight. How do you feel, Augustus?"

"Great. Bloody great. I don't know how I am ever going to keep my hands off you on the ride to Caithness. I'm going to make a besotted arse of myself. If it were just me and my men, we'd simply camp outdoors. But we'll have to stop at inns along the way so you and I can have our own room every night. My men will know and tease me relentlessly."

"I'm sorry. I don't mean to be an imposition."

"You're not. You are the best thing that's ever happened to me. I mean it, June. I love you. I always will."

"Promise?"

"Yes, love. I've been through enough in my life to know the good and bad of what's out there. It is a promise I easily and gladly make. I promise I will love you and be a good husband to you for all the days of my life."

She curled up against him and smiled. "And I promise you the same as your wife."

She cleared her throat.

He arched an eyebrow. "What is it, love?"

"I only ask because I am scientifically curious…"

He laughed. "What are you curious about, *Tallulah*?"

She grinned at him. "The book says that a man's eye is drawn to the female bosom, continually drawn there because his eye must complete the image of what is hidden to him beneath her gown."

He was glad she didn't mind his teasing. In truth, the night they met would be one of the sweetest memories for him. "That's true. And?"

"Now that you've seen…me…" She glanced down at her chest. "Which is better?"

"You mean the fantasy or the reality?"

She nodded.

He kissed her on the lips. "With you? Always the reality, love."

He set about proving it to her.

CHAPTER SEVENTEEN

Caithness, Scotland
July 1821

PARTING FROM HER sisters and aunt had been very difficult for June.

Despite how kind Augustus and his men had been to her the entire journey to Caithness, she still missed her family terribly. Perhaps the reason was because her meeting Augustus and marrying him had all happened so fast. Probably too fast, but she had never doubted the choice she'd made. Over their weeks of travel, she had grown to love him more than she ever thought possible.

She had also grown to appreciate how deeply he loved her in return, all the more heartwarming because he was such a deliberate, thoughtful man who never acted rashly.

As they approached the Earl of Caithness's castle, a magnificent gray stone fortress situated on a hill overlooking the sea, she saw every man's expression lighten and felt their hearts fill with joy.

They had traveled through valleys and glens she truly believed must have been inhabited by faeries, for they were so green and beautiful. They had ridden past soaring crags and waterfalls, stopped to water their horses beneath azure skies where hawks circled overhead and had rested on hillocks filled with wildflowers that were more beautiful than any she could ever create in her dreams.

She turned her head to the sun to feel its warmth and the salty bite of the wind upon her cheeks. The water glistened in the distance, sparkles of light mixing with the white foam crests roiled by the wind. When they paused a moment to take it all in, she heard the distant *whoosh* of North Sea waves gliding to shore and a pounding echo as some crashed into the hollow caves along the water's edge.

No wonder Augustus and his men spoke of this place as nourishment for the soul.

"We're home," Augustus said when they entered Dornach castle's courtyard, and several grooms came rushing out of the nearby stable to meet them and take their horses.

Augustus greeted them warmly as he swung off his beautiful gray, Titan, with agility. Jock and Angus were in tears as they dismounted and hugged the stable lads. The informality surprised her but pleased her very much. Everyone in the castle was treated as family.

No doubt, a trip to the village later would yield the same results, hugs and cheers and tears all around as these men reunited with their kinsmen, and she was introduced to them all.

Augustus had a tear in his eye and a broad grin of delight when he came to her side to help her off the sweet roan he'd purchased for her in Taunton.

"It is breathtaking," she said, returning his smile with a warm one of her own. She tingled when he wrapped his hands around her waist to scoop her off her mount and felt the emotion of his return home flowing through him when he kept an arm around her waist to lead her across the courtyard toward the massive front door.

But they'd hardly taken two steps forward before the door was flung open, and an old, yet still quite spry man came bounding out.

"Grandda!" Augustus ran toward him and picked him up to swallowed him in his arms. "I missed ye, ye old goat!"

"Laddie!" They hugged each other fiercely.

He then embraced Angus, Jock, and the younger men heartily, and bade them go inside for refreshments. This left only the three of them still standing in the courtyard, for the grooms had already led the horses away. Augustus kept his arm over the man's shoulder as they turned to June. "And who is this lovely lass?"

Augustus winked at her. "An angel I met in Taunton and simply could not leave without her. Grandda, this is my wife, June. Formerly Miss Juniper Farthingale of Barnstaple, England. June, may I present you to the Earl of Caithness, my granduncle who has been more of a father to us all."

June started to bow, but the old man would have none of it. "Come here, ye sweet lassie, and give me a hug. We'll have none of that formality among family."

She gave him a sincere embrace. Augustus obviously loved him deeply, so she would as well. After a moment, the earl released her and began to study her face in earnest. "Farthingale, ye say?"

She nodded. "I was on my way to London to stay with relatives for my come-out but met your grandnephew and knew my heart could only ever be his. It was all quite sudden."

"Sudden?" He turned to Augustus in obvious amazement, then turned back to her flashing a broad grin. "Ye've obviously worked a miracle with my grandnephew. I was beginning to despair he'd ever find love. But I see that he has. Farthingale? Were ye headed to Chipping Way?"

June laughed in surprise. "Yes. To my Uncle John and Aunt Sophie's house. Do you know them?"

"Aye, surprisingly well ye could say. And speaking of surprises, I have one for ye. Robbie's still here, and he's also brought his new bride up to meet me. Ye might know her, June. She's yer cousin Heather."

Her eyes widened in delight. "Heather's here?"

"Aye, she and Robbie went into the village, but they'll be

back shortly. They went with Malcolm and Anne. Malcolm is Robbie's elder brother. Ye might know Anne, for she's the sister of the Earl of Wycke, who is now married to yer cousin Honey."

Augustus groaned. "No more talk of family connections. My head will split if I have to conjure up a family tree."

"Weel, ye'll be listening to one more. I hope ye'll have the chance to stop at Coldstream Castle when ye head south again. You'll enjoy meeting Augustus's brother, Thad. He's married to Penelope Sherbourne. Do ye know her lass? She's yer cousin Poppy's best friend."

Augustus burst out laughing. "Bollocks, no wonder I fell hard. I had no chance. I was destined to love a Farthingale, wasn't I?"

"Aye, laddie. I'm glad ye took action and did no' let her slip through yer grasp. These Farthingale lassies are something special. Someone would have taken her in her first season out. Ye were right to act without delay."

"I know, Grandda," he said quietly, but June felt the intensity of his words.

They turned to walk inside, the earl still chatting away. "Robbie and Heather told me about that book. She's a sweet, little pixie. Robbie is mad crazy in love with her. Ye can see she loves him just as deeply. Tell me, lass. Did ye have that book when ye met Augustus?"

She laughed. "*The Book of Love*? Yes, I did."

"That's how we met, Grandda. She was trying to use it on me. Quite clumsily and obviously, I might add."

The earl arched an eyebrow. "Ye married the lass and look besotted. I'd say she did a grand job with it, not clumsy at all."

"Thank you, my lord." She gave a playfully deferential bow.

They entered the dining hall to join the others, but the earl held her back a moment. "Do ye have that book with ye now?"

"No, I gave it to my sister, Willow."

He sighed. "Too bad. Now that my lads are all well settled, I could have used it for myself. I lost my wife a few years back, you see. It was an arranged marriage but turned into a love match. I grieved deeply when I lost her. Since we had no children, these lads became ours. But they doona need me anymore. They all have good, loving women to look after them now."

"After Willow, that book is meant to be passed on to our youngest sister, Cammy." She nibbled her lip, taking his request with all seriousness. "It isn't mine to give away, but I will ask if you might have it after she is settled."

"Och, no. It's all right, lass. I'm an old man. Let it pass on to someone young and hopeful. I've had an extraordinarily rich life. No complaints and no regrets." He escorted her to a seat beside him, then took his seat at the head of the table. "Enjoy the repast. Yer rooms will be ready shortly. I'm sure ye're all tired from the long ride north."

Augustus settled beside her and took her hand in his under the table, as though they were young lovers sneaking a touch. "Aye, Grandda. June and I could do with a good, long nap."

She pinched his hand. "It is early yet. We ought to take a walk into town and try to meet up with your cousins and Heather."

"The town's big. We'll never find them, and they'll all be back by the time we come down to supper." He cast her a steamy look that—oh, heavens—everyone saw, for Augustus took no pains to hide his intentions. He wanted to get her into bed in the afternoon. She had never heard of such a thing. Wasn't it sinful? Well, divinely sinful.

She cleared her throat. "I suppose I ought to rest since we'll all be staying up late to chat, won't we? I'm looking forward to meeting Anne, Malcolm, and Robbie. Seeing Heather again will be such joy."

They were led up to their bedchamber a short while later, Augustus greeting everyone they passed with warmth. Indeed, to be home again was the best nourishment for his soul. The housekeeper, the butlers, footmen, and maids must have been with the earl for decades, and even though Augustus was no longer a lad, apparently he hadn't aged a day in their eyes. They beamed and whooped in welcome. He glowed with pride when he introduced her to them as his bride.

"It is a pleasure to meet you all." She truly felt welcomed into their Caithness family.

"This is my old room," Augustus said once they were finally alone, but not before their travel bags had been brought up and a tub brought in and filled with steaming water. They had also been left ample provisions, including scented soaps that bore the Farthingale label.

"Oh, these are Honey and Belle's soaps. They are our Oxfordshire side of the family. It seems their soaps and fragrances are popular not only in England but as far north as here. Mmm, this one has a trace of vanilla, I think. Lovely."

She looked around the cozy room, taking in the decent-sized bed and the sparse but very well-made furniture. Table, chairs, and writing desk. There was only the one wardrobe, but she had brought so little clothing with her, she was sure it would all fit in there with Augustus's uniforms. "It's charming. I'm going to love it here."

He led her to the window to show her the view, which was spectacular. Below them was a garden filled with colorful flowers in full bloom. Beyond it, in the distance, was the broad expanse of the North Sea.

She had grown up in such a place, close to the sea and surrounded by beautiful greenery. What could be better than this? In a place so wild and beautiful, in the arms of this man who held her so lovingly.

After a moment, he turned her to face him and began to undress her. "I'm sure we'll both be more comfortable without our clothes on." He cast her a wicked smile.

She glanced at the tub. "Shall I go first, or would you—"

"Together. We'll get in there together."

"You're serious?" She laughed. "Why, General MacLauren. Is there no end to your depravity?"

"Apparently not when it comes to you." He removed his clothes and then resumed stripping her bare. His breath caught, and he eyed her with a ravenous hunger. "You are so beautiful, love. I dubbed you Spectacular June when I first set eyes on you, and you are still that to me. Even more so with each passing day."

He took her hand and sank into the tub, settling her astride him. She laughed as water splashed and sploshed over the rim, since they hardly had room to fit together. They managed somehow, soaping each other and sloppily rinsing each other off with playful abandon that quickly turned hot and fervent.

"Oh, my," she purred as Augustus began to suckle her breast, and heat shot through her. The tub water had cooled, but he was steaming it up again with the heat of his magnificent body. She grasped his shoulders, holding tight to his taut muscles. He still put her in a swoon whenever he removed his shirt, and she caught sight of his hard, rippled torso.

They coupled in the water, in the too-small tub that made her feel so decadently naughty. They were terribly misbehaving, slipping and squirming and sloshing more water out of the tub than remained in it. "Augustus," she squeaked, then sighed with pleasure as his mouth closed on her other breast. "Oh…my…"

His eyes were smoky and stormy.

He was no less affected than she was.

She liked this power she had over him.

Nor could she deny that this water coupling was quite exciting. Her skin was pink from the water's steam and glistening with droplets of water that streamed down her body. Some of those droplets budded on her breasts.

This drove Augustus wild.

She loved this hot need she roused in him and loved the protective way he held her as he buried himself inside her. This strong instinct to protect her was as ingrained in his soul as their need to mate.

Despite the awkwardness of their positions, or perhaps because of it, she felt a splendid pressure build inside her. It built quickly and with uncontrollable intensity, suddenly toppling her over that precipice in a burst of ecstasy more powerful than any she'd ever felt before. "Augustus! Oh, my heavens. *Augustus*."

He covered her mouth with his, laughing and groaning against her lips to quiet her as he reached his release as well. His liquid heat poured into her in the throbbing waves of his release. He caressed her cheek and grinned like a conquering hero as the force of his release subsided, and he pulled out of her. "Blessed saints, that was good."

"An understatement, I would say. Augustus, I'm still breathless."

He caressed her cheek again. "So am I, love."

They soaped each other again and quickly rinsed off, this time clean and staying that way. She knew by the still-conquering smirk on his face they would not be getting much sleep after falling into bed tonight. She did not mind. He was home and happy and had shared his heart with her, opened it wide, and made her an important part of it.

They dried each other off, then reluctantly dressed again.

June spread the drying cloths on the slate floor beside the hearth where the tub had been placed and began to mop up the water. Fortunately, none of it had seeped onto the carpet that covered most of the floor.

"Oh, we've made such a mess," she said, twisting the soaked cloth over the tub to squeeze the water back into it.

Augustus helped her wipe it up. "I'm certainly not complaining. I like having a wanton for a wife."

She gasped, her eyes now alight with mirth. "You fiend. Who drew me into the tub? I would never have known such a thing was possible if not for your wicked seduction. Augustus, you must make me a promise."

She tried to maintain a serious expression.

"Anything, love? What must I promise? Never to do this again?" He appeared dismayed.

She burst out laughing. "Of course not. It was wonderfully naughty. You must promise we shall do it again soon."

His features relaxed, and there was a wicked glint in his eyes.

"Oh, this I gladly promise you." He put his arms around her and lifted her up so she was pressed against him. He dipped his head and kissed her fervently on the lips. "I also promise to love you always. June," he said with a catch to his voice and kissed her again. "I'm so incredibly happy."

She clung tightly to him, her heart full of joy. "So am I, my handsome test frog. So am I."

Also by Meara Platt

FARTHINGALE SERIES
My Fair Lily
The Duke I'm Going To Marry
Rules For Reforming A Rake
A Midsummer's Kiss
The Viscount's Rose
Earl Of Hearts
If You Wished For Me
Never Dare A Duke
Capturing The Heart Of A Cameron

BOOK OF LOVE SERIES
The Look of Love
The Touch of Love
The Taste of Love
The Song of Love
The Scent of Love
The Kiss of Love
The Chance of Love
The Gift of Love
The Heart of Love
The Hope of Love (novella)
The Promise of Love (2021)
The Wonder of Love (2021)
The Journey of Love (2021)

DARK GARDENS SERIES
Garden of Shadows
Garden of Light

Garden of Dragons
Garden of Destiny
Garden of Angels

THE BRAYDENS
A Match Made In Duty
Earl of Westcliff
Fortune's Dragon
Earl of Kinross
Earl of Alnwick
Pearls of Fire*
(*also in Pirates of Britannia series)
Aislin
Gennalyn

DeWOLFE PACK ANGELS SERIES
Nobody's Angel
Kiss An Angel
Bhrodi's Angel

About the Author

Meara Platt is an award winning, USA TODAY bestselling author and an Amazon UK All-Star. Her favorite place in all the world is England's Lake District, which may not come as a surprise since many of her stories are set in that idyllic landscape, including her paranormal romance Dark Gardens series. Learn more about the Dark Gardens and Meara's lighthearted and humorous Regency romances in her Farthingale series and Book of Love series, or her warmhearted Regency romances in her Braydens series by visiting her website at www.mearaplatt.com.

www.ingramcontent.com/pod-product-compliance
Lightning Source LLC
Chambersburg PA
CBHW070344200726
48294CB00003B/785

* 9 7 8 1 9 6 0 1 8 4 9 7 9 *